Chaos at the Lazy Bones Bookshop

Books by Emmeline Duncan

FRESH BREWED MURDER

DOUBLE SHOT DEATH

FLAT WHITE FATALITY

DEATH UNFILTERED

CHAOS AT THE LAZY BONES BOOKSHOP

Published by Kensington Publishing Corp.

Chaos at the Lazy Bones Bookshop

EMMELINE DUNCAN

Kensington Publishing Corp.
www.kensingtonbooks.com

KENSINGTON BOOKS are published by

Kensington Publishing Corp.
900 Third Avenue
New York, NY 10022

All Kensington titles, imprints, and distributed lines are available at special quantity discounts for bulk purchases for sales promotion, premiums, fund-raising, educational, or institutional use.

Special book excerpts or customized printings can also be created to fit specific needs. For details, write or phone the office of the Kensington Sales Manager: Kensington Publishing Corp., 900 Third Avenue, New York, NY 10022. Attn. Sales Department. Phone: 1-800-221-2647.

ISBN: 978-1-4967-4615-3 (ebook)

ISBN: 978-1-4967-4614-6

First Kensington Trade Paperback Printing: August 2024

10 9 8 7 6 5 4 3

Printed in the United States of America

For booksellers everywhere

Chapter 1

Walking into a place where everyone knows your name can be overrated, but today, I appreciated it.

Which is a way of saying today had felt like a week in and of itself.

And it was only Tuesday.

But I couldn't complain. When I'd agreed to take over my family's shop, Lazy Bones Books, in the Halloween-themed town of Elyan Hollow, Oregon, I'd signed on for each fall to be stressful since the town was overrun by our annual Halloween festival that drew visitors from all over.

And while I knew I should embrace moments, like now, to de-stress with friends, it didn't mean I wouldn't worry about my never-ending festival to-do list.

Especially since I'd added a literary festival to the opening weekend.

And I was happy to run a business I loved in my hometown. Elyan Hollow used to be a small riverport town on the Columbia River, about thirty miles west of Portland. After a now-iconic Halloween movie had been filmed in town about twenty-five years ago, we'd started drawing visitors year-round to snap photos of the filming sites, with October being the peak tourist time. Since the town had added a formal Halloween festival and then rebranded to Spooky Season year-round, visitors have flocked to town, especially in autumn when the town adorns itself with decorations, holds weekend activities like children's crafts and movie sites tours, plus traditional seasonal offerings like a haunted house, and other attractions, and events like the annual pumpkin-carving competition that drew everyone from amateurs to seasoned pros.

The festival cumulated every year in a massive trick-or-treat night, including festival booths with seasonal treats, costume competitions, and all of the shops and close-in neighborhoods handing out candy.

Our scenic downtown with small shops has a strong Christmas season, most likely due to our combination of locally made goods, a short distance from Portland, and a unique twist on Christmas. Since we still decorate for the holiday season, just with a combined festive and spooky vibe.

But Halloween was our time to shine, and a good festival could make or break the yearly profit-and-loss statements for local businesses.

"Bailey, do you want your usual?" Ash, the bartender-slash-owner, asked as I walked into her taproom, called Elyan's Mortuary & Deli Bottle Shop, even though she only sells beer on tap alongside a handful of craft bottled sodas and sparkling water.

"What's my usual?" I asked.

Ash laughed. "Sparkling water, but I just tapped a new hefeweizen you should appreciate."

"Can I try it before committing?"

"Of course!"

Ash poured me a sample, and I noted that her pixie cut had been dyed a brilliant deep blue with a spiderweb shaved into the undercut on the back of her head.

"This is a true German-style hefe with perfect banana and clove esters from a newish brewery in Portland," she said. She handed over a one-ounce taster glass.

Ash was determined to turn me into a beer aficionado, and as I took a sip, I acknowledged she had a better sense of which beers I'd enjoy than I did. Which isn't surprising, as Ash used to be a brewer for one of the largest local breweries before packing it in to start her own taproom. Show any interest and she'll happily start lecturing about the different tasting notes in German versus Belgium versus English beers and all sorts of beer trivia.

After discussing the beer, Ash poured me a pint. As she handed it over, she said, "How are things going at the bookshop?"

"We're unbelievably busy. But that's good, right?" My grandfather, who'd started the bookshop and ran it until passing it over to me last year, was in town and ready to help if needed. But I wanted to show him I could run the shop solo and that his faith in me was warranted.

"Better than the opposite."

"True that."

My dog, Jack Skeleton, had been sitting patiently by my side, but he must've decided he'd waited long enough for Ash's attention, so he stood with his paws on the edge of the bar. I'm pretty sure the small fluffy dog in the corner felt jealous of Jack's Great Pyrenees reach.

"Well, hi, Jack," Ash said. She reached out and scratched behind his ears. "If you sit down, I'll give you a treat."

Once Jack saw the dog treat in Ash's hands, he sat down with an angelic look, like he'd never stand, and put his paws on the counter. That must've been a different giant snowy white dog in a jaunty red bandana.

Ash leaned over the counter and dropped the treat, which bounced off Jack's nose. He looked like Ash had insulted his mother, then leaned over and snagged the treat. I'm pretty sure the dog in the corner laughed at him.

"You have the strangest dog," Ash said.

"Careful, he'll hear you!" I said.

Ash is partly correct. Jack is frequently solemn until he's not and unflappably calm until he's not. His DNA test had claimed purebred Great Pyrenees, which surprised me since his fur is shorter than the breed's standard. But he has six back toes and an overwhelming desire to patrol the perimeter everywhere we go. He's a strange dog who always keeps a wary eye out, but those are also Great Pyrenees traits, as they were bred to be self-sufficient livestock guardians, frequently caring for sheep for days on ends in the Pyrenees mountains of France.

Some days, I suspected Jack saw me as his sheep.

"You can't mock the dog," a voice said behind me. "He's an angel."

Colby, aka my best friend, had arrived.

She joined me at the bar, and Jack immediately leaned his head into her hip. Her black hair was pulled back into a swishy ponytail, and her Elyan Community Library polo shirt had an uncharacteristic dusting of glitter.

"Trouble during craft hour?" I asked.

"I told the head librarian that we should ban glitter."

"Glitter is the herpes of the craft world," Ash said. "You're going to find it in the books for years."

"Gross."

Colby ordered an IPA, and as Ash poured it, a man I didn't recognize walked up to the bar. His eyes scanned the list of beers on draft with a quizzical expression. He asked, "This is a deli, right?"

Which was a fair question, given the word "deli" in the business name.

Ash smiled. "Sorry, we only have beers on draft. But you can bring food from one of the cafés down the street or from the food cart out back into the taproom. The cart's pretty awesome."

Colby slid a reusable lunch box to me. I glanced inside to see a few end chunks of gourmet cheese on a gel ice pack.

"Gift from my mom. Just remember to return the container," Colby said. Her parents own the local cheese shop, Ghostly Gouda.

"She knows this is a tough week. She asked me to tell you that you'll love the assortment she's putting together for the party on Friday, so don't fret. She'll do you and the festival proud."

"I don't doubt your parents' cheese skills," I said. So I knew I shouldn't triple-check what they planned to bring, even though I wanted to.

Everything needed to be perfect for my festival, and the three fantastic writers scheduled to come. The weekend would go well. It had to. The three authors onboard were all fantastic, and included a hometown hero returning after a long absence, making the festival feel like fate versus my pet project.

I spotted the notebook that contained my ever-running to-do list as I tucked the cheese into my messenger bag. I nearly pulled it out to remind me there was nothing pressing I needed to do at this exact moment.

It's time to unwind, I reminded myself, feeling like it was another item to check off on my to-do list.

"How's my little sister working out? Do I need to talk to her?" Colby asked. I'd agreed to take her younger sister, Danby, on as an intern for the Halloween season. It was a win-win for both of us: I received an extra set of hands during my busiest times of the year, and she received college credit plus payment for her time.

Except corralling Danby's energy was a complication I hadn't expected. It could be worse; Danby had good instincts combined with the energy of five minor mortals.

"Danby's doing great. You don't need to worry," I said.

"Famous last words," Colby said.

"Oh, incoming," I said. A redhead, about five foot eight and very slender, powerwalked into the taproom. Beside me, Jack let out a slight growl.

"Hello," Ash said when she clocked her.

"Save your breath to cool your porridge," I muttered. Jack pushed against the side of my leg as he shifted to stand between me and the redhead.

Colby looked at me and scrunched her eyebrows. "Someone's been reading Jane Austen. But that phrase means stop talking, not keep your eyes to yourself."

"Fine. Pretend this is a ball, and the woman who just entered said you're not pretty enough to dance with," I said. "React accordingly."

"Ouch, that's mean," Ash said. "It's from that zombies book, right? With the girls trained to fight zombies, but their mother wants them to get married instead?"

Colby shook her head at Ash, but the corners of her mouth edged up as she tried to suppress a smile.

"We should have *Pride and Prejudice and Zombies* showing in the taproom. It'd make a nice shakeup to our usual Halloween fare."

Monday evenings are the slowest in the taproom, and the local movie theater is dark. So Ash shows Halloween movies during the festival on the large screen she can pull down on one side of the bar. She usually shows Portland Thorns games, along with the Timbers and Blazers, plus an annual *Nightmare before Christmas* showing in mid-December.

"So, who is it?" Colby asked as the redhead held out a small black device toward the corner of the room. It beeped slightly, and the redhead stopped and made a note on her tablet.

Ash leaned in as I talked.

"You know the ghost-hunting show I told you about?"

"The one run by people who think the town is haunted versus knowing we accepted our fate and leaned into our spooky-vibe because of our movie, right? I met one of them at the library today," Colby said. She referred to the beloved, family-friendly Halloween movie *The Haunted Hounds of Hamlet Bay*.

"Hello, this place is haunted," Ash said. She motioned to the renovated former fire station turned taproom.

"Who by? Some hunky firefighter who couldn't bear to leave his crew behind after he tragically died in a fire station accident? Or maybe he perished rescuing a cat from a tree?"

"Who was his lost love in cat form, since she was a shifter who got stuck, but he didn't let that come between them," Colby added.

"You two think you're funny, but you should hear the strange noises when this place is quiet. The building doesn't like to be empty," Ash said.

"Good thing you've started renting the upstairs rooms out, then," Colby said. Ash had turned the old firehouse rooms upstairs into a low-key hotel. We'd helped her decorate the four rooms to showcase a hip Halloween vibe without being overstuffed.

Ash raised her eyebrow at me. "Back to what we were talking about. Who is the redhead?"

We all glanced at the woman, who'd moved over to a different corner of the room and was scanning it with a black wand. The couple sitting at the table by her openly stared. She brushed against their table like they weren't even there.

"That's Taylor Edison. She's the research assistant from the ghost show, and she's been scouting locations in town for filming. She stopped by the bookstore a few days ago." She'd been rather snooty and scoffed at several of my decorations. She'd also called Jack, who'd spent most of the visit ignoring her, a dirty area rug, so I was pretty sure we were in a passive-aggressive death grudge match.

"Does the show want to film in the bookshop?"

"That's the plan." Although I still debated whether I should've said no.

Taylor turned and walked up to me. She didn't acknowledge Colby or Ash, just stared at me with her intense brown eyes.

"Do you know who owns this building? It's dripping with paranormal activity," Taylor asked me.

"This is Ash, the owner." I motioned to my friend.

"You're not a bartender?" Taylor's eyes narrowed, and skepticism dripped off her.

Ash motioned widely with her arm. "Yep, this fine establishment is mine. I have the business mortgage to prove it."

"I need to talk to you about using your building as a filming site for my ghost-hunting show," Taylor said.

"Your show? Are you the showrunner?" Colby asked. Her voice was overly chirpy.

Taylor sniffed. "I'm scouting out locations."

"Gotcha. I met someone at the library earlier—Lance Gregory? I thought he said it was his show." From the tone in her voice, Colby had decided to lightly antagonize Taylor, so I decided to follow along.

"That's the show host, but he's not the brains of the show," Taylor said through clenched teeth.

"Did you know Lance is local?" I said. "Everyone in town will be so excited to see him."

"Just because someone grew up here doesn't mean he's a good TV host." Taylor looked down at her tablet. I'm pretty sure she was trying to be dismissive, but it just came out as petty. But I'm biased against her.

"I heard he's done a ton of TV shows, though. He's probably the first star to visit town since *The Haunted Hounds* filmed here."

"Star," Taylor scoffed.

If I was feeling kind, I would've told Taylor that Lance being local would open doors for them. But I stayed silent and let her dig her own proverbial grave.

"If you decide you want to film here, drop off a contract, and I'll happily discuss it with you." Ash turned and took an order for a pint of ale.

I looked at Colby and tilted my head toward the backyard. When I started to walk away, Taylor stuck with me for some reason. Jack wedged himself between us and Taylor moved slightly away but kept pace.

"This town is so odd. But small towns always have that weird, inbred vibe," Taylor said. She was staring at three women sitting in a group of club chairs in the corner, knitting, with pints of beer on the tables next to them.

One of the knitters, Pearl, made eye contact with me, and I nodded hello at her.

I paused.

"Taylor, this is Pearl," I said. "She owns the local yarn shop, Stitch Craft."

The knitters all looked our way, but their hands didn't stop. Colby had started dragging me to a group that met at the yarn shop each week, and over time, I'd befriended several knitters, many of whom were longtime bookstore regulars. They'd always ask me about my WIPs as they entered Lazy Bones. I'd always needed to remind myself they meant knitting "work in progress" projects, not the secret graphic novel I'd been working for ages on the down-low. I'd helped quite a few of them download Libro.fm, an audiobook source they can use and support the indie store of their choice, which I hoped was Lazy Bones Books.

"Is that a spiderweb pattern?" Taylor leaned in, and Pearl held up the lacy black shawl on a circular needle that had to be at least forty inches. Taylor was right; the pattern looked like a spiderweb.

"I'm selling kits for this pattern in the yarn shop if you'd like one." Pearl resumed knitting.

"But I'd have to actually knit it?" Taylor asked.

"That's the point," Pearl said. She nodded at me. "Bailey was reluctant, but she's a pretty good knitter now. You should see her color work. There's a drop-in group on Wednesday nights and Saturday mornings that you're welcome to join."

Taylor scoffed and said, "I'll keep that in mind."

Pearl glanced at me. "Remind me to show you how to fix dropped stitches. I dropped one in the pattern, and look, I fixed it, and you can't tell."

"Awesome." I'd "frogged," meaning unwound and started over, a project last month that made Pearl shake her head in frustration. She was positive I could fix anything with a few knitting tricks and perky can-do spirit.

"Are you coming to the knit night tomorrow?" Pearl asked, but I didn't have a chance to answer.

A man walked in, bypassed the door, and homed in toward Taylor. He looked familiar, but I couldn't place him. Taylor's posture straightened up when she saw him.

"Lance." Taylor's voice had switched from aloof to almost grating.

"Do you have the rest of the schedule set?" Lance asked her. He didn't glance at Pearl, or me.

"I'm working on it."

"If scouting is too much for you, tell everyone now. It's a big step from what you did last season, and you should've had the schedule set a week ago. We can't go into overtime, and this lack of organization could tank the show." Lance sounded blunt.

"It'll be fine." Taylor glanced at him, then looked away.

As soon as Taylor said his name, I realized why Lance looked familiar, although I'd never met him. I'd heard the ghost-hunting show *Gone Ghouls* planned to film in town and it was led by a local boy turned TV ghost hunter. I'd checked out the show and then Lance's bio. He'd worked a few gigs per year in TV for about two decades, frequently as the murder victim on crime shows or in small bit roles. About five years ago he'd picked up a gig hosting a low-budget reality show, and had done several more, with the ghost show being his newest. I hadn't heard of the show, or Lance Gregory, until last week, although I'd heard mentions of one of my mother's classmates in Hollywood. As I glanced at Lance, I was struck again by his even, symmetrical, and dark hair that set off his brilliant blue eyes. He probably looked fantastic on-screen.

"Lance," Pearl said from her spot knitting.

Lance glanced her way. "Do I—I bet we were in high school together, right? You'll be the third person who's recognized me in the past hour. I didn't know so many people had stayed local, versus moving on to bigger pastures," Lance said. His voice had taken on a mix of patience and niceness, but there was clearly an unsettled note underneath. From the angry expression on Taylor's face, Lance's comments about her being unprepared had hit home.

Pearl's eyes went down to her knitting as Lance turned back to Taylor. Taylor's face evened out, like she didn't want Lance to notice she was furious.

"I expect you to email the production team a completed schedule by lunchtime tomorrow." Lance turned and left.

Under her breath, Taylor muttered, "You're not my boss, even if you think you're all that."

Colby nudged me, and as we walked away from Pearl towards the back patio, with Jack alongside us. I glanced at my friend.

"Do you think Pearl knits in her dreams? When I swam competitively, I'd dream I was swimming through the world." I'd swum competitively from ages six to eighteen, training at the community center in the corner of downtown, adjacent to the park featuring the Goblin Gate Bridge. Colby had been a teammate, even though she was two years older.

"You had the swimming dreams, too? I thought that was just me. And what was all of that drama about the show?"

"It sounds they could use someone with your organizational skills," I said.

"Yes, I totally want to plan reality TV shows." Colby's voice was deadpan.

"I wonder if they usually have someone else handling logistics?" While Taylor's attitude had rubbed me the wrong way, I felt a pang of sympathy for her. It'd be mortifying to be chastised in public, period, but would feel especially unfair if this part of the show had been dumped in Taylor's lap unexpectedly. Maybe her attitude is the result of stress.

But she'd called Jack a dirty area rug, so my sympathy was limited.

Colby and I paused in the center of the back patio, scoping out the half-empty seating.

Ash had converted four shipping containers into seating, which lined two sides of the patio. Each had a picnic table inside, topped with a small electric fire for warmth in the winter. But a fire wasn't needed now since the late September weather still felt like summer, although the air was starting to cool as the sun went down. Weatherwise, October in Oregon is usually my favorite month, with sunny days, highs in the sixties, and cool evenings. It's perfect for a monthlong festival.

We snagged the last empty shipping container since they're fun.

Jack collapsed just inside the door of the container, like a fuzzy area rug. A quick glance against the patio showed us the Boorito cart was open and busy. It features expertly done illustrations of skulls and flowers that reflect Día de los Muertos in honor of Olivia's heritage, one of the co-owners, as the daughter of Mexican immigrants. It added a nice contrast to the decidedly American Halloween decorations throughout town. In January, the cart's co-owner, Milana, would hold a low-key Koliada celebration and hand out buns on the fifth, aka the day before Orthodox Christmas. Costumes were optional, but she always encouraged us to dress up.

I scanned the QR code on the table for the Boorito cart. I ordered a torta ahogada for me and Colby's usual carnitas bowl, which was lime rice topped with avocado, crema, carnitas, roast corn, fresh tomato, and cilantro and somehow managed to be almost as addictively good as the ahogada.

Olivia brought our food out. Once she handed it over, she sat down at our table.

"If you're here because you're worried about the catering for your lit festival mystery party, don't worry; we have it under control," Olivia said.

"What, me worry?" I said.

Colby and Olivia laughed.

"I saw you and knew you'd need reassurance," Olivia said. We chatted for a moment, and then a customer walked up to the order window, so Olivia darted away, with her parting words floating on the air behind her.

"It'll be fine, Bailey. The festival is going to rock."

On our walk home, Jack and I took the long way and swung through the park near the center of town. After Jack sniffed every blade of grass along the path, I paused by the Goblin Gate Bridge, which crossed a small creek. I quickly pulled an advance review copy, commonly called an ARC, of a new novel by shop favorite and festival attendee Melanie Wilde, due to come out next winter, and popped it up next to one of the goblins on the bridge, angling it just so. After a few photos, I had one that would work perfectly on the shop's social media accounts. The half shadows cast by the setting sun really added to the photo's ambiance.

When I agreed to take over the shop, I hadn't realized how much of a time suck social media would be. Luckily, the town made an interesting backdrop for content, especially when paired with the advance copies hardworking book publicists sent the store. Showcasing both the town and books worked out perfectly.

Plus, I occasionally managed to snap a fun photo of Jack with books or doing something silly that contrasted with his usual dignified demeanor that made a good post. Also, stacks of new releases on Tuesdays always made a splash, especially on the rare week when the stack was taller than Jack.

After I tucked the book back into my bag, Jack and I moseyed along, stopping to sniff the bench by the duck pond. One corner of the park was fenced off for the annual hay bale maze, which was in the process of being built. The maze changes yearly but is always decorated with pumpkins, skeletons, and Halloween decor.

A man in jogging gear passed us and gave me a smile. He looked around my age, maybe a year or two older, with hair so blond it was almost white. His T-shirt claimed he was an Ironman Hawaii finisher. I didn't recognize him. He was either new to town, visiting before the festival, or not a reader.

Jack watched the new guy head off in the distance with a sad look. Clearly, Jack was starved for attention.

But the next person I saw walking my way on the path made me hold in a groan.

My uncle, Hudson.

Hudson's only eight years older than me, and unlike my mother, he returned to town after graduating from the University of Oregon with a double major in business and urban planning. He came back with a series of plans and argued how my grandfather should sell the shop and reinvest the funds. After being rebuffed, Hudson ended up in commercial real estate development. I'm not entirely sure what he does, but he's gotten several promotions. It's paid well enough for him to buy a charming bungalow on the other side of the park from downtown that was perfect for him, his wife, and his toddler.

Hudson hadn't been pleased when I'd taken over the bookstore last year. He still thought we should close the store, especially since he doubted my business acumen.

Most days, I'm sure he doubts I can color-coordinate clothing.

"Bailey." Hudson nodded at me. His light brown hair rocked his usual short and choppy style, and he wore pristine workout gear. His face wasn't flushed.

Jack ignored Hudson and intently sniffed one of the Gothic light poles lining the path.

"I'm trying to convince myself to go for a run," Hudson said.

"I ran this morning," I said. "You know, a local running group meets on the weekends if you need inspiration. They seem friendly."

"You couldn't pay me to join them. Their monthly scavenger hunt runs throughout town are obnoxious."

"That's the Hunt 'n Run group that meets on Thursdays. This is a serious running group that preps for the Portland marathon together. They even help people create training programs."

"I don't have enough time to train for a marathon."

"My main point is that they welcome everyone."

"I'll look into it. How's the festival planning coming along?"

"Good."

"I look forward to seeing the P&L statements afterward. Well, gotta go." Hudson actually broke into a slow jog as he headed away from me.

I could've told him he didn't need to see the profit and loss statement from the shop, as it wasn't his concern.

Because Hudson didn't know my grandfather and I had signed a formal agreement that transferred the majority of Lazy Bones into my name. He thought I was still playing at being a bookshop manager, with my grandfather pulling the strings behind the scenes. Hudson would flip when he realized the building that held the shop was destined to be in my name, although the same wasn't true of the house my grandfather owned. He and my grandmother had originally written their will to split the house and the rest of their estate into equal shares between their children and me. Hudson would go nuclear when he realized I was the only grandchild with an equal share with him and my mom. But then, I was the only grandchild raised by my grandparents. Hudson would be even more angry when he finds out that, five years ago, when my grandmother died of ovarian cancer, my grandfather had planned on leaving the will unchanged. But he tweaked it a few months ago so I'd inherit the building downtown that houses the bookshop along with his minority ownership share, since I already have the majority interest. My grandfather had promised me that he and my grandmother had talked about the future of the bookshop and, if I'd shown an interest in running it, she'd wanted me to take it over.

I should worry about this later, I told myself, and Jack and I ambled in the direction home.

Chapter 2

Wednesday night. I should be home, getting ready to bank up some sleep and quiet time before the festival kicked off in two days.

Instead, I planned to be in Lazy Bones Books for hours after we closed. I'd briefly left the shop in Danby's hands, gone home for dinner, and begrudgingly walked back downtown with Jack so the TV show could film the supposed environment of the shop during the prime ghost-haunting hours.

'Cause evidently, ghosts come out at night.

Which seems boring to me. If I were a ghost, I'd rather hang out when people are around. Even if I couldn't talk to the living, I could listen to them. Children's story time at the bookstore sounded more fun than chilling in an empty shop at midnight.

Hopefully, being on the ghost-hunting show would be good publicity for the shop. Anything that gets people through our front door helps.

Although I was still skeptical about the *Gone Ghouls* TV show, and not just because I'm skeptical about ghosts. It'd been on for a year, with the first season of six episodes offered on a streaming service I hadn't heard of until Taylor walked through my door with a contract proposal. The show had done well enough to earn a second season, but I had questions. Including if they were willing to create haunted moments if their evening was otherwise dull.

At least the shop looked fantastic, with all the sections stocked and ready for the festival. I'd even refreshed the section names, and I loved how the new CRIME IN STORE sign looked in the mystery and thriller section. I'd gone with HANDLE WITH SCARE for the horror section, adorned with a hand-drawn Freddy Kreuger that I spent an afternoon on.

Danby was restocking the seasonal "Fang Girl" display for vampire novels, which mixed everything from YA, romcoms, dark romance, fantasy, and horror to suit a wide variety of taste. My favorite from the section is *Let the Right One In*, which was displayed prominently. Danby's a leaner version of her sister, with the same thick black hair, light brown skin, and strong bone structure. But Danby is more of a free spirit, who plans less than her sister and has an easier time rolling with surprises. I'm happy she asked about interning with me, as she's also a hard worker when she wants to be. And happily, she always does a fantastic job when she pulls on her Lazy Bones Books mantle.

The crew was supposed to arrive at six, and I stepped outside a few minutes past the hour. No crew.

The man I'd seen running in the park the other night was leaning against the wall next to the covered staircase leading up to the office space above the bookshop. We rented the space to Evelyn Jones-Wong, a lawyer specializing in what she called everyday law, which she'd told me once involved wills and estate planning, family law, and small business matters. All civil law.

He tucked his phone into his pocket and briefly made eye contact with me, giving me the opportunity to take in his stormy blue eyes that matched his natural-looking platinum hair. He smiled, then headed up the stairs to the law office. He moved with ease, like an athlete. Like he really had done the Ironman I'd noted on his T-shirt the first time I'd seen him.

One of Evelyn's clients? Or something more? I was still getting to know my tenant, who was a bit older than me, probably in her midthirties. She hadn't mentioned a husband or partner.

A plain white van pulled up outside of Lazy Bones. A man hopped out of the driver's side as a side door opened. I glanced at Jack. "If they don't find anything, they can always film you walking around the shop at night."

Jack basically glowed in the dark. We'd gone hiking through the Mosier Twin Tunnels last winter, and he'd photographed like a ghost dog, especially when cracks of light filtering in from outside caught him.

I glanced at the van again as the driver and a woman piled a few bins and black bags on the sidewalk. "I wonder if the locals will think there's a police stakeout on the mean streets of Elyan Hollow." We were lucky we didn't deal with much crime in town, just the occasional shoplifter and minor property crime. We were far enough away from Portland to avoid most of the urban problems, although I suspected they could be on our radar soon. During the Covid pandemic, we'd grown from people leaving the city to telecommute. At least some of the new transplants had stayed since we're within commuting distance of Portland and its suburbs, which include a few giant tech companies and famous shoe companies. However, we still feel like a charming small town. The catch-22 occasionally crossed my thoughts, making me think about how small-town life within an easy distance of the city appealed to some people, including me. But growth put us at risk of the city problems people moved here to avoid.

The driver walked up. He was tall, over six feet, with gray hair pulled back into a ponytail.

"I'm Bill from *Gone Ghouls*."

We shook hands. "I'm Bailey. This is my shop."

"This is my wife, Jill." He motioned to the woman organizing a couple of black bags on the sidewalk. "We'll set up the video cameras and audio equipment while the rest of the crew arrives."

The two set up their gear while Danby and I watched from behind the counter.

"Bailey, I can stay tonight," Danby said. She held up her backpack. "I have homework I can finish."

"If you've been getting behind on your schoolwork, we should reconsider your internship hours." The thought of losing Danby's help made me feel sick.

"I'm not behind—I can use the time to get ahead, so I'm worry-free this weekend," Danby said. Part of me suspected she was saying words she knew I'd love to hear. "I'd feel better if I get a rough draft of my history paper done now so I have time to revise it all next week. Plus, you'll pay me for staying, so it's like getting a study bonus."

I could feel myself weakening. "Are you sure? It's my shop."

"It's just babysitting TV people. What's the worst that could happen?" Danby asked. "Go. I've got this. Take a break now since you won't get one this weekend."

"Do you need a dinner break?"

"Let me run to the cheese shop; then I'll take over." She took off for her parents' shop, and I was sure she'd return with a gourmet dinner and snacks for the night.

Lance and Taylor walked in like they owned the joint. Besides me, Jack stiffened. His eyes followed them, although he didn't move.

"Yeah, this will work nicely," Lance said. "Except for the Halloween decorations, it still has that small-town feel it had when I was a kid. I can't believe it's still here; I'd thought bookstores went the way of the dinosaur."

Maybe it was a good thing Danby was taking over tonight since I wanted to throw a stuffed ghost at Lance.

"We can play up how they went with a Halloween theme to appease the ghosts that haunt their shop."

I snorted loudly.

They both looked at me.

"Do you have a problem?" Taylor said.

"My shop isn't haunted, but have fun trying to prove otherwise."

Danby came back with a bag from her parents' cheese store.

"The store is closed," Taylor said in a haughty voice.

"This is one of my employees, Danby. She is your contact tonight and has my full authority to make decisions for the shop." My voice was firm like they shouldn't even try to argue with me.

"We won't need your help," Taylor said.

Danby shooed me out. "I'll take care of them."

"Remember, what Danby says goes," I said.

Jack and I walked home, but I felt like I should go and kick them all out of my shop.

The way of the dinosaur, indeed.

Thursday morning

My phone beeped at 5:00 a.m. with a text from Danby.

Need you at the shop.

I dressed hurriedly, although Jack dug in all four paws until I tied a red buffalo-plaid bandana around his neck. I'm pretty sure he gave me a side-eye for heading downtown earlier than usual, but he followed alongside. He'd picked up on my urgency and only insisted on stopping once for a quick pit stop by his favorite tree. Every dog in the neighborhood loves that spot.

Thankfully, I'd already told Colby I needed to skip our usual Thursday morning bicycle ride since I'd assumed I'd spend the night at the shop instead of leaving it in Danby's hands.

When I walked into Lazy Bones, I gasped.

The store was in shambles.

Two of the bookshelves were knocked over, and several had been moved. Broken glass littered the floor in front of the register.

The HANDLE WITH SCARE sign with my hand-drawn Freddy Krueger was split into two pieces.

Danby wrung her hands. She looked up and made eye contact.

"I'm so sorry," Danby said. "I fell asleep in the office and woke up when I heard a crash. I rushed out to find all of this."

"How? An earthquake would've caused less damage."

"There's something else," Danby said.

Her tone caught my attention. What could be worse than what I'd already seen?

She pointed to a box behind the counter with a jumbled skeleton.

Stanley.

He should be sitting on a chair near the register, allowing me to make my favorite "well, if you think you've been waiting long" joke on busy days.

Stanley wasn't supposed to have a broken leg and a broken arm. His spine was supposed to be in one piece.

I turned and glared at Lance and Taylor, who were standing together near the door to the stockroom, looking at a tablet. "You destroyed my shop and broke my skeleton?"

Taylor waved her hand at me. "It's not a big deal. We can reimburse you so you can buy a new one."

"Not a big deal? Our busiest time of the year starts this weekend. People come here to buy books. Look at the state of the store. Do you think elves will magically show up and clean this place up?"

Taylor held up her hand. "It's just mass-produced material clutter."

"Let's not get dramatic and overreact," Lance said.

"And where did the broken glass come from?" I looked around at some of the "mass-produced clutter" that was handblown candleholders from a local artist.

"Just chill—" Taylor said.

"Get out!" I yelled. I pointed at the door.

"You're overreacting," Lance said.

"Both of you, out!"

Jack gave a slight growl as I ushered Taylor and Lance outside, even though they argued with me.

"I don't want to see either of you in my shop ever again," I said.

"You need to chill," Taylor said.

"If either of you enter my shop again, I'll call the police and will have you formally trespassed." My tone was low. No one could accuse me of getting hysterical, although something told me screaming at Lance and Taylor would feel recuperative.

Lance touched my arm, and I shook him off. I snapped at him, "Don't you dare touch me!"

"You're overreacting to all of this."

"Keep out of my way and out of my shop, else you'll regret it," I said. I stalked back into the store.

Inside, the camera operator was packing the last of their gear in black carrying cases. His wife was helping Danby move a bookcase back into its correct place. She began checking the books and sorting them into piles while Danby swept broken glass into a pile. The woman from the film crew moved and held the dustpan for Danby.

The camera operator turned to me. His name flashed into my mind. Bill, and his wife was Jill.

I was close to telling them to leave, but then Bill spoke while Jill continued to help Danby. Jack walked over to his bed and lay down, but he kept his eye on me.

I looked at his paws, but he seemed to have avoided the areas with broken glass, though I told myself to double-check later.

"We're so sorry," Bill said. "This is unacceptable, and I don't blame you if you want to kick Jill and me out, too. But I think I might be able to fix your skeleton if you give me a chance. If it's okay with you, I'll return with supplies later and see what I can do. If I can't, I'll ensure our producers reimburse you for the skeleton in addition to the rest of the damages. Plus, I'll forward you the video footage of Taylor knocking over your bookcases and damaging your store."

I paused.

Evelyn, the lawyer renting office space above the shop, walked in the open front door. Her perfectly shaped dark eyebrows were raised as she glanced around.

Bill continued, "If worse comes to worst, and you need to threaten to sue, the footage will help. And the producers won't want the negative publicity of lawsuits, and even the threat of the lawsuit will make them want to settle."

"I don't know what Taylor and Lance were thinking. They're not usually this stupid or destructive, although in their defense, this was an accident. They know no one will want us to film in their home or business if we act like wrecking balls," Jill said as she sorted a stack of books. I realized she was alphabetizing them. She put a handful of novels back on the shelf, swapped two around, then sorted through another stack and put a few more books on the shelf.

"And that's the major reason our producers should handle this quickly," Bill said.

"If you need legal help, let me know, Bailey," Evelyn said. "My threatening-letter skills are unparalleled, but I suspect this gentleman is right. No one wants to be known as the TV show that walked into a bookstore and destroyed it. We could spin it as one step away from a book bonfire if they dig in their heels."

"Thanks, Evelyn." Mostly.

Evelyn pitched in, along with Bill and Jill, as Danby and I set the shop to rights. In addition to Stanley, Taylor and Lance had broken three glass pumpkins blown by a local artist, smashed multiple candles and candleholders, somehow bent a handful of cards on the stand next to the register, and cracked the glass of the print of the bookshop on the day it'd first opened decades years ago. However, Bill said he thought the print underneath was intact as he bagged the glass.

I kept a running list of the damages we'd found, and Jill paperclipped their producers' business card to my notepad.

"Taylor should be the one smoothing all of this over," Jill said to Bill as I walked by. I listened in as they shelved books.

"Maybe she wants this show to explode in Lance's face so she gets his job," Bill said.

I returned to the stockroom to pull out a few more glass pumpkins and a handful of orange and white pillar candles to replace one of the broken displays. But I didn't have any excess gift items in the back, just extra books.

I knew I should've declined the ghost show, but I hadn't listened to the little voice deep inside myself screaming no.

We had the store mostly set to rights by the time we were scheduled to open. I'd vacuumed the store, hoping no one stepped on any missed fragments of glass. But my eyes kept scoping out the open spots instead of festive Halloween products. And before opening the shop, I checked: Jack's paws were glass-free. Although he pulled his paws away from me, annoyed because he was trying to nap.

Poor Stanley was tucked in a box in the stockroom, maybe destined to meet his final resting place in the afterworld of discarded skeletons.

Before they left, Bill and Jill paused by the door. "I need to pick up glue and a few things, but like I said, I'll be back later to fix the skeleton," Bill said.

They drove off in the van with the show's equipment. Danby stood next to me as we watched them leave.

"I'm so sorry. I didn't realize earlier they were destroying the store. I thought the thumps were sound effects since they were faking a ghost when I checked on them. It was ridiculous, and when I laughed, Taylor said I was harshing their vibe."

"It's not your fault." I shouldn't have left Danby to handle the film crew. "It's my store; I should've been here to handle things." Including busting heads, if needed.

Milo, one of the shop's long-standing sales associates, walked up. "Did something happen?"

I glanced at Danby. "Will you tell him the story while I grab breakfast sandwiches?"

After taking their orders, I headed down the street to the Walking Bread. A bacon sandwich isn't a cure for life's ills, but it'd be a good start today.

Chapter 3

Friday morning

I groaned when my alarm dinged, but I complained every morning when I had to wake up to an alarm. And at least it wasn't a text about the shop being destroyed by ghost hunters, so that's a win compared to Wednesday.

I rolled out of bed, pulled on my favorite athletic-cut bikini, and covered it with board shorts and a rash guard. I refilled my water bottle, slid on my water sandals, and was standing on the front stoop eating the last bites of a banana slathered with peanut butter when Colby rolled up precisely at 6:30. It was her week to drive.

The drive down to the waterfront only took a few moments. We both rented space in the back shed of the small Elyan Hollow Marina to store our stand-up paddleboards, and it took us only a short time to retrieve them and head out onto the river.

The cove at downtown Elyan Hollow's waterfront is protected from the harsh currents of the Columbia River because of a Bardsey Island offshore. We paddleboarded toward the center of the river, then turned when we were close to the dock jotting off the island toward town, and paddled parallel to the shore.

Once, this area had been wild. But a series of dams upriver had slowed the Columbia down, though it was still dangerous, with strong currents. And it held its own share of secrets. We're about twenty miles downriver from Tena Bar, the sandbar where a child found part of D. B. Cooper's loot from his still-unsolved airplane hijacking, which involved Cooper parachuting out of a jet, never to be seen again. As if the universe wanted to keep the story weird, the eight-year-old found the loot nine years after the hijacking.

At least there weren't pirates watching us today. In August, the island, which has a campground and a series of walking trails, hosted a pirate's festival. Three pirates joked about stealing our boards and making us walk the plank. They would've been scarier if they'd been out on the water instead of sitting on the dock, still buzzed from the night before.

We turned, got close to the end of the island, and headed back into the calmer waters of the cove. Colby was leading us today, and I noted the strong shoulder muscles of my friend. She's several inches taller than me, maybe five foot nine, with a muscular build earned with a steady dedication to working out. It should've felt at odds with the love of books and storytelling that led her to become a librarian, but it worked. Colby always wanted to control her own narrative.

Colby and I had been friends as children, even though she's two years older. We'd drifted apart in high school without any hard feelings. When we'd ended up at the same college, our friendship blossomed. Then, when Colby graduated from her master's in library science program and scored a job in Elyan Hollow, it felt the universe had confirmed we were supposed to be BFFs.

Colby quit paddling, and I pulled up alongside her. We sat down on our boards, watching the river.

"Want to head out to Scappoose Bay to paddle when your lit festival is over?" Colby asked.

"That sounds like the reward I'll need to get through this weekend." Scappoose Bay is just east of Elyan Hollow and is a fantastic area to kayak or paddleboard.

"You know you've got this. The festival is going to be fantastic."

"It'd better be, else Hudson will never let me live it down." My uncle, Hudson, thought the lit festival was doomed to fail. I remembered last year he'd even brought a few offers from a developer who wanted to buy the bookshop's building, which had led to my grandfather throwing him out of the house and the two of them not talking for over six months. They'd slowly reopened the doors of communication. My grandfather had signed the store over to me during those six months, and I'd asked him if he was doing so because he was angry at Hudson. He said he was doing it to protect the store, since if something happened to him and the decision came down to Hudson, my mother, and me, he trusted I'd have the shop's best future in mind.

My relationship had always been awkward with Hudson, who was sometimes the adored uncle who'd felt like an older brother when I'd followed him around as a toddler. But he'd also thrown a fit when I'd called my grandfather Dad. As a compromise, my five-year-old self had started calling my grandparents Captain and General Nana because of some long-forgotten book I'd been reading.

Colby and I stretched on our paddleboards as the water lapped around us. Then slowly headed back to shore.

Back to the real world.

It was time to get to work.

After a run home to shower and get dressed, I thought we were ready to leave for work, but Jack gave me a long-suffering look and walked over to his bin of bandanas. He brought me an orange-and-black buffalo-check scarf, which I tied around his neck.

You gotta love a dog who insists on accessorizing. I suspect Jack's love of bandanas is because, when he wears one, strangers squeal about how handsome he looks and pet him.

"Are we ready? Do you need a bow tie?"

Jack ignored my humor, so we were ready for our daily walk to the bookshop.

Nerves jangled in my stomach as we cut through a few residential blocks on our way downtown. Most of the houses had been decorated for Halloween. Some just had pumpkins on their front steps or maybe a few silly headstones in their front yard. But a few went all out on a spectrum from creepy, like the one with an ELYAN MORGUE sign strung across the front of their house with stuffed body bags across the lawn, to charming, with blow-ups of kid-friendly cartoon characters.

We avoided the block with the six-foot spider that moves since Jack hates it with passion.

The film crew was leaving the Haunted House B&B on a side street from the main drag, and I glared their way.

"Who are you angry with?" Kristobel, the owner of the Bone to Be Wild pet boutique, stopped to fawn over Jack, who took it in his stride.

"It's nothing."

"Is that the film crew? I heard they absolutely destroyed your store."

Kristobel walked alongside Jack and me. Jack turned his head to sniff her pocket, so she must have some dog treats she'd yet to share.

"If the film crew asks to film in your store, say no," was all I said.

"I already turned them down." She waved and continued walking to her shop.

My heart thumped a few times as I unlocked the front door of Lazy Bones and headed to the alarm.

On Wednesday, once Danby and I had reset the store, and after I'd sent her home midmorning since she'd been at the store all night, I'd sent out a series of SOS texts and emails.

Thankfully, my pleas for help worked. I'd acquired merchandise to mostly fill the gaps. One of my college friends who works in animation has a side hustle of art prints, and he dropped off a series of skeleton warrior prints that he'd been working on for several years. The one of the skeleton riding a horse while carrying an extra-large sword had been my favorite when he'd shown me drafts, and I was glad he'd finally decided it was ready to print. The local glassmaker had dropped a few more pumpkins and skull blown-glass holders, and he promised to try to make more for us quickly. The tea maker we were using in October's order boxes had dropped off their Spooky Season cold brew tea along with some of the Halloween mugs she'd ordered for her own small storefront, while a local linocut artist dropped off a new selection of seasonal cards for the rack in the front of the shop.

Knowing my community would rally around me lessened some of the sting.

Thankfully, the gaps in the shelves were less noticeable, although I could see bare spots when there should be small surprises to make a customer's day.

Like the gap where Stanley the skeleton should be sitting.

At least the children's area hadn't been touched. The kids' corner held several beanbag chairs along with one of my recent projects: an old cigarette machine repurposed as a toy dispenser that took special tokens in return for small toys and stickers.

Our special section by the register, where we lean into the iconic Halloween movie *The Haunted Hounds of Hamlet Bay,* was also in good shape. Local children, including my mother, had been extras for the movie. At least, my mother claims she's in the zombie scene and has a photo of her in makeup that she claims is from the set. The memorabilia is surprisingly popular, with the maps and short bound guide to filming sites being two crowd favorites. I always include a few books that mimic the movie's vibe, from graphic novels like *Beasts of Burden* and a mix of middle-grade adventure and horror novels that are currently popular.

Since I had time before the shop was scheduled to open, I climbed the steps up to the small office above the workroom in the back of the store. I could understand why Danby didn't hear the devastation the film crew had wrought below since it's surprisingly quiet up here, even when the shop is hopping. A bolted door leads to the hallway next to the law office's front door.

I double-checked the gift bags I'd put together for the authors and ensured each author's schedule was correct. I'd also included a downtown map highlighting the venues and the bookshop, a reusable stainless-steel water bottle with the store logo, and a selection of snacks. I'd drop these by the Sleepy Hollow B&B later this morning since all three speakers had suites for the festival. All of the authors were scheduled to arrive over the course of the day.

I took a moment to close my eyes and take in a deep breath, then let it out slowly.

The festival was going to be awesome.

Even with the damaged merchandise, we'd have a good festival season, keeping the shop afloat for the rest of the year.

I'd barely flipped the OPEN sign before the first customer strode in. She glanced around the store and asked, "What do you have that's like *The Haunted Hounds of Hamlet Bay* but a book?"

I showed her the dedicated Haunted Hounds section and explained each book in depth since she acted put out at the thought of reading the back covers.

"My son will love these!" She bought a stack of books from the display and a pack of cold brew tea for herself, along with one of our branded mugs.

My day felt normal, on the whole, even though the nerves in my stomach kept fluttering. Midmorning, I sent my mother a text:

Remember, my inaugural literary festival is this weekend!

About twenty minutes later, my mother responded:

We'll try to make it out, but Laurel has a soccer game, Ryan has a soccer game and a birthday party to attend, and we have a few other things scheduled. Gotta run! Patients to see!

My younger half-siblings play in competitive soccer leagues that involve a mind-boggling amount of travel. Laurel's team even attended an out-of-state tournament against the best clubs in the country last year. She scored the winning goal in the championship game, getting her attention from college coaches despite only being twelve. At ten, Ryan seems equally dedicated to the sport. Their dad had played college soccer, and they seemed to enjoy following in his footsteps.

And my mother tried to make the most of their games and events. She'd missed all of my swimming meets. She missed my high school graduation because she'd been doing her residency after medical school across the country and couldn't return in time. I couldn't begrudge my younger half-siblings their very different life since they didn't get to grow up at the bookshop like I had. Their relationship with our grandfather had a different flavor, fueled by the rare weekend visit and holidays. But sometimes, I wished I occasionally cracked my mother's top ten list of things she cared about, although I'd long again come to terms with the fact that I'd never be first on her list.

And I'd always known that if you looked at the pattern of my mother's life, including her stellar university grades, acceptance to medical school, and an excellent residency, followed by her marriage and perfect two kids, I took the shine off of the story. Or, in an even worse take, I was the adversity she had to overcome.

And my younger half-siblings didn't have Colby's parents in their lives. They'd enthusiastically celebrated all of my minor successes.

Midmorning, Clarity Blooms, the owner of the Eye of Newt Apothecary, floated into the shop. I've always doubted that's her birth name, and she's vague about her past, which I do my best to respect. In some ways, she felt ageless, but if someone pinned me down, I'd guess she was in her late forties. She favors yoga headbands, flowing scarves, and airy cardigans that drape to her knees. When I'd run into her at the yoga class in the local community center, she'd been decked head-to-toe in pricy name-brand yoga gear that showed off a toned figure. So I always wonder what, exactly, made her tick.

Clarity had volunteered to host one of the authors' events at the lit festival at her "apothecary." It carried products my grandfather called woo woo but fit the books' vibe, so I'd gone for it.

Plus, Clarity is always kind, and I was sure she'd do her best to make the event successful. She'd also been one of the strongest voices supporting the fundraising aspect of the festival, since she was also a supporter of the Tots Book Bank.

Clarity stopped and looked at one of the witch romances on display by the front counter, advertising the author, Melanie Wilde, who was attending the festival. "You should carry some spiritual nonfiction. I can make recommendations."

"Our shop's focus is fiction, but we're always happy to special order titles for you."

"I just wanted to double-check that the food at my event is vegan."

"Yep, everything is vegan, and we have a few excellent gluten-free options, too."

"Good."

We chatted until she left with a paranormal rom-com. Right before lunch, one of my booksellers arrived, freeing me to take care of a few last pieces of festival business.

With Jack beside me, I loaded up the collapsible cart and pulled a few boxes of books to the B&B hosting our author reception, along with the author gift bags.

"I really should've driven," I told Jack.

I'm pretty sure the look he gave me said, "You'll live, human."

Chapter 4

My nerves jangled, but I knew they'd settle down once the festivities started. According to Colby, the pine knee-length dress I'd bought for the event brought out the gold flecks in my hazel eyes, which I don't see, but I trust my best friend. And I liked the way it swished around my knees.

I paused as I stood on the steps of the Sleepy Hollow Inn, soaking in the atmosphere. The inn is a giant Victorian house with a carriage house in the back. Nine en suite bedrooms inside, and tasteful decorations along the windows and front steps. A small WELCOME, SPOOKY SEASON LIT FESTIVAL sign was on the front porch, with a couple of pumpkins with book images carved into the sides and electric candles flickering inside.

It was time for the opening reception for my literary series.

After months of planning, it was go time.

I missed having Jack at my side. When I'd left home, he'd been snoozing on his dog bed. He would have loved to attend the reception: lots of new people to pet him and buffet food set out on a table for him to snag with all four paws still on the floor, showing the world the danger of having a tall dog.

The Sleepy Hollow Inn was the perfect place to host the opening reception. We'd invited the authors from the festival and sold a limited number of tickets to readers who'd enjoy an upscale yet low-key event.

The B&B is immaculate, as always. The living room opened into a formal dining room with a parlor across the wide hallway, which gave us enough space to spread out while ensuring the event felt intimate.

Marion, the owner of the B&B and a longtime friend of my grandparents, had set up the food and drinks in the dining room. She'd had her staff move the usual mix of two- and four-top tables into the garage and set up a buffet table and a handful of cocktail tables. Plus, a vintage bar trolley for Elyan Dreams Wines, a local winery that also ran a small tasting room downtown called Wine Ghouls, whose employees were on hand pouring glasses of their Pinot Noir and Pinot Gris.

The food was all acquired from local shops. Colby's parents had given us a great deal on a couple of cheese plates from their shop, served with house-made crackers. They'd picked up our bakery order for us and, with Marion's help, were putting the final touches to the cheese plates they'd artfully set up between the platters of baguette slices, salad skewers, assorted salami from the local butcher, fruit trays, and assorted desserts. One of the salted chocolate hazelnut cookies was calling my name. Still, I needed to focus on making sure we were ready.

When I'd dropped by at lunch, I'd unpacked books for each festival's author on a table in the living room. The juxtaposition made me smile. I'd set up the books by local boy turned famed horror writer Rex Abbot in the center since he was our biggest draw. His newest bestseller, *The Waiting Room of Lost Souls*, was flanked by two of his greatest hits, *Brothers of the Forgotten Castle* and *Dead Awake*. *Brothers* had even been turned into a popular movie. They looked amusing next to the colorful Halloween-themed picture books, *School for Unruly Ghosts* and *Haunted Bus Ride*, both written and drawn by Tariq Ehsan, who lived in the Midwest but had always wanted to visit Oregon and jumped at the chance to come. To his book's other side was the popular witch romance series by shop favorite Melanie Wilde, including *Witch Knickers* and *Bewitch Me Gently*, which always made me smile. Two years before, we'd hosted Melanie, and she'd been the perfect bookstore guest: charming, thoughtful, and punctual. She'd joked the only divas in her life were the ones on the pages of her books.

Rex agreeing to attend the festival was huge for two reasons. One, his books were guaranteed bestsellers across the country. Whenever he announced a new book, pre-orders would flow in from our regulars in the shop and worldwide through our website.

Two, Rex had grown up in Elyan Hollow and graduated from the local high school. But he hadn't done a book event here until now. He seemed to have left town after graduating from high school and never returned. So this festival felt like a homecoming.

I shifted one of the picture books to angle it so it'd photograph better in the overhead light, then snapped a photo with my phone and stopped to eye the display again.

"It looks perfect," Marion told me. She put her arm on my shoulder, encompassing me in a subtle cloud of rose and bergamot, which smelled like home with a warm cup of Earl Grey tea. Marion had given me a bottle of her signature perfume a few years ago, but it didn't smell the same when I wore it.

"I just hope the literary festival goes well." I wanted to readjust one of the books but couldn't with Marion holding me in place.

"It'll be fantastic. You brought in wonderful authors, the programming looks perfect, and I'm sure it'll raise funds for the Tots Book Bank." I'd gotten members of the town's council and local business groups on board with the festival if it raised money for a local literary program that gave backpacks of books to every child in Head Start and kindergarten in the county to help them start a home library. The organization accepted donations of new and used books, so I collected donations year-round at the bookshop. Colby and I organized regular volunteer nights to clean the used books at the nonprofit's offices.

Marion's assistant called her name from the doorway, and with a final squeeze she left me to stare at the display a moment longer.

It did look good. And the festival was going to be fantastic.

I turned, and a man walked into the room.

My breath caught. Rex Abbot. The hometown hero.

Rex looked like his author photo, which isn't always the case. Although he didn't quite have the same level of brooding intensity in real life. His dark brown hair was cropped close on the sides and longer up top, but the curl on top looked almost purposefully messy, and there were a few strands of gray at his temples. His eyes had a touch of the same wary look that hinted he didn't miss much that the camera had picked up on. He was also dressed like his author photo in an espresso brown shirt with the sleeves rolled up and dark jeans.

"Mr. Abbot?" I said as I walked up. "I'm Bailey Briggs, the organizer of the lit festival. It's nice to meet you."

He blinked when he heard my name. "Bailey?"

"Yep, of Lazy Bones Books." I held out my hand.

"You can call me Rex." His handshake was firm. His silver watch was the same brand as the pens on my wish list. The ones are too expensive for me to do anything but dream about.

"I hope your room here is to your liking? Do you need anything?"

Marion walked up behind me. "And if you need anything, just ask me. Bailey has been run off of her feet with this festival."

"The welcome basket was a nice touch."

Marion's smile would make a princess on tour proud. "Bailey put a lot of thought into those. I just made sure they were delivered."

She'd also bedazzled the gift bags with washi tape and sparkly ribbon, but mentioning that would feel like a distraction.

Rex turned. His eyes took in his books on display and lingered on *Brothers of the Forgotten Castle.*

"I hope you're okay with the display." I could hear my voice's nervousness, and I told myself to chill. Even if I didn't feel confident, I should act like I didn't have a concern in the world.

"It's fine. It's just odd seeing *Brothers*, sometimes. If I wrote it now, it would be a much better book."

"Is that true for most authors?" Marion asked. "I feel that way about my paintings. Over time, my technique has gotten more polished and technically better, but I sometimes feel I've lost some of the passion of my youth, although it's been replaced by a different, perhaps deeper, depth of feeling."

"I wouldn't say I've lost passion, just naivety," Rex said. "But you're right. I couldn't have written that book now; in some ways, I was braver before I was published, at least when it came to books. I had a lot to learn."

"That's true for all of us," Marion said.

I stepped away from the discussion when another one of my authors walked in. Melanie Wilde also looked like her photo on the backs of her books. Straight strawberry-blond hair. Short-sleeved black dress that showed off her petite figure. Celtic-inspired jewelry, just like the heroine of *Witch Knickers* made and sold in her charming magical shop.

Melanie basically oozed charm and had a matching smile.

Then the tornado walked in.

The biggest difference between Tariq Ehsan's author photo and meeting him in person was his authentic self was perpetually in motion. His photo was a minuscule snapshot in time when he'd barely managed to keep still. His wife felt like an oasis of calm in comparison.

I introduced the three of them.

"It's so lovely to meet you," Melanie said. She shook hands with the Ehsans.

"We both love your books." The three started talking.

I glanced around to see if there was anything left to do.

Attendees started showing up promptly at seven. The event looked like my dream: people discussing books while nibbling on cheese and drinking local wine. The authors circulated amongst the crowd, although it was easier for Melanie and Tariq to initiate casual conversations. Rex looked awkward, maybe because some of the people had known him in high school. But he had to know the festival would have a high school reunion element. After a while, he relaxed, and a few genuine smiles crossed his face.

Then Lance and Taylor from the ghost-hunting show walked in.

I glanced at Marion. "Do they have tickets?"

"They're staying here, and we'd decided B&B guests are welcome to attend," Marion said.

"They trashed my store." At the worst time of the year, no less.

"I know. But you don't want to fight with the film heathens and ruin this event."

"I didn't know they were staying here."

"We had a last-minute cancellation, and they snagged the two rooms on the third floor. So far, they've been normal guests. But I've told my staff to keep an eye on them."

Lance walked through the event and said hi to a few people before he snagged a glass of wine while Taylor made a beeline for Rex, who was talking with my grandfather.

Rex looked slightly annoyed when Taylor interrupted his conversation, but the expression quickly smoothed away.

"We should catch up," Lance said to someone, then walked over to me.

"So this is your event?" Lance asked me.

I wanted to order him to leave. Instead, I gritted my teeth. "Yes."

"Looks like you had a good turnout."

"Yes, we sold out of tickets." And book pre-orders for the events in general exceeded my initial goal.

"Good thing I'm staying here, then. I wouldn't have wanted to miss Rex's triumphant return home."

"Did you get the TV show to film in town because of Rex?" I asked.

"No, that was just luck."

As Lance spoke, I noticed how clean his pronunciation was, with a low, soothing voice that worked well on camera.

"Do you recognize this?" Lance asked and showed me a creased snapshot. A toddler in a floofy pink party dress, cowboy boots, and a backward baseball cap sitting in a child's lounge chair in the corner of the bookshop, reading a picture book upside down.

I knew the photo; it's one of my grandfather's favorites.

Except the composition was subtly different, like it was the exact moment in time but captured from a slightly different angle.

"That's me," I said. "Why do you have this?"

"I—"

"Lance, I didn't know you'd be at the reception." Rex had joined us.

Lance tucked the photo in the chest pocket of his blue oxford shirt. "As I was saying to Bailey, all of this has been a lucky coincidence. It's been a while since we met up."

Rex seemed tense. "I've been busy."

Danby hustled up to me. "Can you come over to the bookseller's table?"

I followed her over and helped her reset the tablet so we could accept a credit card payment from a man buying a copy of each book we had on display.

When I returned to the crowd, Rex and Lance were gone.

Chapter 5

Saturday started off perfectly. I'd forgone my usual morning run since I knew I'd be scurrying around all day, and my grandfather had promised to hang out with Jack and take him for his daily constitutional. As I got ready to leave, even my wavy bob was behaving for once. I packed an extra Lazy Bones bookshop T-shirt in my bag in case I needed a midday wardrobe refresh. I stopped myself from adding a second pair of jeans, deciding if an emergency required that dramatic of a wardrobe change, I'd just scurry home.

Jack snoozed in the backyard while my grandfather drank coffee on the porch.

"You sure you don't need my help?" my grandfather asked.

"Tara and Milo are handling the bookstore, and you know they're capable of keeping it going." My grandfather had hired Tara over twenty years ago when her youngest started kindergarten, and she'd probably forgotten more about the shop than I'd ever learned. Milo had worked part-time for the shop for the past four years, mainly on the weekends.

"Call me if you need me."

"Of course."

I headed to the library first since Tariq was reading at the usual Saturday morning story time. And he was perfect, from his funny character voices to his reading speed and his comments on the illustrations. Afterward, he sat cross-legged in the reading area and chatted with the kids.

One kid, maybe about four, gazed at Tariq very earnestly. The kid finally asked, "Do you like baseball?"

Tariq was equally serious back. "I love baseball."

"He's so good at this. Not everyone has this level of magic with kids," Colby said as we watched from the side. "And I'm glad you're holding his craft hour at the Pumpkin Plaza."

I read between the lines of Colby's comment. "You're still finding glitter?"

"I'm pretty sure we'll be plagued by glitter for the rest of the decade, if not longer."

After the library, I headed to the noon event at the Eye of Newt Apothecary. Melanie was scheduled to mingle with readers. We'd dropped off books for sale last week, and Danby was scheduled to pack up and return any unsold copies to the shop after the event. The shop was offering tea and tarot card readings to attendees, along with light, healthy snacks, which were mainly hummus cups with cut vegetable sticks or crispy GF crackers, fruit cut into fancy shapes, plus cupcakes and banana bread made from almond flour that were naturally gluten-free and vegan, which were two requirements for the apothecary. The cupcakes had cheerful witch hat cupcake toppers poking out of the frosting on top.

Melanie mingled, looking stellar in another stylish dress, this time in dark green, with a different set of bronze Celtic-inspired jewelry.

I snagged a cup of black tea, which turned out to have notes of pear and something floral. Not too bad, but it's not quite my favorite matcha.

"Do you want me to read your tea leaves?" Clarity asked.

I shook my head. "That sounds dangerous."

But when I finished my tea and started to put it down on the tray of dirty dishes, Clarity grabbed my cup and gazed into it. She eyed it, then looked at me, then eyed it again.

"Your hard work is going to pay off in a way you can't even imagine and will shine a bright light into your secret life," Clarity said.

"I'll just be happy if the festival is a success." And no bright lights need to be shown in my shadowy secret life, mainly my graphic novel in progress. "My secrets aren't that dark and don't need illumination, which makes me realize I was quite boring."

"Oh, the festival isn't in doubt. But I see your dreams are on the way to becoming true."

Then Clarity's face turned sad. "You didn't tell me you only have one living parent."

"Umm . . ."

"But remember that just because you'll never meet doesn't mean you can't find answers to help you move on."

Melanie broke in, and I almost could've kissed her. "Bailey, can you help me with something?"

One of the attendees wanted one of Melanie's books that we didn't have in stock, so I agreed if the customer ordered a copy through my shop, I'd have it sent to Melanie, who promised to sign it and send it to my shop for the customer to pick up. I ran the order through my phone, happy I'd added an app to process credit card payments during events since I didn't need to lug around an extra tablet or send patrons to the shop.

And then five more customers wanted to order the same book, too.

After I finished the order, the event was winding down, so I got ready to head to the next event setup. As I swung my messenger bag over my shoulder, I noticed Clarity watching me from the side of the store with an uncharacteristically solemn look.

It gave me shivers.

I turned and marched in the direction of the Pumpkin Plaza.

We were scheduled to use the Pumpkin Plaza, aka a two-square block in the heart of downtown that served as a focal point for the festival events, starting with a children's craft hour with Tariq Ehsan.

The city had set up canopies, providing welcome shade on a day slowly heating up.

Tariq and his wife were waiting for me when I entered the Pumpkin Plaza.

An art director visiting the store told me once that the artists she worked with had two of three qualities: being a pleasure to work with, talented, and on time. Finding someone with all three attributes was like finding a unicorn, so she juggled those three attributes depending on the project's needs.

Something told me Tariq was the elusive mix of those three elements as we quickly set up the tables for a children's craft hour. Tariq had brought homemade thick cardboard ornaments shaped like ghosts, school buses, and pumpkins that matched his stories. Along with markers and stencils so the kids could draw on the ornaments. Plus, he had a stack of coloring and activity pages based on his picture books. Some were modified for small children, and a couple looked perfect for adults, and I wouldn't be surprised if a few parents grabbed a sheet and colored with their kids. Or kept one sheet for later.

Adult coloring books are a steady seller in the store, after all.

Danby helped me set up a table with two of Tariq's books, and I put up a small sign with the book prices. My phone was already primed for credit sales after Melanie's event.

And I noticed no glitter in sight. Colby would approve.

Tariq paused by me.

"All of this is amazing," I said.

"I used to be an elementary art teacher," he said. "I learned a lot of tricks when it comes to art projects for the under-ten set."

"Do you miss teaching?"

"Some days, yes, although I do some work with aspiring adult illustrators now, which is less messy, but I miss the chaos of a classroom of kids. And I get to live vicariously through my wife, which makes me not miss school politics."

"Is your wife also a teacher?" I sometimes struggle when thinking about my fellow aspiring illustrators since when I do it feels like I'm one of a crowd of thousands, destined to remain in the background, never quite being good enough to make it.

"Yep, my wife teaches high school math," Tariq said. "Speaking of which, I should go help her."

I tagged along and saw Tariq's wife was setting up a table so the kids could add an orange pumpkin ribbon or black string to the ornament when they were done.

Then it was go time, and children started to show up, along with their parents. I recognized quite a few faces from the library store hour.

Tariq and his wife walked around the craft hour, helping kids and giving them positive feedback. My intern, Danby, was a natural with the children as well.

"This is so much fun," a woman who'd come with three kids under ten told me. She bought copies of both *School for Ghosts* and *Haunted Bus Ride*. "Please do this often."

I laughed. "Hopefully, this will be a yearly event, and if we can draw a steady crowd for children's events, we can definitely plan more."

"Having a library story hour and free craft hour was a great idea," she said.

"I wanted to make sure all of the kids in town felt welcome to come. Not everyone can afford books, but everyone should have access, and that includes the chance to meet author-illustrators."

"Three cheers for libraries. You should see the stacks of books my kids bring home. But I'm carefully building a library of their favorites, and I'm sure these will be at the top of their list. They love Tariq."

We chatted for a while longer, and after two hours it was time to clean up the Plaza and get ready for the main event.

Rex's talk.

The marquee event of the entire literary festival.

* * *

When Tariq and his wife offered to help us clean up, I waved them off and ordered them to get a coffee or late lunch.

"You deserve a break," I said.

"We'll be back for Rex's talk. His books are some of our favorites."

They left.

Danby and a couple of members of the city's park and rec department helped me break down the craft set in the Pumpkin Plaza and prepare it for our marquee event of the day: Rex Abbot's talk. A few eager locals even helped us put out chairs, then claimed their spots in the first few rows. The sunny weather in the seventies made this feel like a workout as I set up a signing table off to the side, along with a cup of ultra-fine tip Sharpies for after the event. By Rex's request, I'd set up a sign requesting everyone bring two books max to be personalized.

A guy from the rec department brought out a wooden podium while his coworker set up the AV system. We tested it.

The cordless microphone worked. So Rex would only be stuck behind the podium if he wanted to be. I'd never seen Rex speak, and I wondered if he was the type that liked to roam or if he had notes and stood in place. He'd seemed quiet in person, but some people sparkle more when they're speaking in front of a large group versus mingling.

"You'll want a similar setup tomorrow, right?" the rec guy asked.

"More or less, except we'll need a table up front for all three speakers and a fourth spot for the moderator." The head librarian had agreed to moderate our Sunday morning panel of all three guests.

"No problem."

The crowd filtered in, and by the time it was five minutes all the chairs were filled and people were standing along the back and sides, ready for the event.

But Rex wasn't in sight.

I checked my phone; no messages from Rex. I texted him:

Five minutes until show time. Are you near? Do you need help finding the Pumpkin Plaza?

But no matter how often I checked my phone, Rex didn't reply. I called him, and it went to voicemail.

"Where is Rex?" Danby said. Her anxious tone mirrored the nerves flowing through me.

"No idea." I walked to the front of the crowd, feeling like I was letting them down.

I picked up the microphone. "I'm sorry, everyone. Rex seems to be running late."

There were a handful of grumblings from the crowd, and someone called, "When will he get here?"

"That's an excellent question and I wish I knew the answer," I said.

Tariq glanced at Melanie, then nodded to the microphone at the front. They walked up together.

"May I?" Tariq asked, and motioned to the microphone.

Might as well. I handed it over, knowing that Tariq was good with crowds.

Tariq's voice was calm as he spoke into the microphone. "I don't know about you, but I'm excited to hear from Rex."

The crowd whooped and agreed.

"While we wait, let's talk about story inspiration with the amazing Melanie Wilde. If you haven't read her books, you should because they're hilarious and built on a foundation of heart. I'd love to hear about how Melanie created the magical jewelry shop in her books, which is a place I'd love to visit. Does her witch have any potions that would help with writer's block? Because there are times I'd love extra help."

He handed the microphone to Melanie, who smiled as she accepted it. "I'll answer your question, Tariq, as long as you also talk about how you created your school for ghosts, which is hilarious but also shows some serious world-building chops for a book that's only thirty-two pages and what, six hundred words? Well, to answer your question."

Tariq and Melanie spent the next hour talking about the unique worlds they'd created in their books, then talked about their favorite Halloween movies and got the audience involved in a discussion that left everyone laughing. I called and messaged Rex multiple times, but he didn't answer. I debated emailing his publicist, but there was nothing she could do to fix this particular problem. I checked in with the bookshop and Marion; no one had seen him.

Some of the energy that had made my heart race and want to freak out when Rex didn't show settled. At least I had Tariq and Melanie to work the crowd. And they were awesome.

At the hour, I thanked Tariq and Melanie for their impromptu talk, and the crowd dispersed. Although a few joined Tariq and Melanie at the signing table. I was sure a few had run to and from Lazy Bones to buy books for the authors to sign.

"I have books for Rex to sign," a fan told me. "One's even a first edition of his debut from over twenty years ago."

"I'm so sorry Rex is not here to sign them. I'm not sure how we got our signals crossed. But we have another panel tomorrow morning, and I'll see when Rex can do another signing then. Hopefully I'll try to set up something in the store during the afternoon." Even if I had to sit on him and force him to sign books.

Because that wouldn't be awkward at all.

"What if I can't make it?" Disappointment rang through her voice.

"If you leave them at the bookshop with your name and contact info, we can get Rex to sign them, and you can pick them up at the shop."

"But it's a first edition."

"I understand if you don't want to leave it with us, and I really want to find a solution that works."

After I talked with a few more disappointed fans and made a quick heads-up call to the bookshop's current staff to inform them of the incoming sad readers, Colby met me at the entrance of the Pumpkin Plaza.

I couldn't believe Rex didn't show, especially after dipping out of last night's reception early.

I should have done a better job planning or stuck with authors I knew would appreciate the chance to attend versus the hometown hero.

"Take a walk with me?" I asked Colby. I needed to burn off the anxiety that'd fueled me for the last hour, and she nodded.

We were quiet as we marched toward Goblin Gate Park; Colby kept up with my frantic pace without comment. There wasn't a line for the pumpkin maze, a series of hay bales set up in the corner of Goblin Gate Park, so we decided to visit the maze for our annual visit.

At least there's a solution to the maze, although I wasn't sure I'd find a solution to the flaky-Rex problem.

The volunteer by the entrance was a regular at the bookshop, and she waved us through after I handed over a token for both of us. Every year, the festival drops off ten tokens at participating businesses, giving us access to the Haunted House, the Ghost Train, which is really a tractor pulling "train cars" through town, and the maze. Plus, a handful of one-off events around town, like photo ops in the Pumpkin Plaza.

The pumpkin decorations piled on a pirate skeleton near the front of the maze were cheerful, and the signage WILL YOU FIND YOUR WAY OUT, OR WILL YOU JOIN ME HERE FOREVER? felt like silly-scary. No one would actually get lost forever in here.

"I can't believe Rex didn't show up. He's supposed to be my biggest draw." We'd paid his travel expenses. The least he could do was show up on time. He'd approved his schedule beforehand, so it's not like any of the events were a surprise.

And I had the email confirmations as proof. How should I approach this? Have a serious talk with Rex? Call his publicist? Short-sheet his bed in the B&B? The last thought made me half-smile to myself.

"He didn't communicate with you at all?" Colby asked.

I shook my head. We turned left at a crossroad decorated with a mermaid with a cauldron. The mermaid must go above water to use it unless its hybrid mermaid witch magic allows for fires underwater. Each intersection has a unique decoration that serves as an identifier to help the maze staff make their way through quickly, and this was a creative choice.

My voice still sounded edgy. "Rex didn't answer my texts or phone calls. You know, we paid for him to come to this. Airfare. Hotel room. We're even paying him an honorarium to cover his meals and the time he's giving up here."

"Maybe something happened."

"Or he decided that the readers of Elyan Hollow aren't worth his time. We've invited him for events before and he always said no."

I paused to take a photo. The afternoon light made one of the hay bales with a pumpkin on top cast an eerie shadow at odds with the cheerfulness of the rest of our surroundings. Like the shadow was something dark creeping up on an otherwise cheerful world.

We chatted, and I took a few more photos as we made our way to the maze's center.

"How close are you to having a rough draft of your supersecret project?" Colby is one of the only people who know about my graphic novel in progress, although I have yet to share any of it.

"I have eighty pages of thumbnails detailing the action, but I'm nowhere near drawing finished art yet. I'm still trying to get the story right." Thumbnails meant I'd drawn crude drawings that followed my script and showed the action, but I hadn't focused on the clean, crisp drawing the eventual graphic novel would need. I'd already created a series of character sketches, showing my main character from every angle.

"Let me know when you want feedback."

We entered the maze's center, which had a couple of benches.

A figure in a red-and-blue-plaid shirt, dark jeans, boots, and pumpkin head was slumped against one of the benches.

"That's a weird ambiance choice," Colby said.

"That's not a decoration." The maze designer had shown me her sketches and mood board for this year's decorations last June. Something this realistic wasn't part of her plan. She leaned toward a family-friendly, retro feel.

I forced myself to move forward. Touching the body made me feel queasy, but I still forced myself to touch his wrist, noticing the sleek silver watch.

Just like the watch Rex wore last night at the opening reception at the B&B.

The wrist was cold. Too cold. And the smell around him made me queasy. I stepped back and forced myself to call 911.

"I think I found a dead body."

Chapter 6

The 911 operator initially assumed I was calling in a prank. But Colby took over and in her best librarian used to wrangling children voice told her who we were and why we wouldn't lie, and asked for paramedics.

"You don't want to be the nine-one-one operator who didn't believe one of her fellow town employees and left a dead body for young children to stumble across, do you?" Colby said.

A moment later, Colby turned to me. "Help is on the way."

We stood vigil as we waited. Maybe we should've tried to pull the pumpkin off his head to do CPR and mouth-to-mouth, but it felt too late. The thin red mark across the victim's neck, right under the pumpkin covering his face, kept popping into my mind. I wanted to turn away like Colby, but part of me feared he'd stand up.

I would've loved for this to be a Halloween prank. Someone scaring kids with a pumpkin head mask.

"At least I know why Rex Abbot didn't show up," I said. A mix of emotions flowed through me. Including horror with a tinge of guilt since I was the reason Rex was in town.

"Are you sure it's Rex?"

"That looks like the same Montblanc watch Rex wore at the reception." Classic brown leather band, sleek face. Quiet, and quality, luxury.

"Montblanc?"

"They make pens, too, that are supposed to be amazing to write with. I've debated buying one, but I can't spend that much on a pen, no matter how awesome." I paused. "I'm going to need to cancel the reception tonight."

Tonight's murder mystery party at Ash's taproom was supposed to be a fun way for attendees to mingle with the authors while solving a fictional murder.

I hadn't planned on stumbling across a real body.

The fictional party sounded much more fun.

The first firefighters showed up, followed quickly by a police officer and then a couple of paramedics. Colby and I were ushered to the other side of the clearing.

One of the police officers had us recount discovering the body, then asked us to wait. So Colby and I sat on a bench within sight of the body and watched as the area was enclosed in crime tape.

A woman with a toddler walked around the corner, and the police officer quickly headed her way. I heard him say, "We need to clear the maze," into his walkie-talkie before ushering the woman away.

I glanced at Colby. She stared at the hay bale wall across from us like she could read something in the bundles. Not that long ago, the hay had been growing on a farm somewhere in the Oregon sunshine.

Now the hay encircling a crime scene had a front-row view of the county coroner, assorted crime scene techs, and police officers doing their thing. A drone buzzed around, and I wondered if the police were mapping the crime scene.

It felt like days had passed, but it was only about an hour later when a man dressed in a rather tight Elyan Hollow Police Department polo tucked into dark cargo pants walked up. He wore a badge on a chain around his neck. His face rang a bell in my head. I'd seen him in the bookshop, trying to wrangle a couple of toddlers. His wife was a shop regular. She'd been front row at Melanie Wilde's readings the year before.

I hadn't realized he was a police officer, not that it would've mattered.

Colby and I both stood up.

"So you two found the body," he said. "Remind me of your names?"

"Let's start with your name," Colby said. "And why do we need to talk with you? We've already told the police officer what happened, and I'd really like to leave."

Colby looked as stressed as I felt inside, with the way she couldn't stay still and kept twisting her wedding ring or watch.

He stared at Colby momentarily, then pulled a card case out of his pocket. He handed over a business card to both of us.

I read the card. "Andrew Whitlock, Detective, Elyan Hollow Police Department."

"We have enough crime in town to have detectives?" I said.

"We're not as busy as Portland. But yeah, there's enough to keep me busy. We haven't had a murder for a few decades." Detective Whitlock's tone had gentled, and I wondered if he was trying to build rapport.

Or if it had dawned on him that we were freaked out after discovering a body, even though I suspected we were holding up remarkably well.

"I'm Colby Snow, which you might know since I've seen you at the library before," my friend said.

"You work there, correct?"

"I'm the Youth Services and Outreach Librarian."

Detective Whitlock made a note and then looked at me. "And you?"

"Bailey Briggs."

"Briggs . . . any relation to Hudson?"

"Yes."

The detective eyed me again. "You're his sister's kid, aren't you?"

I nodded. I assessed the detective's age and decided he could've been in school with Hudson.

The detective made another note. It's always a weird feeling when people know, or at least think they know, the details of my past. Like back when we'd had sex ed in high school and the teacher had mentioned that teen mothers tend to end up in poverty and everyone's gaze had swiveled to me.

"Is there any particular reason the two of you were in the maze today?" the detective asked.

"We come every year, but today . . ." I told Detective Whitlock about Rex not showing up to his scheduled appearance, and it ended with me guessing the body had to be Rex. I mentioned the watch. "Who else could it be?"

"You didn't take the pumpkin off of his head?"

"I just couldn't. It turns out I'm not brave."

After a few more questions, a uniformed officer escorted us out of the maze.

Chapter 7

By the time we exited the maze, it was almost time for the evening reception in the taproom to start. I debated calling Ash but hightailed it to the Elyan Mortuary & Deli instead.

One of Ash's bartenders was at the door, ready to make sure attendees had tickets, next to the CLOSED FOR MURDER WITH THE SPOOKY SEASON LITERARY FESTIVAL sign, with a QR on it in case anyone wanted to buy tickets at the door. Someone had carefully written: *We'll open to the general public at 8 PM* in a black Sharpie on the bottom of the sign.

I winced at the sign.

"Do you need a character envelope?" the bartender handling the door asked. Every attendee would get a character to play for the murder mystery game portion of the evening.

"No thanks." I'd planned on working the book table and letting the attendees investigate their fictional murder to their hearts' content.

Should we refund the tickets? And what should we do with the catered food? I felt tired and sluggish but knew I needed to make decisions.

Melanie Wilde was already there, chatting with Tariq and his wife at a table. They wore name tags. I guessed Tariq had handled their name tags, given the stylish flourish of all of their names.

Ash waved me down. "Do you know what's going on at the maze? I heard the police closed it down. And are you okay? You look off."

I tried to tell her. I needed to cancel tonight's event and maybe the whole literary festival. I needed to admit that by inviting a hometown hero to town for the inaugural literary festival I'd somehow caused his death.

Because there's no way that was an accident.

But before I could get the words out, a man strode into the taproom. He looked calm and confident.

Not just any man.

Rex Abbot.

Colby walked in behind him, and she also froze when she caught sight of Rex. When she could move, she made eye contact with me.

Rex walked up to me, as I stared at him.

"You're not dead," I said.

Rex blinked twice. Yep, still alive. "You are correct."

"Then who died in the hay bale maze?" As soon as I spoke, I wished I could unsay the words.

"Someone died in the maze?" Ash said behind me.

I nodded and glanced at Rex's wrist. He wasn't wearing a watch.

Rex stared at me. "Someone died in the maze and you thought it was me? Why?"

"You didn't show up for your talk earlier, for one," I said. A spark of annoyance from this afternoon cut through the devastation weighing me down. "The whole reason I went for a walk in the maze was to calm down, not to stumble across a body."

"You found a dead body?" Ash asked.

"Yep, I thought it was a decoration and would've kept walking," Colby said from a half step behind Rex. She weaved around him to stand beside me.

"Of course you two found it together," Ash said. "Do you guys need anything? Especially strong pint of beer? I might have some tea in the back. Aren't people who find bodies supposed to get extra tea with a ton of sugar?"

"Maybe in an English murder mystery," I said.

Rex's gaze hadn't moved from my face. "Are you sure you're okay?"

I straightened up. "I'm fine."

Was I? And what about tonight? My three guests of honor were here. We may not need to cancel.

But my thoughts kept returning to a key question: Who had died? I'd been so sure it was Rex.

On the far side of the room, Olivia was setting up the catered food from Boorito. Mila carried a tray, and the two worked to get the food set up.

"I guess the evening event should go on as scheduled." Maybe the death in the hay bale maze didn't have anything to do with us. Although the watch the victim was wearing still bothered me.

"There's no reason to cancel, I don't think," Colby said.

"It's hard to know what to do."

"As tragic as an accident in the maze is, it has nothing to do with us, right?" Ash said. "So let's get this party started."

Ash let me into her back storeroom. I grabbed the bin of pre-ordered books I'd dropped off yesterday. After putting down a black tablecloth printed with white skulls around the border, I set up a book station at a table facing the bar. We'd already packed and labeled the pre-orders in orange gift bags with books inside, with extras like bookmarks and a handful of candy packed in each Halloween-themed treat bag from the local candy store. Like trick-or-treating for adults, book-style.

"Can we help with anything?" Tariq asked.

I forced a smile. "Just work the crowd."

"I love meeting with readers," Melanie said.

As we spoke, I could feel Rex Abbot staring at me from beside the bar. He held a tall boy of flavored sparkling water.

"I need to ensure the food is ready before we open the doors," I said. Why was Rex staring at me so intently? And why had he missed today's talk?

I headed to the food table. It looked like everything we'd agreed on: two types of tamales, both chicken and a vegan option, chili verde that would have deliciously tender pork, plus fresh tortillas, beans, rice, guacamole, chips, and salsa, plus a couple of salads. All were made in-house, or rather, in the commissary kitchen space Boorito rents. Olivia had set the vegan options and salads up on a table next to the meat options with signage about allergens, with a collection of desserts on the third buffet table.

Usually, Boorito's avocado salad would call my name and I'd return for round two with the main courses. But my stomach burned when I looked at the food, and once I checked to make sure everything looked as it should I turned away.

Everyone who bought a ticket got a free drink of their choice in addition to the food, and the usual water station was set up. So there wasn't anything left for me to do.

So I returned to my book table, ready to meet the readers who'd paid to come and deserved a good experience.

Rex stepped in my way.

"I'm sorry about missing my talk today. I honestly thought my talk was scheduled for tomorrow afternoon," Rex said.

The words "If you checked your schedule, you'd know that you only have the Pastries & Panel event at the Pumpkin Plaza," were on my tongue. But I switched to saying, "I called you multiple times." Not to mention multiple texts, one email, and direct messages on multiple social media accounts, although I doubted Rex ran those himself.

"I had my phone on do not disturb. I'll add you to the list of people who can call through."

But it was too late for that. "Disappointed fans brought books for you to sign."

"I'm happy to sign them tomorrow. And I'd like to talk—"

"Are you Rex Abbot?"

I knew that voice. Detective Whitlock, whom I'd formally met earlier in the maze.

Rex turned. "Yes, I am."

Detective Whitlock looked at me. "You misidentified the body."

"I didn't mean to." I looked away from him, and Rex was in my eyesight when the detective spoke.

"What was your relationship to Lance Gregory?"

Rex stiffened. An odd look passed through his eyes before his face closed off. A swirl of emotions flowed through me.

"Lance? The body is Lance?" I asked. Lance's face when he showed me the photo of me as a toddler flashed through my mind. "How'd you know the body was Lance?"

The detective glanced at me. "That's what the ID in his pocket said, but we're waiting for a formal identification."

I mentally compared Lance to Rex. The clothing was similar. And had Lance been wearing Rex's watch? And why?

"You were seen arguing with Mr. Gregory in downtown."

"Yes, after I kicked him out of my shop." The impact of the words hit me as they left my mouth. Would the police think our argument was the prelude to me murdering Lance?

"Why?"

"His crew damaged my store when they were there overnight filming." I stared back at the detective. "I know you've been in Lazy Bones with a couple of kids. Do you remember the skeleton by the register? Stanley? They broke him in half and knocked over a couple of shelves, which damaged some books and smashed some glass items for sale. They even managed to break the glass of a picture frame. So it's not like I didn't have provocation before threatening to formally trespass them for the store."

"You must've been furious."

"Sounds like Lance's regular MO. He was always good at tearing things down," Rex said quietly beside me.

The detective's gaze swiveled to him. "What's that supposed to mean?"

"Lance tends to act without thinking through the consequences."

"Have you known him long?" Detective Whitlock studied Rex.

The detective was burlier than the writer but a few inches shorter and maybe a decade younger. I edged backward, not wanting to stand between them.

Rex finally nodded. "We were in the same grade here in Elyan Hollow, so I knew him growing up. I ran into him occasionally when I lived in Los Angeles, but I would call him an acquaintance."

Yet they'd left last night's reception at the same time. Something in Rex's words rankled me, but I couldn't parse through it because the detective turned to stare at me and said, "You must be furious with Lance and this, what did you call it, film crew?"

I made my tone sound measured, trying not to hint at the anger deep inside me. "I wasn't happy they damaged retail items before the biggest retail days on our calendar. But I'm working with their production company to get reimbursed for the damages. One of the crew members is assisting me."

"Just to clarify, Gregory was in your store officially? For a TV show, you said?"

"You know he's the host of that ghost-hunting show filming in town, right?"

"No, what's this about a show?"

I explained the basics of the show, as far as I knew. "The bookshop isn't the only place they've approached, so who knows what else they've done in town and who they could've offended."

"Have you heard other complaints?"

Rex broke in. "Is Bailey being arrested? Regardless, Bailey, you should talk to a lawyer before speaking more with the police."

Evelyn, the attorney renting the office space above the shop, walked in. I waved her over. "Actually, this is my lawyer." Sort of.

I stepped over to her and gave her a quick summary of what was happening. As we talked, more people entered, all reading their character sheets.

"I can help you for now, but I don't practice criminal law," Evelyn said. "If you need it, I'll get a recommendation for the right sort of lawyer."

Evelyn turned and looked toward Detective Whitlock. "Do you have any more questions for Bailey, Detective?"

"Where was she when the murder was committed?"

"Has the murder already happened? Where's the body?" one of the attendees asked. She was the co-owner of the local winery. She turned to Detective Whitlock. She pointed at the name tag on her chest. "Who are you? I'm Police Chief Charger of the local police. I'm clearly grizzled and on the verge of retirement. Oh! Look at your badge? Were we supposed to bring props?"

"No, you're not the police chief, and impersonating a police officer—" Detective Whitlock's voice was sharp.

"It's a game," I broke in. "This event is a murder mystery party, and this attendee is playing Detective Charger."

The real-life detective turned his gaze to me like he thought I was lying.

Surprise! I was telling the absolute truth. "Everyone here, except for the authors and people working, were given character names and backstories." I turned to the winery owner. "This is Detective Whitlock, who works for the actual Elyan Hollow Police Department."

"I'm the local district attorney!" Another attendee walked up. "I'm up for election, so I must schmooze everyone here. Who wants to donate to my election campaign for a drink token, wink wink."

Clearly, our attendees hadn't come because they had acting chops to exercise, although their enthusiasm was impressive. A few more people gathered around us.

"I'm a librarian! I'm very anti-censorship and think everyone should read whatever type of books they like," said a man who definitely was not one of Colby's coworkers, because I've met all of them.

"Detective Whitlock isn't part of the game, but Police Chief Charger here is, so you two should talk."

I ushered the attendees away from the actual detective investigating a real murder. I acted confident, like I had everything in control, even though I felt like the ground beneath me was shaky. Part of me noted that Colby had taken over my book table and was handing out the pre-order bags. She checked off a name, so hopefully, the book bags were going to the right people.

Evelyn followed alongside me. "According to your game, I'm the plucky owner of a nearby coffee cart who keeps sticking her nose into murder investigations. But I'll stay out of character until we have the police dealt with."

"What should I do now, Evelyn?" My body wasn't sure how to react. I still felt tired, but seeing Rex had brought on a second wind of energy that was starting to recede.

"You haven't done anything wrong, and nothing requires you to speak with the police. You did your civic duty, called nine-one-one, and gave the police your statement about finding the body. You can go on with your life. If the police ask you to visit the station, call me, and absolutely do not go with them unless they arrest you. Then, go quietly, don't answer any questions or say anything, period, and call me. Seriously, do not say a word except, 'I'd like to call my lawyer.'"

"That's more than a word."

Evelyn tilted her head slightly as she stared at me. "You take my point, right?"

"This is reassuring."

Evelyn half smiled at the sarcasm in my tone. "I'm giving it to you straight. And I know someone we can call on your behalf if you're arrested. She's a pit bull, adorable when she yawns and acts playful, but watch out when she growls. The local police won't know what bit them. But hopefully, it won't come to that."

"I did yell at Lance."

"I know. That's why I dropped down to your shop the other day. But you didn't threaten to kill him, and you were provoked. Besides, threatening to have someone formally trespassed is different than murder."

"I did tell Lance to stay out of my way, else he'd regret it," I said.

"Oh my, I've been poisoned!" a loud voice yelled in the center of the room, and a woman dramatically fell to the floor.

Detective Whitlock started to walk toward her. I stepped in his way. "That's part of the game. She's the murder victim for the party."

"This is ridiculous," the detective said.

Looks like the real-life detective wasn't going to sign up for a murder mystery party anytime soon.

Rex and Evelyn joined us. Rex subtly edged between me and the detective, not unlike Jack when he's not sure about the person I'm chatting with.

"Detective, I suspect a murder mystery party isn't the best place to interview witnesses and other upstanding community members," Evelyn said. "I'm sure there are more productive investigative paths you could be following right now."

The detective bristled at Evelyn's tone, and after a final glance at me, he said, "This isn't over, Ms. Briggs."

And he left.

Chapter 8

After the murder mystery party at the taproom, which included two dramatic Poirot-style denouncements that were wrong, followed by Melanie solving the puzzle to applause from the crowd, I felt a feeling of relief. The event had gone well. Multiple people told me they hoped Lazy Bones would throw regular murder mystery parties, which I said I'd consider.

"Just think of all the fun we could have with a Christmas holiday-themed party. Who killed Santa Claus?" the winery owner said.

"And who deserves a lump of coal in their stocking?" Her friend, who'd made one of the wrong denouncements, wanted another crack at solving a murder.

"Think of the fun we could have with murderous leprechauns for Saint Patrick's Day?"

Some attendees ordered more beers as the taproom opened to the general public, and Ash was grinning widely as she served them. "I'm game to throw another party if Bailey will spearhead it," she promised.

"We need to talk," Rex told me as I packed a few odds and ends into the foldable cart Danby had used to drag event supplies and books from the bookshop to the taproom.

All I wanted was to unload my gear, not talk to anyone, and go home to crash. Maybe when I woke up tomorrow, I'd discover this had all been a dream. Even though "it was all a dream" is the type of plot line I'd scoff at in a story. My voice sounded tired to me as I said, "Not now. I better see you at the Pastries & Panel event tomorrow morning in the Pumpkin Plaza. We can talk then."

"I'll be there."

Ash waved as I pulled my cart out of her shop and headed to Lazy Bones. Rex stood near the doorway, watching me. I turned away.

I dropped the cart off in the closed bookshop, which was clean and ready for tomorrow. I quickly unloaded the cart and loaded it with the boxes of books I'd need tomorrow morning, knowing that even though I just wanted to go home, it'd be better to take care of this now.

Despite the feeling of lead in my legs, I swung by the Pumpkin Plaza instead of taking the shortest route home. The first Saturday of the Halloween festival is always the annual "pumpkin"-lighting ceremony. Sunset is at about six thirty, when the ceremony starts, even though it's not fully dark. Children under twelve bring the carved pumpkins they want to enter in the pumpkin-carving contest. They all light the pumpkins as a group, with parental supervision. Then, at 7:30 p.m., the twelve-to-eighteen crew bring in their offerings, with the adults bringing theirs at 8:00 p.m. The judges photograph the pumpkins, and photos of the winners show up in the Chamber of Commerce office downtown. They're also published in the local paper and announced on social media.

I snapped a few pumpkin photos to upload to the shop's social media accounts while tagging the festival. I'm always impressed by the creativity of the teens and adults and the charm of the pumpkins carved by kids. I almost entered my headless horsemen entry last year. But I displayed it at the Sleepy Hollow instead, where Marion used it in multiple Halloween posts. I especially appreciated her photo of it partaking in the daily wine and cheese hour.

The blue-ribbon winner for adults this year was incredible. The artist re-created most of *The Starry Night* but replaced the building with a ghost.

When I caught sight of my grandfather, who was looking at the children's pumpkins with Jack beside him, a feeling of relief flowed through me. He looked the same as always, with his green-plaid flat cap covering his white hair, and a battered waxed canvas jacket that I'm pretty sure is older than I am. The only thing missing from the image was my grandmother, and I felt one of the pangs of loss that always hit me when I thought of her. When I clocked who was standing with him, I almost swerved away, but my grandfather saw me and smiled.

"Bailey!" My grandfather motioned me over.

"Hey, Captain."

Jack danced in place when he saw me, his front paws flailing a few times, then settled against my side. Even though I should've walked straight home, Jack's presence made me feel calmer. At least he always thinks the best of me.

Hudson glanced over, and I had the feeling I was interrupting something.

"That's my daughter's," Hudson said, and motioned at a pumpkin with a classic smile with one tooth. It was way too steady to have been carved by a four-year-old, so he or, more likely, his equally type-A wife helped.

"It's nice." I didn't say I preferred the charm of the misshapen carving next to it, which was clearly done by just a child.

"How'd the murder mystery party go?" my grandfather asked.

"It was excellent. The attendees enthusiastically embraced their roles and seemed to have a great time. I've had requests to hold more parties like it," I said.

"I heard there was some sort of accident in the hay bale maze today," Hudson said. "It's good it didn't get in the way of your little festival."

"About that . . ." I told them about finding the body.

"Are you okay?" Hudson asked with genuine concern in his voice. The side of him I'd adored as a child peeked out. The part of Hudson that, until he'd hit high school, had been happy to play board games or go for a bike ride with me. Before he'd starting worrying about his image. I wasn't entirely sure how my practical grandparents, who'd happily driven the same car for over twenty years because it still worked, had produced a son who valued the outward signs of success, like his ever-changing leased luxury car.

Yet Hudson had moved back to Elyan Hollow, so maybe I was reading him wrong.

"Yeah, but I'm exhausted," I said.

"Good job powering through this today," my grandfather said.

Jack leaned harder against my leg like he was trying to reassure me, too.

"Lance would've been in school with my mother," I said.

"Hmm, he was, I think," my grandfather said. He glanced at Hudson, then back at me. "I feel like there's something I should know about him. Your grandmother would know what I'm trying to remember. There was something about Lance. He might have been the kid that was bullied? Or am I mixing him up with someone else?"

"Do you mean the one who had his nose broken and needed plastic surgery to fix it?" Hudson asked.

"Maybe."

If my uncle was right, you couldn't tell now that Lance had broken his nose. It'd been straight, almost too perfect. But he'd a nearly too-flawless, almost generic handsomeness to him.

But it shows you can't always tell someone's past from their exterior.

My grandfather walked home with Jack and me while Hudson went to talk to a few friends he'd spotted. My thoughts were whirling as we walked through the neighborhood streets of Elyan Hollow. Everyone's porch lights were on, and at the minimum, lit pumpkins sat on the front stoop of every house.

It was the formal pumpkin-lighting night, after all. Everyone in the neighborhoods surrounding downtown would have jack-o'-lanterns on their porches from now through Halloween.

But my mind kept going back to the horror from earlier today.

I'd been so sure the victim was Rex.

But one question kept pinging at me: Why now?

At least I was home. And the flickering lights of the pumpkins I'd carved were beacons in the night, as all shone with electric candles as we climbed the steps up to the wide front porch.

"Do you need anything?" my grandfather asked as we entered the house.

"No, I'm ready to drop."

I headed to the stairs to the upstairs bedrooms with Jack at my heels while my grandfather headed toward the back patio. He has an outdoor reading nook, and I frequently find him there at all hours.

I still used my childhood bedroom. Although I turned it into a lounge slash studio space and moved my bed into the room next to it, which had an attached bathroom instead of sharing the hall bath. The smallest room on the floor was a guest room. My grandfather was still installed in the same primary bedroom suite he'd been in my whole life, which had a private seating area and a large bathroom. The finished attic has a couch and a second guest bed tucked under the sloped ceiling, and it's a great spot to read in the winter.

Hudson was right; this was an awfully big house for my grandfather these days, even with me in residence. Someday, my grandfather might prefer a one-story ranch with a smaller yard to maintain. Or even a condo.

But we were comfortable. And importantly, my grandfather wasn't ready to make any changes. And I was there if he needed someone around.

However, if I was arrested for a murder I didn't commit, that would force a momentous change on all of us.

Jack was sacked out on his bed when I was done in the bathroom. I should have headed to dreamland. Instead, I crawled into bed with my laptop. My body was tired, but my mind was still whirling.

Between a web search and the library's online portal to news archives, I found some early career articles about Rex. He'd been young when his first book came out, only twenty-four, and one of the horror magazines had devoted a lengthy feature on him and his debut novel.

"I wrote the first draft of *Brothers of the Forgotten Castle* between my sophomore and junior years at Berkeley. I spent the next six months revising it while studying, and signed with my agent during my final semester before graduating," the article quoted Rex. "I'd expected the process of finding an agent to take ages, but everything fell into place like destiny."

I scanned a few more articles about Rex but didn't discover much. He'd kept his private life in the background, although I did see a snippet about him marrying a Hollywood screenwriter. When I searched her name, I found her active social media presence, which included recent lovey-dovey photos of a man who most definitely was not Rex.

Divorced, most likely. It looked like she had a steady career as a staff writer on TV shows, which didn't tell me anything about Rex.

I sent Rex a quick email reminding him we needed to schedule a time for him to sign stock at the store, then went back to my web browser.

When I searched Lance's name, the same headshot and thumbnail images of his Hollywood career showed up from the last time I searched. I'm a bookseller in a small town, but something told me Lance's career wasn't overly impressive. Although it had been somewhat steady, which had to be a sign of success. Based on my experience watching shows like *Barry*, many people don't get as far professionally as Lance. But was one to two single guest appearances per year on TV shows enough to live on? Had his recent step into hosting become a more stable career? Had he still been looking for his big break? One that now most definitely would never come.

Lance showing me the photo of me as a toddler kept flickering in my mind.

I almost texted my mother and asked the question that kept flitting around my mind, but I couldn't bring myself to put the words down in any permanent form.

Was Lance my father?

Chapter 9

Sunday morning. I usually sleep in as long as Jack will let me on Sundays, with my goal to have a lazy day, but not today.

Today was the final day of the festival. The first thing on the schedule was the "Pastries & Panel" event at the Pumpkin Plaza, with donated baked goods and carafes of coffee and tea provided by Wicked Treats and the Walking Bread. Once the panel was over, Rex and Tariq were done. Danby was scheduled to drive Tariq and his wife to Portland, where she'd pass them off to the youth librarian from The Dalles, a town in the desert side of the Columbia River Gorge, where he'd do a school visit before flying home.

Two hours after the panel, Wine Ghouls was hosting a lunchtime cheese and wine tasting, with Melanie as guest of honor. The shop is owned by the local Elyan Dreams Wines, and they get excellent reviews for their wines, and they'd worked with Ghostly Gouda to find the perfect pairings.

Continuing with the festival after Lance's death still felt awkward, even if he'd had nothing to do with the event. But I still found myself walking downtown, ready to keep trucking on.

Despite what he'd said, was it just a chance that Lance and the film crew had been in town at the exact same time Rex made his triumphant return home? I stopped on the sidewalk. Had Lance's arrival been part of a plan that backfired, leading to his death?

Had seeing Rex been a coincidence? Or had Lance followed Rex here? Or the reverse? Despite repeat offers, Rex had avoided local events, even though my grandfather had used the bookstore's resources to offer to host a bookstore signing for years, always leading Rex's publicist to graciously decline.

Rex had also turned down a distinguished alumni award from the high school a few years ago.

So why now?

Or had Rex known Lance would be in town and that's why he decided to come?

Or was it all chance?

Instead of heading straight to the store, since I had an extra forty minutes, I headed to the Sleepy Hollow Inn and paused on the porch. The inn is a few blocks down from the marina along the waterfront and faces the Columbia. I watched a barge navigate the river for a moment, heading to the heart of the river on the other side of Bardsey Island from town.

The cove in town is protected by the island, and I felt like Elyan Hollow had been sheltered from crimes of the outer world . . . until yesterday when Lance died.

Marion was in the front room of the B&B as I entered.

"How are you? I heard about yesterday," Marion said. She gave me a hug.

"It's hard to believe that really happened," I said.

She studied me for a moment. "Do you need a day to decompress?"

"No, I want to see the festival through." I needed a bit of normalcy, which, amusingly, was a festival that was anything but my ordinary weekend.

"Do you need breakfast?"

"I could handle a cup of tea."

Marion sent me into the dining room, where Melanie and both of the Ehsans were sitting at a table, all sitting by mostly empty plates. Based on the remnants, it was Spanish omelet day at the B&B, along with their usual seasonal fruit salad and other usual fare.

"Bailey, come join us!" Melanie waved me over.

"How are you today?" I asked.

Melanie grinned. "Ready to rock the panel, of course."

After adding hot water to a mug, I snagged a bag of Rose City Genmaicha green tea from the selection on the table and sat down with two of my writers.

The third, wayward writer wasn't in sight.

"The mystery party was such a great idea. It was the most fun I've ever had at a book event," Melanie said.

"She says that because she solved the murder," Tariq said.

As we chatted, it felt like Tariq and Melanie had known each other for their whole lives.

Tariq's wife looked at me. "Are you okay? Yesterday must've been rough."

I was starting to get tired of being asked that. "I'm fine. Hopefully, the police will figure out what happened quickly so we can all return to normal. So I'm focusing on what I can control, like ensuring today's panel goes off without a hitch."

"The best-laid plans of mice and men," Tariq said.

"I know perfect doesn't exist, but I want to ensure the attendees have a good time."

"What can we do to help?" Melanie asked.

"Just show up on time. And hopefully, Rex makes it. Although you two can clearly put on a good show without him. You saved me yesterday."

"I'll make sure Rex arrives on time," Melanie said. "I promise, even if I have to drag him there myself. It wasn't fair for all the readers who showed up yesterday to hear him. I was sad to miss him since I've always loved his books."

"Did he say why he didn't show?" Tariq asked.

I shook my head. "Just that he thought his event was today."

Melanie shook her head. "If his schedule is similar to the one you made for me, there's no excuse. Our obligations were clear."

"Definitely," Tariq agreed.

"Maybe I'll go check on Rex now," I said. I finished the last of my green tea. I went off to metaphorically gird my loins, which is an expression I've always remembered since someone in my high school English class misread it out loud as "lions."

I walked up to the Rip Van Winkle suite in the B&B, which is separate from the other rooms, with no shared walls between it and its closest neighbors, and overlooks the backyard. It's supposed to be so quiet that guests should feel like they could sleep for twenty years.

A voice said, "One moment!" to my knock. When Rex opened the door, he looked surprised to see me. He wore a navy blue button-down and jeans, but his hair was slightly damp with curly ends.

"I'm making sure you're ready for the panel," I said. I glanced behind him. I'd been in the suite before and knew it had a couch and coffee table in the main room and a desk, which now held a laptop and open notebook. The bedroom and bathroom were off the side.

"Yes, I'll definitely be there. And I'm planning to stay in town for a few days, so to answer your email, which I read a few minutes ago, I can sign at your store this afternoon and also drop by anytime during the week at your convenience."

"Can I get that in writing?" I asked.

Rex's chuckle was slightly sarcastic, but he said, "Come in; I'll email you."

He walked over to the desk and started typing on his laptop.

I glanced around. Rex was tidy; I'd seen guests who could somehow walk into a hotel room and make it look like a tornado destroyed it within half an hour. The notebook, fancy pen, closed binder on the coffee table, and novel caught my eye. One of the coffee cups was on a coaster next to the book. I took a closer look at the pen without being obvious.

It had to be a Montblanc 'cause of the star on the end of the cap. It was the same brand as his watch from the opening reception, although it wasn't one of the pen models I sometimes looked at and dreamed of buying. A glance from my spot near the door toward the bedroom didn't tell me much other than it looked like he'd made his bed. He'd used the in-room French press and kettle in the seating area, and it was neatly sitting on its tray on the bureau, still half-full. The laptop bag next to the desk was the same brand of messenger bag I use, and it looked broken in but cared for. And it had the brand's old logo, which they'd changed a few years ago.

"Done. I emailed you." Rex stood up from the desk.

I checked the work account on my phone, and Rex's email was there.

"Got it. Just remember to watch the time." Inspiration stuck. "Can you set an alarm on your watch to remind you?"

Rex shook his head. "When I flew here I had my watch but must've misplaced it. Hopefully, I'll find it since it was a gift from a dear friend."

Interesting. Had Lance stolen it? Or had Rex given it to him but didn't want to admit why?

"Do you need breakfast before the panel? It's Spanish omelet day, which is always a hit. We'll also have pastries at the event—"

"But I'll need to speak, and I don't want to spray crumbs over the audience. And I've always been a fan of Tortilla Española, so stopping by the breakfast downstairs sounds like my best bet."

"You have time." And it would give Melanie a chance to herd Rex to the event.

We walked out of his room and headed to the stairs. "Do you speak Spanish?" I asked.

"Enough to get by. Why?"

"Tortilla Española." I'm not an expert, but his accent sounded decent.

"I spent a few months in Spain a couple of years ago. Have you traveled? Or spent most of your time in Elyan Hollow?"

My back straightened. Was Rex accusing me of being a hick or something? "I haven't traveled as much as I'd like, but I did go on a backpacking trip through Italy and France after I graduated from college."

"What'd you study?" Rex asked.

But we'd reached the dining room, so I avoided his question. "Here you go. I better see you at the panel."

"Rex, come join us," Melanie called out. "Remember, Bailey, I'll ensure he arrives on time! Even if I have to drag him down the street by his ear."

I waved goodbye to everyone as Rex joined Melanie and Tariq and headed downtown.

As I walked to the bookshop, I felt relieved that Melanie had volunteered to usher Rex to the panel. I loved the visual image of petite Melanie dragging a much larger Rex by the ear through town.

The park and rec department was already setting up the plaza as I walked up, pulling my cart of books. They'd done an excellent job cleaning up after last night's pumpkin-lighting event. Nary a scrap of garbage in sight.

Setting up the book table felt automatic, and once again, I loved the contrast of the three different styles of books. Hopefully, I could hold a similar festival next year with an equally compelling trio of writers. While I didn't dream of this festival becoming the next San Diego Comic-Con, maybe it could be a well-respected genre festival with authors, and especially readers, clamoring to attend.

The platters from the Walking Breads and Wicked Treats looked drool-worthy, with a nice mix of sweet and savory, with a bonus tray of cookies from the same dedicated GF bakery that'd catered the event at the apothecary. Morning Broo provided several carafes of coffee along with cream, oat milk, sugar, and monk fruit sweetener.

Attendees trickled in, and with ten minutes to go a sight made me smile: Tariq and his wife walked up, followed by Melanie Wilde, who had her arm locked around Rex's elbow. Like he couldn't escape without having to carry her along with him.

"And here's the Pumpkin Plaza, just two blocks from the bookshop!" Melanie roared as she escorted Rex to the speakers' table in front of the growing crowd of attendees.

I wondered if she'd given him a steady stream of commentary describing the town as she'd led him to the event. The Ehsans were chatting with each other.

"That's hilarious," a voice said next to me.

Colby. She was eyeing Melanie and Rex, who marched arm in arm to the speakers' table.

I smiled. "All three speakers are here, so today is a win. What else can go wrong?"

"You spoke too soon," Colby said. "My boss just texted me, and she broke her foot. She's at the ER."

I felt like the world screeched to a stop with a loud record scratch. "You're joking."

Colby's boss was supposed to moderate today's panel.

"But I have good news. My boss emailed me the list of questions she developed for the talk. You're lucky she had the presence of mind to forward them. But I'd expect nothing less from the Automaton."

I could breathe again. "Your boss isn't that bad," I said automatically.

And I realized there was an obvious solution to this problem. I looked at my friend with my best big puppy dog eyes. "So we just need a poor sucker used to talking to groups to fill in."

Her gaze back at me was level. "That's right."

"I'll buy you a beer."

"No, you'll buy me dinner."

"Deal. This will make a change from herding children."

I led Colby to the speakers. "This is Colby Snow. She's one of our beloved local librarians and is filling as a moderator today," I explained quickly, and the writers took it in their stride.

At 10:00 a.m. exactly, I introduced the authors to the crowd, which had filled the plaza, with people standing around the edges.

"And now I'll hand things over to our moderator, Colby." I handed the microphone to my best friend and retreated to the book table.

Colby was the perfect moderator, asking questions without answering them herself and asking follow-ups that kept the focus on the panelists. During the Q&A, when a man started rambling on with his own answer to one of the questions asked midway through the panel, Colby smoothly cut him off and paraphrased his ramble to make it sound like a question. Rex was clearly trying not to laugh next to her.

"Thank you, everyone, for attending the inaugural Spooky Season Literary Festival. We hope to see you again next year for a weekend of literary thrills." The crowd applauded at Colby's final words.

A line quickly formed at the book table, along with signing lines for each author.

"It's been years since I saw Rex," one of the people in the book line said. I glanced her way. A woman about my mom's age. So, probably someone they'd gone to high school with.

"Were you friends with him?" the woman with her asked. She looked younger, maybe midthirties.

"No, he wasn't that warm of a guy, to be honest. He was polite. But I remember trying to talk to him once when we had a class together and he just gave me one-word answers."

"Did you know the murdered guy?"

"Oh yeah, Lance was a trip. Everyone loved Lance," the woman said.

I ran a credit card payment.

"Christmas is sorted!" said the customer. She walked away with a stack of books and got in the line for Tariq, although I knew she'd end up in all three lines given her purchases.

The woman who'd gone to school with Rex picked up two of Melanie's books. "I adore these so much," she said. She handed them over for me to scan.

The woman with her added, "They're so funny, but they also hit me in the feels."

"Will you get Melanie to come back when her next book is released?"

"Melanie knows she has a standing offer to come here for each new release. She's an Elyan Hollow favorite." And she knew she was invited to sign stock if she was in the area, but couldn't squeeze in an event.

"How do we find out when she'll be here next?" the woman who'd been in school with Rex asked.

I handed over a bookmark and pointed out our email address. "We send out a monthly newsletter with event announcements and post them over social media, too, so consider following us there."

The woman handed over her card. "I'm a social media consultant, and I grew up here and just moved back. I've always loved your shop, so let me know if you ever need an assessment. I'm happy to give you some tips for free if it means you'll keep bringing my favorite author to town."

I smiled and tucked the card into my pocket. "Thank you. I appreciate it."

They left to get into Melanie Wilde's line and I helped the next customers, who were buying a stack of Tariq's books.

Today's panel was successful, even if it differed from my plans.

Thankfully, Colby filling in was a good switch versus yesterday's chaos.

Chapter 10

Danby and Colby helped me load up the cart after the crowds had mostly left the Pumpkin Plaza. A few groups remained around the periphery, chatting. The bakeries convinced the last few people to take doggy bags of the remaining pastries home, and the park and rec department quickly cleared out the tables and chairs, leaving the plaza pristine, like we hadn't even been there.

Both Snow sisters offered to help me return the cart to the shop, but I waved them off. "I've got this."

They walked off in the direction of their family's cheese shop.

The shop had a few customers as I took the cart inside, unloaded some of the boxes of books, and added more of Melanie's titles, along with more Lazy Bones bookmarks and business cards. I took a moment to drink a water bottle, then headed to the wine-tasting room.

I was almost done, and even the harshest critic would have to admit the festival was a success.

The Elyan Hollow winery is just outside of town, and its branding is upscale, with only shades of pumpkin orange on its logo hinting at the town's Halloween focus. But they'd embraced the Halloween theme in Wine Ghouls, with tiny skulls and ravens on the wine barrels used as tables throughout the shop.

Melanie was early to the wine tasting, and she'd brought along the last of her swag, a mix of bookmarks and stickers. "I underestimated how many readers I'd meet," she said.

"Which is always a good problem to have," I said. I set up a table with Melanie's books for purchase, and she arranged her book swag next to it.

"Are you enjoying the festival? Any suggestions for next year?" I asked.

"It's been a blast. You could've assigned me another event or two, like a second event yesterday, in addition to my apothecary pop-up. Maybe one for aspiring writers? Or for teens who are aspiring writers or closet bookworms? Tariq, by the way, is a delight. Good call inviting him."

I folded my cart and stashed it under a table, and we both looked at the display.

"Looks good. Although I question how many people coming will buy books 'cause it feels like everyone in town already bought copies at my earlier events," Melanie said.

"It pays to be optimistic. And you can sign the unsold stock, and once I post on social media about it, I expect online orders will spike."

We chatted about social media and web sales for a moment.

"When we upped our social game, sales skyrocketed," I said.

"It's so nice that you get to talk about books you love. As an author, I struggle with being too self-involved and promo-ish. And I know that I'm way more likely to buy a book you write a review for than I am to buy a book based on a self-promo post, so it's a weird cycle," Melanie said.

"My inexpert advice is to keep being genuine," I said. "Readers like it."

The owners of the wine shop walked up and congratulated Melanie on solving the murder mystery at the party last night, which made me think of finding Lance, and the hopeful mood building inside me withered. But I made myself smile.

And thankfully, the wine store staff had everything ready to go on their side. The profits from the wine-tasting event were earmarked for the Tots Book Bank, and as the room filled, it was lovely to see the community coming out for the fundraiser. I sold a couple copies of Melanie's books, not as many at previous events, but enough to make me glad I'd set up shop. Especially since we also got a few pre-orders of her next book, out in six months, that I ran through my shop's system from the tasting room.

Then, I heard something that made me pause.

"Didn't Lance's parents move not long after he graduated high school?" someone said behind me. I tried to look busy as I listened in.

"Yeah, he was their youngest, so when he graduated, they were the happiest empty nesters I'd ever seen. They sold their house within a year. It was one of those oversized Victorians on Branch Street, so it was way too big for his parents. It's now the Haunted House B&B. They moved down to Medford, I think, once he retired from managing the paper mill."

The Haunted House B&B? The one I'd seen Lance leaving?

If Lance's father had managed the paper mill, which was owned by a large timber company, his family must've been affluent, at least for Elyan Hollow. Their house was in an upscale section of town. Although I didn't know if it had been as swanky over twenty-five years ago, back when we'd been a small port and timber town on the Columbia River. Before we'd become Halloween central.

And if the first thing his parents had done was sell their home once he graduated, there might've been practical reasons for Lance to not come back to Elyan Hollow. He could've visited his parents and family for the major holidays, just at their new home.

"What happened to Lance's older siblings? There was what, five of them?"

"Yep, all sisters, except for Lance. Last I heard, the twins opened one of the farms where people order boxes of vegetables—"

"A CSA?"

"That sounds right. They're somewhere out in the countryside, growing vegetables. One of Lance's sisters went in the military, and I have no idea where the other two ended up."

"The parents sure were proud of Lance."

"They thought the sun rose and shone out of his—"

"No swearing in public," another voice said.

So the man said, "They thought Lance could do no wrong. He was high-spirited; I'll give them that. But I won't be surprised if all of his sisters did better in life. One of them—I can't remember her name—was darn sharp."

Someone walked up to me to buy a book. When I finished the transaction, the people I'd been eavesdropping on gossiped about the new café opening downtown.

"It's nice to see some of our kids move back to town and open businesses. I remember when we feared the town would decay, and now it's getting more vibrant by the day."

"I thought you hated the Halloween theme."

"It's goofy, but it's worked."

Rex half smiled at me as he walked up like he was slightly scared of me.

And I blinked. Rex wasn't scheduled to be here.

"You know, I don't think we had any sort of wine bars in town when I lived here. But the Oregon wine industry was just starting to take off then." Rex glanced over at the bar, where a group of attendees were getting the next samples of their wine flight.

"Wine Ghouls opened two years ago, although the winery is older." I realized Rex wasn't holding a wineglass. Had he snuck into the event?

"If it isn't Rex Abbot." One of the older men who'd gossiped about Lance walked up. "It's been years. You won't remember me, but my twins were a year ahead of you."

"How are you doing," Rex said as they shook hands. We quickly collected a handful of people my grandfather's age or slightly older.

"Are you back in town long?" a woman asked.

"For a few days. I'm still figuring out my exact plans." Rex looked stiff, like he was trying to be friendly but wasn't comfortable. I could relate.

"You're in LA these days?" the man asked.

"I was, but I sold my condo over a year ago. I've been house-sitting for a friend near SF, but they're returning home from an extended assignment abroad, so I'm figuring out my next steps."

"SF?" someone asked.

"Sorry. San Francisco."

"If you need a real estate agent . . ."

I tuned them out when a reader walked up. She scanned the books.

"Don't you have any of Rex's books?" she asked.

"I'm sorry. This event is for Melanie, so I only brought her books. I would've brought some of Rex's if I'd known he'd be our surprise guest." I glanced at the writer, wondering why he'd shown up. Maybe Melanie had made an impression on him while she dragged him from the Sleepy Hollow Inn to downtown?

"I'll be at Lazy Bones to sign books this afternoon," Rex said, startling me and the reader.

She blushed like she was unexpectedly talking to one of her idols.

"We agreed on three o'clock, correct, Bailey?" Rex said.

I nodded. "Yep. I'll head to the shop, and we'll be ready for you to sign."

"I can't wait!" the woman squeaked, and then practically ran across the shop for a sample of life-fortifying Pinot Noir.

"Rex, we need to talk more, but the wife is motioning to me like she needs something," the man said. "The wife likes books like this, but I'm more of a nonfiction reader."

He walked away.

The wife? It made me want to roll my eyes.

"The twins that guy mentioned? They were nightmares," Rex muttered to me. "But maybe they grew up."

"Or they're just older nightmares," I said. "Were you friends with Lance?"

"Friends? Sort of. You know the people in your social circle, but you never try to spend time with them one-on-one? That was always Lance and me." Rex bit his lip, then said, "Although I was shocked to hear about his death, of course. I didn't expect it."

Yet they'd been close enough to leave the Friday night reception together.

"Bailey, can you take a photo for me?" Melanie asked.

So I walked over to take a photo of Melanie surrounded by a group of women, all holding copies of her books. The man with "the wife" looked on with a patronizing smile, which made me wonder if some of the attendees were treating this as a see-and-be-seen event rather than a literary celebration.

Which might be a good sign for the future. As long as most of the people came because they loved the authors in attendance or wanted to learn more about them.

After I handed Melanie her phone back, I noted a new person walking into the wine tasting.

Taylor.

She saw me and held up her torn ticket. The first half had gotten her in the door, and she could redeem the rest for a tasting flight or a single glass of wine.

"I am dying for a glass of Pinot," Taylor said.

I flinched at her words.

Taylor half turned away from me. "You have no idea how hard these past few weeks have been, and Lance's death has caused utter chaos in my life."

The callousness of her words made me blink. My voice went lower as I said, "Can't you at least pretend to be sorry he's dead?"

"You have no idea what my life was like while working with Lance," Taylor said. "I'm going to go get that wine I paid for."

She flounced off.

As I looked around the wine-tasting event, I thought it was what

I'd hoped for when I put together the festival. I should be operating on the equivalent of a runner's high today, with everything having worked out despite a few hiccups. Once this event was over, the festival was done.

Despite the hiccups along the way, it'd been a success.

But I still felt like the sword of Damocles was above, ready to descend at any moment.

Chapter 11

After a successful wine-tasting event that felt like the perfect sendoff to the festival, I repacked my cart, now half-full of signed Melanie Wilde books, and scurried back to the bookshop.

Hopefully, my social media blast about Rex's impromptu afternoon signing at the shop would catch the attention of festival attendees who'd missed the morning panel at the Pumpkin Plaza.

My usual weekend employees, Tara and Milo, worked the shop as I dragged the cart in. They'd done the opening tasks for our regular noon opening, and a handful of customers were browsing.

"I've set the signing table up here. Is that okay?" Milo asked. He motioned to a table near the Crime in Store section.

"Perfect." It was the same spot we set up signings after in-store events. Although I'd started holding the events in Ash's taproom when we expected a large crowd.

After I shoved the cart into the back room, Milo and I finished setting the table up, adding a seasonal tablecloth, this time with an orange-and-black haunted-cemetery vibe. I added a cup of thin Sharpies, which Rex's publicist had requested we have on hand for his signings. After pulling a loaded library cart of Rex's books next to the table, we were ready to rock and roll.

Provided Rex showed up.

"So, did Abbot have a good reason for not showing yesterday?" Tara asked me.

"He said he thought his event was today versus yesterday." Did I believe Rex's excuse? I still needed to figure it out. The only thing I'd decided was that I simply didn't trust him.

And I really hoped he showed up today. Otherwise, he'd make our shop look even more unprofessional than we already did.

Since we had half an hour, I ran out to Morning Broo to get drinks for all of us, which I was paying for out of our petty change. One of the perks of being the boss is treating your hardworking staff occasionally.

"Bailey!" Olivia from Boorito was ahead of me when I joined the three-person line in the coffee shop.

"Hi, Olivia."

She linked arms with me. "You didn't tell me about all of the excitement yesterday. No wonder you looked so sad at the beginning of the mystery party. I just thought you were stressing yourself out again for no reason." Olivia's look my way was sympathetic. Someone entered and stood behind me in line.

"I can't believe someone was murdered in Elyan Hollow," Olivia said.

The woman in front of Olivia turned. "I heard it was a mob hit. The guy who died got on the wrong side of some Hollywood big shot with a super sketchy past, and he ordered the dead guy to be taken out."

"I doubt it," I said. We all took a step forward in line, with Olivia still alongside me. But if mob rumors were going around town, it could be time to set up a bookshop display revolving around Mario Puzo's *The Godfather* and similar crime fiction.

"No, I heard it from my sister, and she's friends with one of the police officers' wives, so it has to be true," the woman insisted.

A man sitting at the table closest to the line said, "I heard he got into a screaming fight with one of the store owners downtown."

Olivia laughed. "Yes, he fought with Bailey here, but there's no way she topped him in the maze."

Everyone stopped and looked at me. "I didn't touch Lance."

A deep voice behind me said, "It seems unfair to speculate."

Rex.

He looked at me. "I have time to get a coffee before the event at your shop, right?"

I nodded. "Plenty of time. I'm actually getting pregame coffees for my staff."

After I gave the barista my order, Rex said, "Let me buy the drinks for your shop."

"Instead, let me buy yours. We usually buy a coffee for our guests."

"Let this be a small act of atonement for not showing up at the right event yesterday," Rex said. He turned to the barista. "What are your pour-over options?"

While Rex and the barista discussed the shop's selection of beans, and Rex ordered a quad shot sixteen-ounce Americano instead, I could see a couple of locals whispering about me.

Or maybe they were talking about Rex.

But I suspected they were talking about the likelihood of me murdering Lance.

We had a line out the door for Rex's signing, although the crowd wound down after an hour. Multiple people had asked me to take photos of them with Rex, and he'd diligently posed with a slightly stiff smile.

He'd surprised me by asking the last customer in line to take a photo of me and him by the festival display in Lazy Bones.

"My publicist asked me to get a photo to send to *Publishers Weekly*. So check their newsletter next week," Rex said.

He sat back down, and I set him up to sign the rest of his books we had in stock.

"We have more on order, and I wish they'd arrive so you could sign them," I said. Signed copies are always popular with our customers.

Tara appeared at my shoulder. "Milo and I can handle the rest of today if you want to take off. You deserve a break. Maybe a nice nap."

I laughed and, a few minutes later, left, knowing my staff would put a few of the signed copies for sale in the shop and carefully store the rest in the back.

I realized I was free.

I should start the wrap-up work from the festival, like sending out emails to the apothecary, taproom, and winery. I should run the financials from the events, even though I'd be shocked if we hadn't turned a healthy profit.

But I needed to take an hour to myself. So I rushed home, packed my sketchbook and pencils into my bag, slid treats for Jack into my pocket, and walked to my favorite spot along the river path not too far from the marina, maybe half a mile downriver. But it always feels like a world away. I climbed up the embankment to a rocky outcropping, to my favorite spot overlooking the river. If people passed by on the trail that continued for about a mile until it climbed up to a small parking lot, they would only see me if they looked at the exact right spot.

Jack sprawled on his side next to me, indifferent to the view of the barges emerging from the tip of Bardsey Island in front of us. A small wild area of tall trees separated us from a neighborhood of established homes.

I cracked open my sketchbook. I'd been working on a story idea for a few months but was too mentally exhausted to focus. Instead, I sketched a few thoughts from the festival. Melanie with her Celtic-inspired jewelry. Tariq discussing baseball with a four-year-old in a Cubs jersey.

I hadn't been there long when Marion texted me, and after I sent a quick response back I sketched a figure with a pumpkin head walking down Main Street.

Like Lance when I'd found him. Was there a reason for the

pumpkin? Or was Lance the unfortunate victim of someone suffering a mental break?

Rustling in the trees behind me caused me to tense up. Next to me, Jack lifted his head but didn't bother getting up.

Rex stepped out of the trees. His eyes widened when he saw me, and his mouth briefly opened like he was going to say something.

I held my sketchbook to my chest.

Rex spoke. "I'm impressed this spot still exists. I used to come here to read."

"Yep, it's clearly still here." My words felt even more awkward than usual.

"I remember sitting here, dreaming about becoming an author like the books I read," Rex said. He gazed out at the river.

"You mentioned you were in school with Lance," I said. "Do you know if he and my mother were friends?"

Rex's eyes stayed on the horizon. "I'm not sure anyone was truly friends with Lance."

I slid my sketchbook back into my bag and added my pen case and water bottle. "We need to get going," I said.

With Jack at my side, I walked back into the real world.

At about seven, I left Jack at home and went to my final errand of the day. Marion was waiting for me on the front porch of the Sleepy Hollow B&B. "You sure you're up for this?" she asked.

"Of course."

We walked up to the third floor, to the Irving Nook, which Lance had rented. The police had already visited and said it was cleared, so I'd agreed to help Marion pack Lance's belongings for his next of kin. She wanted a second person on hand as a witness, and ideally, one who didn't work for the inn.

The Irving Nook was smaller than the suite we'd rented for Rex for the festival. But it was comfortable. The brass bed frame of the queen bed looked retro chic, and the orange-and-black Pendleton blanket gave it a Western classic meets Halloween vibe. The wing-back chair in the nook under the dormer window looked perfect for reading, and an antique dresser held a stocked coffee-and-tea tray complete with kettle and French press. Three jars of locally ground coffee beans waited, never to be brewed. Lance had left a stack of books and a cheap pen on the desk, but that was about it.

"Did Housekeeping service the room on the day Lance died?" I asked. The bed looked pristine.

"Sadly, yes. My poor cleaner was terrified to talk with the police. But she rallied, and thankfully, the detective who talked to her was gentle."

"Did she say if anything was out of the ordinary?"

"No, she just made the bed. Lance left towels on the floor, so she replaced them." Like many inns, the Sleepy Hollow had discreet signs in the bathroom that told guests if they left their towels on the floor they'd be replaced while encouraging the guests to hang towels to signal their willingness to reuse them.

"Give me a minute to take the photos," I said. Marion stepped back into the doorway as I photographed the room, just in case Lance's family had questions or thought something was missing.

Lance's black roller bag was open on a luggage stand in the small closet. A handful of crisp button-down shirts in grays and black, along with a pair of jeans and a navy pair of khakis, were on hangers above the suitcase, along with a gray tweed sports coat. Two lightly scuffed brown oxfords were lined up beneath the luggage rack. He'd probably traveled with two pairs of shoes, these oxfords and the boots he wore when he was found.

What would it be like living out of a carry-on-sized suitcase for a few months? I'd had an extended backpacking trip in Europe once, but I'd lived in merino T-shirts, my favorite cardigan, and jeans. I hadn't needed to dress up or be on camera.

His navy-blue toiletry bag hung from a hook in the bathroom, and he'd left a toothbrush and electric razor next to the sink.

Nothing felt surprising or unexpected. He'd traveled light. All of it was all signs that Lance had been going about his day, planning to return to his room at the end of the day.

And nothing in here seemed to be as expensive as the watch he'd been wearing when he died. His suitcase was a basic black roller bag that looked battered, like it was often used.

Marion pulled the suitcase out and moved it onto the bed. It opened like a clamshell, and I photographed the pile of packing cubes inside. One of his packing cubes was held together with duct tape. Together, we folded the clothing from the closet, and as Marion packed it into a cube, I snooped through the others.

The duct-taped cube was boring and full of socks and boxers, neither of which I wanted to handle. But I checked, and nothing was hidden inside. Another cube held basic T-shirts in charcoal and navy, like the one I'd seen Lance wearing in the taproom. A thin black wool sweater rounded out his clothing.

I paused and touched the bottom of the bag, which shifted. I stacked the packing cubes on the bag and pulled on the bottom, which came up. It was a thin sheet of plastic the size of the bag, and I wondered if Lance had added it or if it'd come as part of the suitcase.

There was an expanding file folder below it, and I pulled it out.

"What's that?" Marion asked as I unwound the string from the button on the side to open the folder.

There were six sections inside, and the first was a series of printouts of buildings in an old mining town in Colorado. Sticky notes attached to the pages made me think this was Lance's research file for the filming sites. He'd made extensive notes of local legends.

Section two was full of printouts and notes about an old Edwardian seaport in Washington, about a four-hour drive away. My grandmother had taken me there once, and I had a fond memory of drinking a giant strawberry ice cream soda and walking along the pier in Port Townsend.

But the third section made me gasp.

"Is that Taylor?" Marion asked.

"I think so." I felt slightly sick and quickly flipped to the next page. Lance had photos of Taylor kissing a man I didn't know. They were standing outside of what looked to be a motel room. The time stamp on the final photo showed the man walking away from the motel room several hours later. He looked like he was in his mid-, maybe late, thirties, with sandy blond hair.

The last page was Taylor's résumé, which made me pause 'cause it felt like an odd juxtaposition.

Or maybe it paired perfectly.

Taylor's résumé told me a couple of things. One, she'd studied acting at university in LA.

And her only listed work experience was as an intern for a production company. But a handwritten scrawl to the side said: *Her parents?*

The second section had a packet about Bill and Jill, with the word "boring" scrawled on one of the résumés. They'd both worked steadily doing camera and sound work in the film industry.

The final section was almost empty.

It just had a color photocopy of the photo that Lance had shown me at the opening reception. Toddler me, reading in the bookstore.

"Why did Lance have that photo?" Marion asked.

"That's a question I want to answer," I said. I turned and looked at Marion. "You were close with my grandparents. Do you know who my father is?"

Marion brushed my shoulder with her hand as she said, "I honestly don't know."

"Do you have any suspicions?"

She rested her hand on my shoulder. "I wasn't close to your mother when she was a teen. I'd babysat her occasionally when she was small, but she, like most teens, was focused on her friends. And she was bound and determined to be class valedictorian. She didn't have time for chatting with her parents' friends."

This was just one example of my mother's focus, as she'd managed to hold on to her top spot in her class despite everything.

"When Liz told her parents she was pregnant, she refused to tell them who her father was. Which concerned your grandparents, but they didn't have any reasons to doubt her when she said everything was consensual. And she said it would be best if the boy wasn't involved."

"That's a big decision," I said.

Marion paused. "If Lance was your father—and I'm not about to claim he was—his parents wouldn't have been thrilled he'd become a teen parent. I saw them occasionally at parties and events, and they were proud of Lance. They saw him as an intelligent, high-spirited boy bound to conquer the world."

"I wonder what they think of his Hollywood career. And they must be devastated now." I couldn't imagine getting a phone call saying that your healthy, adult son was murdered. "Wait, you just said 'they saw him as.' Did you disagree?"

"Teens are complicated. You were fairly easygoing, but you had moments when it seemed easier to boot you into the river than get you through to a functional adulthood. Lance was a good athlete and popular, but there was always something about him I didn't trust. Seeing these files makes me think I was right."

"We should tell Detective Whitlock about the file folder," I said.

"He's going to be mad he missed it," Marion said.

"Unless someone snuck in here after he left? But why?"

Marion called the detective as I glanced around the room. A memory of seeing Lance in town flashed through my head. He'd had a black backpack that looked more professional than student. That type of bag usually has a laptop sleeve and is big enough to carry a jacket, notebook, and water bottle.

I checked under the bed and through all of the nooks and crannies of the room.

No bag.

And no laptop or tablet.

Or charging cords for a phone or any other electronic device.

Marion said, "I'll see you soon, Detective," and hung up her call.

She turned to me. "What's wrong?"

"Lance has to have owned a laptop, yes? Where is it?"

"We should assume the police took it," Marion said.

We finished packing the rest of Lance's things in two cardboard boxes, and I left to carry the first downstairs. Marion planned to double-check the corners of the room to ensure we hadn't missed anything.

"Is that Lance's stuff?"

I looked up to see Taylor blocking my access to the top of the stairs.

"Can you move out of my way, please? As you can see, I'm carrying this downstairs." I shifted my grip on the box.

"Lance had something of mine. Can I see if it's inside that?" Taylor didn't move.

"What do you think he had?"

"Just let me check."

Marion joined us in the hallway. "Is there a problem?"

"It sounds like Taylor wants to snoop through Lance's belongings," I said.

Taylor raised her hand to her forehead and leaned forward slightly. "We worked together, and I'm not sure what will happen now that he's gone."

Given the weepy tone in her voice, maybe Taylor had learned a few things while she studied for her theater degree.

"C'mon, let's get some tea downstairs," Marion said. She whispered, "Wait up here," to me. She escorted Taylor downstairs, and I returned to wait in the Irving Nook. It should feel warm and cozy, but now it felt full of ghosts.

Chapter 12

Just because the festival consumed my weekend didn't mean that the rest of my life had stopped. After my usual Monday morning run along the river with Colby, I'd gotten ready and headed into the shop with Jack at 8:00 a.m. I had an hour to prepare the shop to open. Jack collapsed on his bed for his morning nap while I rearranged the display by the register of festival books to highlight these were signed copies and removed the festival signage from the window.

I reminded myself that the festival had been successful, even if finding Lance would haunt my nightmares for years.

The first delivery of the day came a few minutes after 9:00 a.m. It included Halloween-related items for our monthly subscription boxes, including a big box from Stonefield Beach Teas. So I headed to the workroom, taking care to turn the monitor showing the in-store video feed so I could keep an eye on the front door in case anyone entered. Jack napped on his bed like a lazy security guard who would get up for pets but probably wouldn't notice shoplifters.

Today, I wanted to pack and prepare our Teas & Thrills book boxes. While these go out monthly, I made a special effort with the October boxes, ensuring the products that accompanied the books were seasonal. I added more October one-offs to our website, meaning people who weren't regular subscribers could purchase them, which always sold out.

This year, for the tea box, we had Pumpkin Chai and blood orange rooibos teas from Stonefield Beach, aka my favorite local tea maker based in North Portland. Plus a mix of locally made candies from Wicked Treats a few doors down from the bookshop, all packed into Halloween treat bags, plus a handmade glass pumpkin candleholder with an orange tea light, an illustrated postcard of a haunted house drawn by an artist we carried in the shop, and a couple of seasonal stickers. Plus, two hand-chosen thrillers I'd chosen, one of which was published last week and the other came out tomorrow, so it was in this week's rack of new releases to put out on Tuesday. I'd read advance copies of both books about six months ago and looked forward to hearing our readers' thoughts in our monthly (and totally optional) thriller book club.

Our Chaos & Coffee box would be similar, except with a pound of freshly roasted coffee from Morning Broo, a local coffee shop and micro-roastery that sold their retail packages under the more sedate name Elyan ORE Roasters, which should be hand-delivered to the shop this afternoon, alongside two-ounce bottles of pumpkin pie spice simple syrup. Subscribers for all of our boxes were promised two books and set minimum dollar amount of products. Our customers seemed to like the surprises inside, which didn't mean we didn't occasionally get a complaint email from someone who prefers a green tea harvested only during full moons on Tuesdays but received a fruity black tea when "that's not what I drink."

And once I was done with these, we'd need to compile two different mystery boxes, plus romance, horror, science fiction, fantasy, and "romantasy" boxes, aka fantasy romances. The romance-related boxes would have a "love potion" tea and "mystic forest" candles alongside the same candy bags. The horror boxes would get "ghost cemetery" candles. The mystery boxes received appropriate "mystery" candles with a solvable puzzle indicating the scent inside.

Mid-month, we'd send out a batch of classic boxes, meaning the same genres as above, but with books that'd been out for at least ten to fifteen years, if not longer.

My grandfather had been slightly skeptical when I'd started the subscription boxes. But they'd been an overwhelming success, and it was fun to see the ultimate destinations of each shipment, which included zip codes as far away as Hawaii and Maine along with states in-between, and even a person in British Columbia, Canada, willing to pay the international shipping rate despite being about a six-hour drive away.

Added bonus: our affiliated book clubs drew good numbers, with locals who subscribed to the boxes coming by to chat about the books. The book clubs frequently led to additional book sales since we gave attendees ten percent off during the official meetups. This offset the cost of snacks and lemonade; at least one attendee brought a bottle of wine to share, and some were starting to bring communal snacks. The more they drank, the more they wanted to buy books. Showing that book people are the best.

Midmorning, my metaphorical hackles raised.

Taylor, from the *Gone Ghouls* show, walked in. Her hair was pulled back into a bun instead of its usual blown-out style with curled ends. Her dark brown pantsuit was reminiscent of hard-hitting female politicians on the campaign trail. But something about Taylor felt inauthentic. Like she was playing a role.

I was gearing up to remind Taylor that she was banned from Lazy Bones when she spoke.

"Our showrunner asked me to come in," Taylor said. She sounded formal.

"Okay."

Taylor glanced back at the stack of boxes I was attaching labels to. "What's that?"

I stared at her. "You're here, why?"

"I was asked to come in and formally apologize on behalf of the show and to tell you that the production company will, of course, appropriately compensate you for the damages that occurred while filming here. Here's the card of our showrunner. Email the receipts and description of damages and he'll ensure everything is promptly taken care of."

Taylor paused, then said sarcastically, "Or rather, his executive assistant will. And I'd call first so she knows to look for your name when you send in the email."

"Not a fan of your showrunner?" Or his assistant. I taped up the "Lazy Bones Book Crate" box in preparation for adding a mailing label.

"He's okay. He secured the funding, and the show wouldn't exist without him," Taylor said.

Taylor tapped a quick staccato on the countertop. "But he doesn't pay as much attention as he should. I mean, he isn't on-site because he's battling cancer, so I get it. But he put Lance in charge. But it was clear to everyone that Lance was a has-been or, honestly, a never-was. Our show could make it to the big time with a better presence. Imagine someone younger, like mid-twenties, who understands the current world and what would be attractive to a hipper demographic. Someone who would look good trending on social media."

"Did you have someone in mind?" I wondered if Taylor heard the sarcasm in my voice.

"Everyone associated with the show knew who should've been the lead. Our showrunner admitted to me once that he found Lance's delusions of grandeur obnoxious. He should've hired me, but he tried to claim our financial backers were more comfortable with an older, more experienced lead. Especially since Lance had those attributes and was relatively cheap since it's not like he had other shows knocking down his door."

"Will the show go on without Lance?"

Taylor nodded. "Yes, yes, it will, although we're having an official virtual meeting later today to discuss exactly what will happen. I'm pretty sure we'll use the episodes with Lance, then do a retrospective episode and introduce the new host for our final episode of the season. It's actually a good opportunity for us. Lance's death might help us stand out. The ghost-hunting show where the lead was murdered? A gold mine."

The callous note in her tone made me feel cold like I needed to grab a cardigan. "You do remember your coworker died?" I asked.

"Yes, and I know I sound like a brat—"

I didn't interrupt to say I'd thought of a different *b* word.

"—but this is my career, and I didn't particularly like Lance. He was slimy, and if you think I'm opportunistic, I'm nothing compared to Lance. I'm pretty sure he got this role by blackmailing our showrunner, to be honest."

"Blackmail?"

"Lance wasn't opposed to it. He bragged about how it was leverage to get what he wanted. He wormed his way into a starring role in a TV pilot because he blackmailed the casting director. But the pilot wasn't picked up, and she left the industry, so nothing came of it." Taylor looked at me. "Lance could be charming, but he was also a snake, slithering around, looking for dirt."

That seemed unfair to snakes. The photos Lance had of Taylor kept popping up in my mind. "Did he bully you?"

"He tried to, but I was too strong for him to push around," Taylor said.

Something told me that wasn't the whole truth, but calling Taylor out for lying wouldn't help. "How'd you get a job on a show like this? Have you worked in the industry long?" The content of her résumé came to mind.

"I worked hard to get this, but it was partially luck." Taylor's smile transformed her face into a work of art. "I have a bachelor's in drama. I remained in contact with one of my professors. I babysat for her often, and she introduced me to our showrunner. I was lucky since I don't know many people in the business. I'm not exactly a nepo baby."

Nepo? Oh, nepotism baby. Which is a claim I can't make, as I inherited the family business. Granted, I was the only family member who wanted it and I'd worked hard to get the knowledge to operate it, but I couldn't claim to be self-made. But the barrier to working in, let alone running or starting, a bookstore felt different from Taylor's career.

"And honestly, our showrunner has always said he wants to get me in front of the camera. Fingers crossed, this is my chance."

Maybe when, or if, I got serious about publishing my graphic novel, I'd be as ruthless as Taylor.

But I doubted since most of the writers and illustrators I knew supported each other. Not that all get along, because they're all people with unique quirks and biases, but from what I'd seen, there was minimal backstabbing. Although I'm sure there's plenty of grumbling to trusted friends.

"Did you grow up in LA?" I asked.

Taylor nodded. "In Brentwood. My parents still live there, and it will be so relaxing to stay with them when we're done filming. I can't wait to spend an evening in the hot tub."

"What did your parents do? Were they in the film industry?"

"Tangentially. I don't like to talk about it."

"Did you ever find the lost item you were looking for yesterday?" I asked.

Taylor blinked. "Yeah, I had it all along. That Marion is nice, especially for someone who runs an inn."

Having Taylor around gave my jaw muscles a workout, with all of the unintentional clenchings to tamp down on releasing my true, unaltered thoughts. I only said, "You mean someone with a truly kind heart who has built a business centered around customer service?"

I didn't mention Marion's previous career as an art director for an internationally known ad agency based in Portland.

Taylor glanced away. "The inn is nice and better than the Haunted House dive Lance wanted me to book. You should've seen the fit Lance threw when he heard we'd gone with a different inn." She turned to me with an innocent look. "Did you see anything in Lance's room that the show might need?"

If Taylor had used this approach last night, she could've sweet-talked Marion and me into letting her scope out Lance's boxes.

"Not as far as I could tell. But if you know the show is missing, let Marion know, because we documented everything we packed from Lance's room."

Taylor pursed her lips together, then nodded. "I think that's all. Like I said, call the number on the card."

As Taylor left, I wondered about those photos again. How had Lance ended up with them? And who was the man? Was he connected to their show?

And where was Lance's laptop?

And did Taylor know Lance had the photos?

Since the shop was otherwise empty, I called the number on the card Taylor gave me.

After I got off the phone with the show's peppy executive assistant, I made a second call, which quickly went to voicemail.

I had an idea to explore.

Midmorning, thankfully, during a lull while I worked on our daily book order, Detective Whitlock showed up again. I texted Evelyn an SOS from behind the counter, where I'd been processing an online order.

As I texted, the detective stopped and studied the display of our festival authors. Jack stood up from his bed and ambled over. He leaned lightly against my leg.

"My kids loved the event at the library," the detective said. "They did the craft hour downtown, too."

Was he trying to get on my good side before twisting the knife and getting me to reveal all of my deep, dark secrets, like the time I parked next to the meter and, gasp, didn't pay and wasn't caught by parking enforcement, thereby cheating the city out of one whole dollar in parking fees?

I kept my tone even, like the detective's presence didn't make me want to kick him out and close the store for the day. "It was wonderful to see so many children at the events, both locals and kids from out of town."

The detective moved to the paranormal romance section. "My wife loves these, but I don't get it."

"It's a good thing she doesn't read for you, then," I said.

"That's true."

Evelyn walked into the shop. Her shiny black hair was pulled back into a ballerina bun, and she wore a dark purple fit and flare dress with silver buttons on the shoulders. The only thing that detracted from her lawyer-at-work persona was her bright red sneakers.

"So, what's going on down here?" Evelyn's tone was brisk, and her "I don't suffer fools willingly" vibe was fully displayed.

"I have a few more questions for Ms. Briggs." Detective Whitlock turned to face both of us. The intense professional mask on his face contrasted with the *Ice Planet Barbarians* novel he held.

Evelyn nodded at the book. "Interesting reading choice, Detective. I had you pegged as a nonfiction buff. Or maybe a podcast listener."

He glanced at the book and quickly stuffed it onto a shelf. "My wife's a fan. Back to the matter at hand: I would like Ms. Briggs to take me through her argument with Lance Gregory again."

"Are you trying to pin down a motive?" Evelyn's tone was even drier than before, which I wouldn't have thought possible. I'll have to bring her down next time we need a dehumidifier.

"I'm curious if Lance treated others as poorly while he was in town. I'd like to hear about his actions in Lazy Bones Books to see if it was a pattern," the detective said.

My internal BS meter said the detective was telling us a partial truth. Evelyn looked equally skeptical.

"Let me rephrase." The detective's tone switched into smooth but highly professional mode. "I'm more than aware it's possible Ms. Briggs is one of many locals who argued with Lance, and from other reports, she focused on threatening to have him banned from her store, which I admit is a long way from murder. So, I'm trying to figure out the victim's state of mind in the days leading up to his murder, and this is one of the few places where I can pinpoint his actions. I would like to note I appreciate Ms. Briggs handing over the file folders she found in Lance Gregory's room. Given the chain of custody issues, it most likely will not have any value in court, but it might help my investigation."

Evelyn glanced at me. I realized she wore tiny scales of justice silver earrings. "What's this?"

I explained about finding the folder in Lance's suitcase last night.

Evelyn stared at the detective. "You guys missed it?"

"Potentially. Or maybe someone hid it and put it back into Lance's suitcase when we were finished."

If the detective was right, that would have to be someone onsite. Like Taylor? Although if that file had come into my hands, I would've burned the photos of me.

Rex?

Could he have removed information about himself from the file and then returned it?

"So, if Ms. Briggs can walk me through what happened the morning the film crew was here and give me a sense of the damage, we can all go on our way."

Evelyn glanced up at the ceiling, then nodded at me. She said, "Keep it brief."

As I explained the knocked-over shelves and broken items, a customer came in, followed by a second.

Of course, the lull wouldn't last until I could finally usher the detective out of the door.

"Do you have signed copies of the newest Rex Abbot?" the first customer asked.

"Right over here," I said. Jack stayed beside me as I led them to the large display near the door with a large "signed copies" banner at the top.

"You have Melanie Wilde, too!" the customer said. Proving that no matter how diligently we advertise events, we'll never reach everyone.

When I returned to the detective and Evelyn, Jack sat between me and Detective Whitlock.

My erstwhile attorney said, "Is there anything else?"

"Colby Snow wasn't here the day of the bust-up with the TV crew?" the detective asked.

"I wouldn't call it a bust-up, and no, she wasn't here." Danby had witnessed it, but that wasn't his question.

"I heard you two are pretty close," the detective said.

"Is Bailey's friendship with the town's children librarian relevant, Detective?" Evelyn asked.

"It's just interesting that they found the body together."

What was the detective implying? That we'd killed Lance together?

"Detective, we were being nice and answering your questions. But now we're asking you to leave, and if you want to question her again, I better see a warrant."

Detective Whitlock's gaze back at Evelyn was level. "Thank you both for your time, and I'm sure we'll speak again soon."

The detective left, and the sick feeling in my stomach returned at full force. Would I even be a suspect if someone else had found Lance's body?

"Don't talk to him again without calling me," Evelyn said.

"Nice shoes," was my only reply.

Evelyn glanced at her feet. "Darn it, I forgot to switch to my work shoes. The heels that match this dress are totally boss, but I don't like walking to the office in them."

"Do things look bad for me?" I started to ask, but the customer on the hunt for signed books came up with a stack to buy.

"You scored today," I said. The customer had several books by Rex and Melanie, a local coffee cart mystery, three romances from the just-released table, and two fantasy hardbacks from Portland author Fonda Lee.

"I just saw the signs about the festival, and I'm bummed I missed it," the customer said. "But I was in Paris, so I can't exactly complain."

"That's . . . true?" I still felt like the world was shifting under my feet, and I was struggling to sound coherent. "Would you like a bag?"

"How about one of these tote bags!" The customer handed over one of our new shop tote bags, designed to look like books, with our name on the spine, and I scanned it, then packed their purchase inside.

"I have my TBR list for this week!" The customer walked jauntily as they left, and I wished I had even half of their pep.

When I looked around, Evelyn was gone.

Without answering my question.

Chapter 13

Right before lunchtime, Colby's mother, Tessa, walked in. Looking at her shows me what Colby will look like in thirty years. They have the same sturdy, muscular build, and streaks of gray have just started invading her mother's hair, showing up like salon highlights. Her T-shirt said TAKE IT CHEESY across the chest with the Ghostly Gouda store logo below.

"I brought something for you," Tessa said. She handed over a brown bag with handles with her cheese shop's logo stamped on the side.

"You didn't need to," I said. But I still dove into the bag to find a sandwich wrapped in butcher paper, a reusable container of apple slices, and a homemade chocolate chip cookie.

"I wanted to check in and see how everything is going. Colby told me about Saturday, but not before the gossip mill told me heaps of wrong information."

"What did you hear?"

"That you'd killed Lance in the hay bale maze in a continuation of the fight you'd had with him downtown," she said. Tessa clamped her lips together like she was trying not to smile. "The owner of the bakery saw the fight."

"Ouch."

"And someone else claimed you had a brief but torrid love affair with Lance and killed him when he threatened to leave you."

And that was gross on multiple levels. "Well, I've never killed anybody."

"Just broken a few hearts."

It was my turn to laugh. "Doubtful." My last two relationships, well, my only two real relationships, had fizzled out with a distinct lack of drama.

"Colby told me about how you were the one to realize something was wrong. She was going to walk right past it."

I didn't want to relive that moment. So I asked, "Did you know Lance?"

Tessa shook her head. "I don't think so. He must've graduated and left town a year or two before we moved to Elyan Hollow."

This reminded me that Tessa had grown up in a different part of Oregon. She'd once told me that the tribe she and her daughters were enrolled in had been stripped of their federal status in the 1950s but fought and got it back in 1983. She'd met her husband in college, and they'd eventually optioned their cheese shop when Colby was a toddler.

Our conversation took a brief lull until Tessa asked, "How's Danby doing in her internship?"

While I didn't doubt Tessa wanted to see how I was doing, I suspected she saw it as a great time to check in on her formerly wayward daughter.

"Danby's fantastic. She's a hard worker and dependable. She was a lifesaver during the festival."

At least Tessa and her husband didn't need to worry now. When Danby had done a few boneheaded things four years ago during her junior year in high school, Colby and her parents feared the incidents would follow Danby around for the rest of her life, tanking her future. Even though juvenile records are sealed and her social media prank gone wrong had been stupid and caused about twenty-thousand dollars in damages at the high school, it hadn't been vicious. Just misguided. The vandalism charge had led to Danby owing community service hours and needing to pay for damages, with the monetary award being waived for good behavior.

"I just want her to end up on a good path," Tessa said. "I don't even care what the path is, as long as she's happy and out of trouble."

"Something tells Danby will do great," I said.

"Fingers crossed."

We chatted for a few minutes; then Tessa left. I pulled out the sandwich—Brie with crisp green apples on ciabatta—and took a bite.

Perfection, with a slight note of Dijon mustard.

If only everything in life was as easy as a simple sandwich.

Tara joined me at noon, and I took Jack for a quick stroll. He followed me upstairs to my office when we came back. He diligently watched me eat the rest of the sandwich and cookie that Tessa had brought, then laid down when I started updating our daily order with our primary book distributor, although we have accounts with several.

Tara messaged me that she needed a second set of hands in the shop, so Jack and I headed downstairs to a sight that always warms my heart: multiple customers browsing for books, with a short line at the register.

"I can't believe I'm finally in Hamlet Bay. I just need to find a haunted hound," a teenage girl told her friend as they browsed the books about the film.

And I realized I was getting old since I wanted to ask them why they weren't in school.

Jack walked around the counter as if summoned, and the girl squealed when she saw him.

"Look! It's a ghost dog!" She and her friend fawned over Jack, who let them pet him and tell him he was the best boy ever. They took several photos with him before buying a few books and leaving to search for haunted hounds.

Just as we hit an afternoon lull, Bill from the ghost-hunting show came in, carrying a sturdy tote-like bag divided into sections, with tools sticking out of the top.

After saying hi, Bill held up his bag and said, "Hopefully, I can fix your skeleton."

I left the store in Tara's hands and took Bill back into the workroom. I retrieved the coffin-like box containing Stanley, and together we laid the skeleton pieces out on the table we use for assembling orders and unpacking boxes.

"This specialty glue is designed for plastics, and I hope it'll do the job," Bill said.

"Do you make repairs like this often?"

"I fixed my share of toys over the years for my nieces and nephews," Bill said. "Again, I'm so sorry about what happened."

"Was that normal?" I started packaging new online orders as Bill worked, taking time to carefully wrap the books I'd already pulled in Halloween-themed kraft paper.

Bill shook his head. "No, else I wouldn't be part of the show. Lance had been intense once we arrived in Elyan Hollow, almost feral."

"Why'd the show choose Elyan Hollow?" I asked.

"Well, given what happened, it's obviously cursed for the show," Bill said. "But that's a good question. From what I heard, Lance promised our showrunner that it would have a fantastic atmosphere for *Gone Ghouls*."

Bill aligned one of Stanley's legs and applied tape to the inside. Once it was arranged to his satisfaction, he used the glue.

The scent of adhesive filled the air. The sort of intense scent that I knew would quickly give me a headache.

"I suspected I should've done this outside," Bill said.

I opened the back alleyway door and the window on the far wall and turned on a couple of fans. The fresh air reduced the adhesive scent while Bill stood unmoving, holding the skeleton pieces together.

"Thanks for that, since I can't let go of this until the glue sets."

"Were you part of the first season of *Gone Ghouls*?" I asked as I returned to packaging orders. Most were for signed copies of writers from the lit fest, meaning our marketing, especially on social media, had worked.

"Yep, and it was such an easy season in comparison, even before the whirlwind of this past week." Bill moved on to the next piece of the skeleton.

I kept my voice casual. "What changed?"

"The biggest change is our showrunner is working remotely 'cause of cancer treatments and our production director quit in anger and some of their duties have fallen on Taylor's shoulders. She's trying hard, but Taylor is brand-new to the industry and doesn't want to admit she's in over her head. We should've postponed filming the show, especially when our production director split, since we needed more preparation time. The show has always been bare-bones, crew-wise, but this season has been especially rough."

"Did Taylor and Lance butt heads?"

"All of the time, especially since Taylor clearly wanted Lance's job," Bill said. "While Lance was good at what he did, at least he usually was. He truly was talented on screen. Not everyone has that magnetism."

"Do you know what changed when you came to town?"

"Jill and I have been debating that since we're trying to make sense of everything that happened. Lance wanted to seem like a big deal, like a star, and now that he was in his second season of a show, he thought it was the right time to return to his hometown. I think he was annoyed when someone else took most of the light of his triumphant return."

"Lance was jealous of Rex?" That made sense, maybe. Rex was well-known, at least in book circles.

"And something upset him a few days before he died, but I'm not sure what happened. Lance got even more intense, and he and Taylor argued like a pair of pubescent nitwits."

Taylor. She just felt untrustworthy to me. "Is it hard to get a job like Taylor's?"

"Do you want to become a production assistant?" He looked at me with raised eyebrows.

"I'm happy running my bookstore. But I'm always curious."

"I'm pretty sure Taylor networked herself into the show and sees it as the first stepping stone on her way to greater things. She wants to take over Lance's role. She will be disappointed since our show-runner texted me earlier that he found a replacement for our final stop in Shaniko. And it sounds like he might be sending a production director, which we could've used weeks ago. We could already be done filming, and maybe Lance would still be alive." Bill's voice held a note of genuine sorrow missing from my conversations with Taylor.

"What's the next step with your show? Do you start putting the clips together into a show?"

"Oh no, that's not my role. The footage goes to an editor next. Some shows have a team of editors, but we'll probably have one who will take the footage and turn it into about six episodes. Do you know the voice-over the show has? That will be recorded after the episodes are edited together."

"So you'll be done with the show after this?"

"Yes, after Shaniko. Have you been there?

I shook my head no.

"It's a ghost town in Central Oregon that will give us some interesting footage if everything goes right."

"Then you're done?"

"Yep, and Jill and I will have a few weeks off before shooting a travel show next, and hopefully, it'll be less dramatic than the scenery we're supposed to highlight."

As Bill tried to put Stanley back together, I packed a stack of orders and piled them into one of our outgoing mail bins. With the book boxes I'd done this morning, we had an extra-large shipment. The sort that boded well for this spooky season.

"I think I'm done," Bill said.

Stanley was back in one piece, and when I looked at the spot where one of his legs had been broken I couldn't even see the line.

"Maybe let him continue to dry overnight, just in case the adhesive needs more time to set," Bill said. "Although you can try to move him now if you need to since the glue is supposed to cure fairly quickly."

"Let's give Stanley the best chance of future life possible," I said. Even to myself, I sounded a tad ridiculous.

I made a DON'T TOUCH! DRYING SKELETON sign and left it beside Stanley as Bill packed up.

"Thanks for fixing Stanley," I said.

"I'm just glad I could try. I noticed it when I was buying a book last week, and it seemed like an important part of your shop. I couldn't fix the broken candleholders and still feel sick about that."

I escorted Bill out, thanking him again.

Something he said stuck with me.

If Lance had been jealous of Rex, that would be an incentive to attack Rex. But Lance was the one who died.

Unless Rex had just been defending himself? But if that was the case, why not call 911?

Chapter 14

The Haunted House B&B owner responded to my voicemail by texting me in the afternoon. Tara said she was fine watching the shop, so I left Jack with her and walked to a street near the Sleepy Hollow Inn without the river view.

What would it be like to walk up to your childhood home and find it turned into a small inn? The Haunted House is smaller than the Sleepy Hollow, with five suites in the main house and a former garage turned into a "carriage house" to the side. It doesn't look as upscale, but I approve of the decorations that leaned more toward silly than scary. I'd checked their websites, and their rooms are cheaper than Marion's B&B, with a simple continental breakfast of local pastries, yogurt, and cereal. The house on the right was a family home, while the one to the left, closest to Main Street, was a CPA firm.

Based on their photo in their website's "about" section, the owners were younger, most likely in their late thirties. Their site also said they'd bought the house to run as a B&B since their dream was to be innkeepers, although he was also a music therapist and she was a programmer.

The carved pumpkins on their front steps were classic, and I noted they'd put in a small open elevator to the side of the porch that would be useful for people in wheelchairs.

I sent a text as I walked up the stairs, and Fiona, one of the co-owners, met me at the front door with a round belly leading the way. Pregnant, I guessed, although I'd never ask since that's one major rule of life: never ask a woman if she's pregnant, even if you can see a baby is coming out.

Fiona immediately led me downstairs, so I only caught a glimpse of the cheerful Halloween decor upstairs. "We remodeled the basement to be a fully self-contained two-bedroom apartment."

"It must feel weird to live in a beautiful house—"

"But being stuck in the basement? Yeah, I know. But it's the best of both worlds, and I can make a mess in the kitchen without worrying guests will see it. And it's let me rent out the kitchen upstairs to a local baker who needs access to a commercial kitchen without needing to rent it full-time, so it's a win-win for both of us. Especially since they always leave it impeccably clean."

"Was that part of your remodel before opening?" The remodel was a guess on my part, but the little bit I'd seen looked fresh.

"Yeah, part of our business license was upgrading the kitchen to a commercial level, even though we don't currently use it other than renting it out."

She led me through the laundry room to a door. She unlocked it with a touch keypad and led me inside.

Their apartment had an open-concept living-dining room, with three doors opening, presumably to the bedrooms and a bathroom. Three guitars were mounted on the living area wall, and there was a rack with two keyboards and a few other instruments next to the couch. A bookshelf was overflowing with books, and I itched to inspect them. They'd forgone the Halloween theme from upstairs for a mix of modern and relaxed that felt comfortable and lived in.

And there wasn't a single Halloween-related decoration in sight.

"My office." She pointed to one of the doors. "I work from home, so I'm on double duty most days. But I'm pregnant, so we'll see how everything goes once the baby arrives. I might see if I can convert the small office upstairs from the reception to my full-time office. But I'm afraid I'd be too close to the action and can't see myself working without interruption."

"Plus, you'd have a baby with you, right?"

We briefly chatted about her nanny plans, and then she looked at me. "So, why'd you want to drop by?"

"I saw the ghost-hunting crew leave here the other day."

"You're the store that had major problems with them, right?"

"Yep, they destroyed half of my shop."

Fiona winced. "Horrible timing."

"You can say that again. I'm curious how your experience went with them."

"Well, they didn't destroy our place, but we only gave them access to our living room and dining room, and my husband kept them from going upstairs when they tried. One of our guests complained the film crew was noisy, and we had to give the guest a free night to calm them down."

"I'm glad they didn't damage anything."

Fiona paused. "For some reason, Lance really wanted to move one of our china hutches, but he couldn't because it's bolted to the wall in case we get an earthquake."

"Interesting."

"You know, I have security camera footage of them filming if you want it," she said.

And with her words, I realized I was a total and complete idiot since I, too, should have security camera footage of the film crew, in addition to the footage Bill had sent, which I'd quickly downloaded from the shared folder he'd linked me to and saved to my own personal cloud storage in case I needed it.

Fiona logged on to her laptop and sent me a link to the relevant footage.

"So what do you do for fun around here? I'm still figuring things out," Fiona said.

"Umm . . ." Should I invite her to our usual taproom meetups? Stand-up paddleboarding? "What sort of hobbies are you into? It'd help if I knew where we overlap."

"Well, I love to read and need to become a regular at your shop. When we first moved here, I was finishing up my master's, so I wasn't reading for fun and was pretty much working all the time. Now that I have more free time, well, until this baby arrives, I'd love to pick up a craft. Or at least meet more locals."

I told Fiona about the knit night, our monthly evening cleaning books for the Tots Book Bank, and our informal evenings at the taproom. "And if you're looking to volunteer, Colby always has ideas. They offer an after-school study club for teens, and if you're willing to help with tech, I bet there's something you could do."

"I love to encourage kids, especially girls, to go into STEM, and I bet I could brush up my high school math skills, too," Fiona said. I sent her Colby's info, which was all her public library info, like her professional email address. I made a mental note to text her about Fiona.

A while later, I said I should run, and Fiona needed to return to work.

"I could let you out the basement door unless you'd like me to show you the china hutch. The one Lance kept trying to move? From the video, it looked like one of his crew was telling him to stop. Although the girl, well, woman, but she was younger than the others, kept coming back to it, which was weird."

On our way out, Fiona motioned to an ornate china hutch against a wall of the entryway. It had been painted a glossy black, and the shelves had curved flare that looked hand carved. The bottom had closed doors with silver hardware. The top shelves were filled with local guidebooks and hiking guides, along with a collection of brochures. The lowest had a basket of reusable water bottles with a *feel free to borrow one, just remember to return it* note.

Plus, several haunted-house figurines and plastic pumpkins added to the ambiance.

"Do you like it? My grandmother picked it up for pennies when a neighbor cleared their barn. It was in rough shape when she gave it to me, but I sanded it down, and a friend helped me replace one of the rotted shelves. I'd planned on staining it walnut, but black fit in well here."

"It fits the Haunted House theme," I said. "It's awesome. I could use something fun like this in the bookstore." Although we lean toward lighter colors in the bookstores to keep the merchandise out of shadows. Their entryway was well lit, so the black worked nicely, especially against the soft pumpkin wall color.

A peek into the dining room made me smile when I caught sight of their glossy black table with matching chairs. The B&B felt younger than the Sleepy Hollow, with a unique take on Halloween, in a good way.

Fiona and her husband were like a younger version of Marion and her deceased husband. They'd also dreamed of opening an inn, and they'd make it happen as a side hustle while working in other fields.

Hopefully, Lance's murder wouldn't ruin Elyan Hollow's reputation, which would crush the dreams of people like Fiona.

Tara and I closed down the bookshop under Jack's snoopervision.

"Oh, good!" I said when I caught sight of the empty outgoing-mail section of the backroom. Our mail carrier had stopped by when I was out.

Before heading home, Jack and I dropped by Stitch Craft, which stayed open an hour later than the bookshop on Mondays. The shop always makes me smile. The light and airy front room makes the perfect backdrop for the curated displays of colorful yarn and sample knit garments. The area to one side of the door is set up with couches and a pile of colorful floor cushions that encouraged knitters to come in and stay awhile and was a great space for knitting classes and formal meetups. Two hallways led off the front room, one to three smaller rooms full of yarn, accessories, and file cabinets of knitting patterns, and the second led back to the storeroom and offices.

My friend Lark and a second sales assistant were unpacking a box of variegated yarn in bright colors. Lots of primary yellows and blues, greens and purple. I took a glance. Fingering weight, meaning the yarn was skinny and used for socks and non-bulky items.

"This yarn is perfect for baby items," Lark told me. Her curly hair was dyed indigo, and she wore it pulled back into a bun with a knitting needle holding it in place. I'd seen Lark knitting the green short-sleeved sweater she wore. I bet she'd purchased her vintage jeans from a resale shop since she once told me she hates buying brand-new clothes. She'd probably sewn the embroidered flowers running up one leg herself. I was also willing to bet the striped socks peeking out under her Birkenstocks were hand knit. She joked once that she should've grown up in a hippy commune but instead was raised by an investment banker.

"Are you here to add to your stash?" Lark asked. "There's a really soft merino in that everyone needs. The colors are to die for."

There is no need to bring death into this. I shook my head. "I'm here to help Pearl with something."

"Head on back to the office, then. But stop by on your way out so I can show you that merino." Lark's enthusiasm for the yarn felt more like sharing than a hard sale, and I knew I'd need to be careful else I'd end up walking away with a bag of merino that I didn't need.

The yarn store has a small storeroom but keeps most of its stock on the floor. The area is more of a workroom, with a table for blocking projects, meaning to soak finished knit projects and then pin them out to dry. Plus, a mini-fridge and microwave were in the corner, with Pearl's office off to the side. She was working on the store's computer when I walked in. Peaches, her dog, looked up at Jack from her basket and hopped over to say hi. Jack stood stoically as Peaches sniffed him, then returned to her bed.

"I'm so glad to see you. I'm so tired of working on the accounts. It's the worst part of running a shop." Pearl leaned back and stretched. Like her employees, she was wearing a hand-knit top, this time a striped cotton cardigan in orange and black with elbow-length sleeves over a black T-shirt with her store logo on the front.

I pulled a printout out of my bag. I'd offered to email it, but Pearl prefers hard copies. "How does this work for your design?"

Pearl wanted a hand-knit stocking that mixed Halloween and Christmas for her winter holiday display. Once she'd explained the basics of her concept, she'd asked if I would draw it for her and then create a knitting chart.

"This is almost perfect," Pearl said. "Can we tweak the pumpkins to be slightly shorter than the trees?"

I made a few notes and promised to bring the new pattern on Wednesday for our usual knit night.

"I bet after this revision this will be ready for a sample knit." Pearl squirmed from side to side in her seat in excitement.

"Did you go to any of the literary festivals?" I asked.

"I dropped by the Saturday talk at the Pumpkin Plaza, which wasn't what I expected. Although the two authors speaking seemed lovely."

"I was lucky Melanie and Tariq stepped up and entertained the crowd."

"Did it go well? I dipped out when I realized Rex wasn't there. I really wanted to hear him. I even brought my knitting so I could give him my full attention."

"You're one of the people who focuses better when their hands are busy, right?"

"Definitely. Listening to an audiobook while knitting makes me much more engaged with the story. I can remember almost everything that happened. I wish audiobooks had been a thing when I was in school. Or ebooks, because being able to change the font helps." Pearl smiled. "I finally listened to Rex's books last year. It's hard to believe we were friends as kids."

"You were?"

Pearl nodded. "We weren't BFFs, but we hung out. Got pizza with people like your mom. He used to read my school papers and help me with grammar."

"So you knew Lance, too, then."

"Everyone knew Lance." Pearl's tone was guarded.

"You two weren't friends?"

"Lance wasn't exactly trustworthy. He'd act nice to your face while stabbing you in the back as soon as you turned away. When I look at the former classmates I see occasionally, I'm relieved he left town. And I'm not the only one who felt that way."

"Oh?"

"He was subtle, but he was the sort of guy who'd stand on the shoulders of someone drowning if it'd help him get ahead. I remember when he cheated off my friend's chemistry homework. Their answers were too close to each other, and the teacher pulled both of them aside. Lance swore he'd never cheat, and the teacher flunked my friend, who'd been getting extra tutoring and was working so hard."

"That sounds unfair."

"My friend quit trying after that. And that was why I kept my distance from Lance."

Jack nudged my hand as if telling me it was time to go home for dinner. My stomach grumbled.

"I'll see you Wednesday," Pearl said.

Jack and I walked home, seeing a few visitors taking advantage of the weekday quiet to take photos of town filming sites, reminding me the spooky season is always the best time of year.

Chapter 15

Tuesdays are always a special day at the bookshop: the week's new book releases go on sale.

This means I get up extra early to reset the sales floor and, depending upon new titles that have arrived, shift books that had been out a few weeks to their sections and to create space for their new neighbors. Some publishers we order from are particular about us never putting books out before their formal release day, so we're always careful to keep the new books under wraps.

New release Tuesday always does well on the shop's social media account, so I snapped up photos of the stacks of new releases and then double-checked everything was ready in my social media planning app.

And Tuesdays are a special day for me for another reason: it's my volunteer day with the library. So once I get the shop up and running and work throughout the morning, I always leave the shop in Tara's hands. I head home for a late lunch, which lets me drop Jack off at home and pick up my Crosstrek. I then head to the library to pick up a collection of books and DVDs I'll deliver to homebound patrons. Jack will spend his afternoon napping and watching for our mail carrier, whom he loves, likely because he'll always stick a dog treat through the mail slot for Jack.

In the winter, I might take Jack with me on my rounds since it'll be cold enough for him to safely wait in the car, but in the warm months, he's happy defending the house. And by "guarding," I mean napping on his bed.

When I arrived at the library, Colby was sitting in the middle of a loud group of toddlers, so one of the library assistants helped me load up my car with this week's deliveries. After double-checking my list, which is frequently the same list of names, I headed out to the neighborhoods of Elyan Hollow. I'd love to do the deliveries by bicycle, but I'd have to buy a trailer to pull the books.

This is always one of my favorite times of the week. It's more than just dropping books off to readers. It's also spending a few minutes chatting and checking in. Most of the people I deliver to are homebound, and it's an excellent way to check in and ensure everything is going okay. I can make notes for the social worker on the library staff to follow up on if anything is off since she's well-versed in community resources.

After my first two deliveries, I smiled when I glanced at the next name on my list: Estelle Sullivan. I pulled up to her tidy bungalow on the outskirts of downtown. I pulled out her stack of books, which included a couple of weighty science fiction tomes and a book of colorful knitting patterns. I headed up the front walkway to her cheerful red front door and knocked.

"Hey, Mrs. Sullivan," I said when the tiny old lady dressed in a navy sweat suit opened the door. She was in her early nineties and had spent her career teaching in the local high school.

"Hey, no walker!" I realized as I stepped into her spotless living room. Full bookcases covered the walls, and a TV perched on the mantle above the fireplace.

"My physical therapy is going well. I hope to be able to walk downtown again soon." Mrs. Sullivan broke her leg at the beginning of summer, leading to some gossip about whether her family would try to get her into a retirement community. But two of her college-aged grandchildren showed up to help out, and Mrs. Sullivan now seemed as vibrant as ever. I still saw her granddaughter around town occasionally, and based on the mix of shoes in the rack by the door, I suspected her granddaughter had moved in with her.

"Just be careful."

"My granddaughter said she'd come with me for the inaugural journey. You know she's staying with me while she studies at Portland Trinity, right? It's not too bad of a drive to North Portland, and it's so much cheaper than trying to rent an apartment. You wouldn't believe the cost of rent these days."

"Actually, I can." I debated renting my own place, but sticker shock kept me at home.

"You're right. You and my granddaughter have a few things in common." Mrs. Sullivan sat down on her couch. "It sounds like your life has been too exciting recently. How do you feel? Finding a body must've been a shock."

"I don't recommend it." I glanced over at the line of photographs on her mantle. Those were all happier memories, unlike me finding Lance.

"I should've gone to the festival but didn't want to deal with people. Once I retired from teaching, I vowed to avoid large crowds. But Rex was one of my former pupils, and it's always lovely to hear about one doing well in life."

"You must have taught my mother then."

"I remember her—she was an outstanding student and took all the advanced-math classes she could, which always endeared students to me. I was about to retire when I taught your mother," Mrs. Sullivan said. "So many students fade into this mass of faces I vaguely remember. But your mother was part of one of my final classes. So that might be why I remember her and her friends so well."

"Did you know Lance Gregory?"

She nodded. "Lance was quite the class clown, always wanting everyone's attention. He was fickle, flitting from one girl to another, but that didn't stop him. Or the girls. He was awfully handsome as a teen."

"Including my mother?"

"Maybe. Lance was the sort that floated between social groups, and he was a grade or two ahead. While your mother was popular with her classmates, she had her own circle. I can't remember if she paired off with anyone. I was shocked when I found out she was pregnant. She didn't seem the type."

I flinched. "That's harsh."

"I just mean that I thought your mother was the type to focus on her schoolwork. She was so driven to be valedictorian, and I thought she was a late bloomer regarding relationships. But teenagers make impulsive decisions. And clearly, you turned out well. It helps that your grandparents were in a position to help, so she didn't have to raise you alone. Not every teen has that level of support. I can think of another girl at school with your mother who desperately wanted to keep her baby. But her parents pressured her to give it up for adoption. I don't think she ever fully forgave them."

"Poor girl," I said. "Rex Abbot was in their class, too, right?"

"Rex was a year or two ahead of your mother if I remember correctly. He was friends with Lance, I think."

"Rex and Lance were buddies?" Not according to Rex. So, if Mrs. Sullivan's memory was accurate, Rex must've been lying through his teeth.

"They were friendly, at least. When I look back, after everything that happened last weekend, I keep seeing the two of them, along with Matt Leverton, who was always bad news. I wasn't surprised when Matt ended up in jail since he always got in trouble. But Rex was smart enough not to get involved. Plus, his dad was in the local police department, and he wouldn't have wanted to get in trouble."

"Rex's dad was a police officer?"

Mrs. Sullivan nodded. "Until he passed away from a heart attack right around his retirement, just a few years after his wife died from cancer. Rex definitely had a tough lot. His home life wasn't easy, and his parents died before his twenty-third birthday. I've always felt sorry for him."

I really wanted to ask if the former teacher thought Lance was my father. But before I could ask, she kept talking.

"I don't think so. In retrospect, Rex had a harsh home life," she said. "I didn't realize it then since Rex seemed like a diligent, slightly shy student. No one would've thought his father was abusive, at least to his mom. He seemed focused on getting out of town.

"If you had told me Rex would become a town celebrity, I would've been surprised, but not entirely. There was always something special about him. Your mother has always been a credit to the school, so no one was surprised when she was accepted to medical school. If you'd told me Lance was most likely to be murdered, I would've been shocked. He was the sort who always landed on his feet, no matter how covered in mud. I would've guessed he was the type to become a politician, which shows my crystal ball isn't very accurate."

Mrs. Sullivan glanced at the clock on her mantle. "Oh, dear, I've kept you long enough." She handed me back a stack of library books, along with a handful of tiny baby hats for Colby's preemie hat campaign for a local NICU ward. The stitchwork was perfect despite the hats being small enough to fit on a plum. The yarn was a cozy cotton so soft I wanted to cocoon myself in it.

"The hats are wonderful."

"Thank Colby for the yarn," Mrs. Sullivan said. "I loved making them and let her know I'll happily knit more."

"You know, we have a group that meets on Wednesday evenings and knits. You're always welcome to join us. I can work out a carpooling arrangement for you."

"Where do you meet?"

"Stitch Craft."

"I love that store, but it's a bit pricy on my pension."

"You can work on the preemie hats with yarn you bring yourself. You don't have to buy anything." Although I knew Pearl preferred us to buy something, she'd agreed to host the knitting club when she realized it had started organically meeting in the bookshop.

And if Mrs. Sullivan was as talented a knitter as I suspected, Pearl might enlist her to make shop samples.

We said goodbye, and I headed outside.

Before I started my car, I made a note on my phone. Matt Leverton. One of the regulars on my route shared that last name. But when I checked my schedule, she wasn't on my list.

But I could look into him later.

When I was done at the library, my phone beeped.

Tara, one of my employees.

Can you close tonight? Family emergency.

I responded right away:

Of course. Be there in thirty minutes.

THANK YOU!!!

I swung by home to drop off my car and pick up Jack, then tried to hustle to the bookstore.

Jack wasn't in the mood to put pep in his steps. But after a few arguments about which bushes needed a good sniff, he consented to walk at a slow but steady pace to the bookshop.

I loved Jack, but I sometimes wondered what it would be like to have a dog with a strong desire to please versus one who liked to shoot skeptical side-eye my direction whenever he disagreed with me. I could practically see him asking, "Are you sure? Because I'm positive you're wrong, human."

Tara had her purse ready so she could dash out the door. "Thank you so much, Bailey. My sister was in a car wreck. She's okay, but I'm going to babysit her kids so her husband can stay with her in the hospital."

"Please let me know if I can do anything."

Tara left at a brisk pace, and I glanced at Jack.

"That's the sort of hustle we needed today."

Jack yawned at me.

Tara had left a note of what she'd done and had yet to start. We still had an hour to close. I should pull some online orders or do something productive.

Instead, I pulled a pad of legal paper out from under the counter. Maybe I could figure out what happened to Lance if I started making notes.

I wrote *Matt Leverton* down on the top of the page and clicked open the web browser on the shop computer.

Although I wasn't sure if looking up a troubled classmate of Lance's would help with his murder. But I did wonder what Lance had genuinely been like. So far, he seemed like a chameleon.

But then, most people have multiple facets to their personalities.

The man I'd seen waiting outside Evelyn's office and also running in the park walked into the shop. He smiled, sporting a pair of world-class dimples, then nodded at me before walking toward the mystery section. He looked casual in faded jeans and a Hillsboro Hops T-shirt.

From his shirt, I knew he liked baseball enough to wear a minor-league T-shirt, and from seeing him running in the park, he was at least somewhat devoted to running and, most likely, triathlons. He snagged one book quickly, then picked up a few books and read the back cover copy intently, like he would be tested on the content later. His white-blond hair stuck up, like it was purposefully messy.

Jack stood in the corner of the horror section, next to a face-out copy of Johnny Compton's *The Spite House*. He glared at his neon-green tennis ball like it had just insulted his mother, and he was daring it to move.

When the man walked around the endcap and saw Jack, he said, "Let me throw that for your buddy."

"No!" I tried to say but couldn't speak in time. The man rolled Jack's ball across the store, and Jack trotted after it. Jack swatted at the ball a few times with his paws, sending it bouncing first toward thriller and then toward romance before he finally picked it up. Then Jack carried the ball to their original corner and resumed their staring contest.

"Please don't throw his ball again," I said.

The man raised one eyebrow as he looked at me.

"Jack's not a normal dog. Fetch isn't really his thing."

"So Jack just likes to get in staring contests with inanimate objects?" the man asked.

"Exactly." However, once in a while, Jack seemed to appreciate me throwing a ball for him in the backyard and he batted it around with his paws a few times before leaving it and running off to sniff something.

He put his books down on the counter. Two mystery novels and fantasy, all of which were on books I'd written shelf-talkers for. He glanced at my notebook, where I'd written a few notes.

"Leverton?" he asked.

"Just a former local that I want to look up," I said, sliding the notebook out of sight. I really shouldn't sketch out my speculations in the store. Scratch that. I shouldn't investigate Lance's death, period. Although if the police arrested me, I'd become involved regardless.

Chapter 16

After I closed up the shop, Jack and I retreated to my office upstairs. I clicked open the security camera footage from the night the film crew was here.

Bill and Jill fussed over the camera, lights, and microphone while Taylor and Lance walked around the store.

Danby walked into the store and went behind the counter, and Taylor turned and said something to her. Based on the way Danby stiffened, Taylor had said something snide.

Danby glared back, and whatever she said made Taylor turn with a huff.

Go, Danby! I smiled. But I knew I should've stayed and sent Danby home. None of this was fair to my intern.

I fast-forwarded, watching the film crew scurry around like ants. Then I saw Taylor walk up to one of the bookcases, and I switched back to regular speed.

The store was shadowy, with just the streetlights from outside lighting the shop. Taylor's white shirt glowed in the darkness. She reached out and shook the bookcase, then tossed a book in Lance's direction.

I compared it to the footage from the TV show, which showed a scared Lance jump when the book Taylor threw crashed to the ground beside him. "The ghost here is furious," he said. "And I think it's just gearing up. The air feels electric, like the ghost has more to say."

"They're all liars," I said. Or at least, their show was fiction.

I switched back to the security footage. Bill and Taylor argued in the footage, and then Lance joined in. Once they started filming, Taylor shook a different bookcase, but it slipped from her hands and crashed into a second bookcase, which then fell toward the register. Books and merchandise smashed on the floor. A box on top hurtled into the photo of the shop's grand opening, breaking the glass of the picture frame.

Taylor stood with her hands on her mouth, like she was in shock. Lance turned and yelled at her.

I turned back to the TV show footage. Lance was staring at the camera. "You know that feeling when the hairs on the back of your neck stand up? That's how I feel—"

The bookcase behind him crashed, causing the chain reaction of destruction. Lance jumped, showing legitimate fear.

"What did you do?" Lance yelled at Taylor.

"It was just supposed to wobble!"

I glanced at Jack. "Do you think we can compensate for mental anguish? Taylor's lack of respect for books hurts my soul." But it looked like the damage had, in fact, been an accident. An avoidable one, since Taylor didn't need to shake the bookcase to create a "spooky" atmosphere. But she hadn't been intent on destruction, even if that was the end result.

Jack looked at me but didn't say anything

I continued watching the footage, then paused.

Danby had rushed down and was talking to Bill and Jill. Taylor and Lance were off to the side, away from the rest of the TV show crew. Lance smirked as she ranted at him. She jabbed him in the chest with her finger, and he smirked harder.

I really wished I had audio of their encounter. But I'm pretty sure Lance said, "You don't want to do that." Although my lipreading skills are mediocre at best.

My phone beeped. Colby.

Taproom dinner?

Jack and I think that's a great idea. I'm at the shop—I can be there in a few.

Save me a seat! I'm just about to leave the library.

I decided to watch the Haunted House B&B footage later since I clearly needed a burrito after this footage to recover. Or maybe some tacos would do the trick.

I didn't really feel up for a beer. Still, I knew I wouldn't be able to resist the siren call of hops after I walked into the Elyan Mortuary & Deli.

"Bailey!" Ash waved me down from the end of the bar, where she sat with a half-full pint of a deep golden beer.

I nestled onto the barstool next to her. Jack flopped down between us. "You don't spend enough time here?"

"Shift beer. Plus, I like to keep an eye on things."

Ash waved down her bartender. "Give Bailey one of the new Ghost grisettes and put it on my tab."

"Ghost grisette?" I'd learned enough from Ash to know grisettes were a type of beer similar to farmhouse ales like saisons or bières de garde. But Ghost?

That better not mean ghost peppers.

"Trust me, you'll love it. I brewed this grisette with an old friend at her brewery, and it's only available here. If it does well, we will collaborate on a whole line of spooky-themed beers. I can't wait to release our Christmas ale, but I need a good name." Ash hummed and half danced in her seat.

"Slay Ride?" I offered.

Ash sat up straight. "That might be perfect."

"Is this a friend you used to brew with?"

"Yep, we're former coworkers. She left not long after I quit to open this taproom, and she's finally gotten her brewery up and running on a small farm in the wine country. She's growing some of her own ingredients, and we're going to collaborate."

"You must miss being a brewer." I couldn't imagine Elyan Hollow without the taproom.

"Yes and no. I was getting bored brewing the same standard beers again and again, and I don't miss the paycheck. Brewing isn't lucrative, and I worked three different side hustles to save up to start this taproom. But I miss the smell of hops, and boiling wort. I miss talking with people who geeked out about beer minutiae as much as my old coworkers did. But I love it here. I feel like I found more friends here—people like you have become chosen family."

My phone beeped with a text from Colby:

Running late. Order me a bowl?

Sure. I texted back.

I scanned the QR code for Boorito, and when their ordering page popped up I glanced at Ash. "Want to join us for dinner?"

After a quick discussion, I ordered a trio of tacos for me (pollo, carne asada, and tripas), a carnitas burrito for Ash, and a pollo rice bowl for Colby.

"Wait, you didn't order anything for Jack."

We both looked at Jack, still sprawled beneath our barstools. "He'll live."

We chatted for a few minutes. Colby showed up, decked out in a navy Elyan Hollow library T-shirt, red cardigan, and cords. Her black hair was pulled back into a messy bun.

"No glitter today?" Ash asked.

"I'm proud to say glitter has been officially banned from the library craft hours. So that might be my lasting legacy." Colby paused by the barstool on the opposite side of Ash. "Should we move to a table?"

We headed over to one of the side tables with four chairs, with Jack reluctantly following. He sat back down with a sigh like he wondered why we were bothering him when he'd be comfortable keeping an eye on the bar.

Pearl from the yarn shop walked in with a couple of her friends, and she waved at us before they sat on the couches a few tables away. Most of the women bought pints of beer, but Pearl had made the responsible midweek choice and opted for a bottle of grapefruit sparkling water.

I should've made a similar decision, but I did enjoy the grisette, which was light and a bit bready, with a pear-like note.

"I'm telling you, my taproom is a de facto community center but with beer. Delicious, delicious beer," Ash said while looking intently at Colby. "And burritos," she added as Olivia showed up with our food.

My world felt brighter as I looked down at my tacos. "I'd love to chat, but a big order just came in. Hopefully, I can catch you later. We should chat 'cause it's been a few days." Olivia put a bottle of avocado salsa next to my plate, patted me on the shoulder, and scurried away.

Jack nosed my hip.

I shook my head at him, and he gave me a look back that said he needed a taco, but he settled back down.

As I added a line of avocado salsa to my tacos, Colby and Ash continued their discussion.

"But people have to pay to stay, which is the value of the library. Our services are free."

"True, although, for the record, as long as someone buys a cheap can of water, we don't kick them out. And you're funded by taxes, so everyone pays, just not at time of service. So we're both serving our community in unique ways, just like Bailey's bookstore adds to it, even though people have to buy her books versus borrowing yours."

A group of guys, probably in their mid-forties, took the table next to us.

"It's nice to see you again," one of the men said.

"I can't believe it's our thirty-year reunion this weekend. It only feels like a decade, max," another man said.

Thirty years. They would be a few years older than my mother, maybe seniors when she was a freshman.

"I can't believe that Lance Gregory died. Do you remember him? He was on the basketball team my senior year, and I loved that guy. He was hilarious."

"Was he Ally's younger brother?" one of his friends asked.

"That's right."

I didn't overhear anything interesting, and Jack and I eventually headed home, me full of tacos and a grisette and him with a couple of peanut butter treats in his stomach. In a typical festival year, tonight would've felt like a win.

Chapter 17

Wednesday started like usual: I went for a run with Colby, who was stressing out about a budget meeting that afternoon, so it was my turn to reassure that she was ready. I ate breakfast at home, including my morning matcha, and walked to work with Jack, who was dressed in a black buffalo-check bandana.

I went about my usual opening routine and checked out the list of book orders that had come in overnight. One gift basket request was based on a copy of Rex Abbot's *The Waiting Room of Lost Souls*. We'd received additional copies of Rex's books in yesterday's afternoon delivery. So I sent Rex an email inviting him to drop by anytime to sign stock and then refocused on the book orders. I printed them and handled the rest of the bookstore business, scanning a few emails from distributors and flagging a handful of emails to deal with and/or read later.

As usual, I flipped the OPEN sign over at 9:00 a.m. exactly, then checked out the stack of orders. Pulling books for four of the orders was simple, and then I looked at the gift basket request.

The gift basket was a new idea I was trying out from this year's Spooky Season Lit Festival through Christmas, with hopes of making it a regular option. Customers can choose the books, and we'll build a gift basket around each person's with a few guided choices depending how much the customer wanted to spend. This customer had asked for tea, no candy, no scented items, and mentioned it was for a Halloween birthday.

After a few minutes, I'd pulled a small art print of a skeleton knight reading a book with a cat in its lap that matched the aesthetic of Rex's book. Plus, a sampler of seasonal teas from Stonefield Beach, one of my Portland favorites, and a loose-leaf tea infuser with a skull charm dangling on the end of the chain. After adding a couple of bookmarks and a pumpkin sticker that said: "Happy Birthday," I packed the items into a cardboard basket lined with orange tissue paper, then packaged the whole thing in a clear bag, which I closed with an orange-and-black-plaid ribbon.

As I was fixing the ribbon, the bell on the front door jangled.

"Hi, welcome to Lazy Bones," I said. I turned.

Rex.

My voice faltered.

"Is that one of my books?" Rex asked. He motioned to the gift bag.

I nodded and told him how the gift baskets worked.

"Would you like me to personalize it?"

I untied the ribbon, slid the book out, and handed it over to Rex, along with the sales slip. I pointed out a line highlighted in orange. "You can see the recipient's name here."

Rex looked at the title page. "I signed this on Sunday, but you have the same-colored Sharpie, so I added a message without it being obvious they were signed at different times."

Jack leaned against Rex, and after he signed, Rex gently petted Jack. My dog looked like he could stand there all day as long as he continued to get attention.

"We received more of your books if you're up for signing," I said.

"Bring 'em on."

I dragged the boxes of Rex's books out from the back and set him up with a few thin Sharpies. "Thanks for signing all of these.

We're creating a special page on our website for them." And I'd promote them as perfect Christmas presents since what's more seasonal than terrifying the pants off of your loved ones with scary books?

Although, as Rex set about signing books under Jack's supervision, I thought about how his books aren't usually gory. They frequently put characters in situations with no good choices and then add monsters, which may or may not be metaphorical. Rex is a fan of the "humans are the worst monsters" trope, which he made feel fresh whenever he used it. I realized this was one of the many reasons I enjoyed his books. He played with tropes in unexpected ways that kept my attention as a reader.

"What are you doing for lunch?" Rex asked me.

My face felt hot. But then the door jangled. Danby was ready for her internship hours.

Saved by the intern.

"I need to get Danby started," I said.

"I can chill if you're in the middle of something," Danby said.

"Rex is just signing," I said. I turned to the author. "I'll be back in a moment."

Danby and I went into the back room. I clicked the shop monitors on so we could keep an eye on the front door.

"Now that the festival's over, I have a new project for you," I said. While I was employing Danby to work in the shop, her internship hours needed to involve special projects versus her acting like a sales associate.

"I can't wait," she said.

"In our lead-up to Black Friday, and the rest of the shopping season until Christmas, I have an idea for a 'Frostbite' snowman theme—"

"Like a cheerful vampire snowman with two eyes made of coal and a set of fangs?"

"Exactly. And I want to create a bunch of Frostbite-themed promos and a handful of giveaways. For example, posts advertising our Bookish Advent calendars starting in early November and promoting our signed books and seasonal offerings. . . ." We discussed the concepts, including how to subtly work in the number of shopping and, therefore, shipping days before the holiday. I set Danby up with the folder of images I'd created, with instructions to create a content calendar and mock up a few social media posts.

Getting Danby set up to focus on the future made something echo in the back of my brain. We—mainly Danby's parents and Colby, but also me to a lesser extent—were focused on helping Danby get her life "back on track" after she floundered a bit in high school. But nothing she had done had irrevocably destroyed her future, even if she wasn't following the straightforward path her sister had blazed.

Danby was like my mother if you put a minor criminal conviction on par with an unexpected pregnancy. They'd both done something that added a few extra challenges to their lives, but with the help of their families, they were thriving despite the setback. If there had been any echoes from their misstep, it had faded into the distance without notice.

But why had Lance died here? Neither Lance nor Rex had spent much, if any, time in Elyan Hollow as adults. If someone was going to harm Lance, why here?

I paused.

Had someone mistaken Lance for Rex?

They were both white men about the same height, in the general 5'10" to 6' range, making them taller than average but not exceptionally so. Plus, people change as they age. Had someone heard Rex was in town and vaguely recognized Lance enough from their high school days to attack him by mistake?

Had this been the first time someone from their past had confronted them over something that, to the murderer, felt meaningful? Something that stayed with them long enough to snap? Or, even worse, infuriated them enough to lure Lance into the maze and kill him?

I shivered. I'd always felt safe in Elyan Hollow. It wasn't perfect, but I'd gone for runs at night with a few safety precautions, like letting Colby or my grandfather know my intended route, ensuring my phone was charged, and bringing a small flashlight and a whistle.

Had I been mistaken all of this time?

Were there buried secrets in town worth killing over? Or had Lance been in the wrong place at the wrong time?

Chapter 18

After quickly stopping home to eat dinner and pick up my knitting bag, Jack and I headed downtown.

I'm still amazed that Pearl lets me bring Jack into Stitch Craft, but he's good at finding a spot by the seating area and sprawling out on the floor next to the red velvet couch. Anyone who wants to leave has to step around him. He's better behaved than Pearl's Jack Russell, Peaches, whose favorite game is to steal skeins of yarn out of attendees' bags and run around the store with them.

The last time that happened, Jack opened one eye when he heard Ash shriek but didn't bother to stand up as Ash chased Peaches around the store. Pearl had eventually, and begrudgingly, replaced Ash's slobber-stained merino wool.

And all of the regulars zealously keep their knitting bags tucked up next to them, out of the reach of the Jack Russell.

Colby had happily agreed to pick up Estelle Sullivan for tonight's knit night, and they weren't in the shop when Jack and I arrived. So I sat on the velvet couch, and Jack collapsed beside me.

Pearl walked by, and I handed over the folder with the revised pattern.

"Thank you, Bailey," she said. Pearl headed to the register, where a short line of customers waited.

As I arranged my yarn to get ready to start knitting my rather basic sailors cap in a navy, which I could work on while talking, I glanced at the display closest to the seating area, which Pearl had refreshed since the last week.

Halloween galore. Pearl leans toward color work knits, meaning projects with knit designs in more than one color with multiple strands of yarn. Several cowls in three different lengths of stranded Halloween-themed colorwork hung around a mannequin wearing an orange sweater with a bat motif around the bottom. Several hats were displayed on the short shelf, including a simple black-and-orange-striped watch beanie and a slouchy hat with ghosts and bats. A couple of hooks on the corner held scarves with baskets of orange and black yarn beneath them.

The shop displays will eventually be sold, and, back when I was a newbie dragged in against my will, I'd looked at a handmade shawl once, feeling sticker shock when I saw the tag. But then I'd learned to knit, and once I factored in the time and cost of yarn, the staggering price made sense. It reminded me of the meme that you could buy something for $9.99 or spend $100 to make it yourself. But there was something satisfying about wearing your own hand-knit items, and I hoped this hat would be my grandfather's Christmas present.

Jack and I were the first to arrive but not the last. Pearl joined us, along with Evelyn, the lawyer renting office space above the bookstore, Olivia from Boorito, Marion, Ash, and Lark, Pearl's mainstay assistant in the yarn shop and my friend. The lone man in our knit nights, Jonah, slid into the spot next to me. Jack ignored them, although he lifted his chin when Colby stepped around him to sit on the couch parallel to me. Colby had brought Mrs. Sullivan, who greeted everyone with a smile as she sat down and started to work on a fuzzy green baby hat.

Evelyn had brought a bottle of Pinot Noir, and Marion brought a Chardonnay, so Lark broke out the shop's six-ounce mason jars with a "crystal" design 'cause we were fancy.

"I'm so happy I found these jars for the shop when I was thrifting," Lark said. She handed them around.

I opted for a small glass of Pinot from Oregon but not from our in-town winery. Marion and Lark went with Chardonnay. I jokingly raised my eyebrows at Colby when she joined Pearl in a mug of peppermint tea.

"I'm just not feeling it," she said.

As we chatted, Olivia said, "Bailey, you need to give us the scoop on what's going on with the murder."

"Umm . . ." Remembering Lance brought so many conflicted feelings. The horror of finding him, knowing he could be my father. I really didn't want to talk about it.

But this was a knit night. I should've known Lance's death would be the conversational point.

"It's hard to believe someone from here was on an actual TV show and managed to get killed in our pumpkin maze," Olivia said. She quit knitting her red-and-green-striped hat and bounced in place. "Do you think they'll make a TV movie about his death? And what was he like? You talked with him."

"I don't know if it's relevant, but I can give you some of the dirt on Lance as a teen," Mrs. Sullivan said.

"That's not fair," Pearl said. "He's not here to defend himself."

"What happens at knit night stays at knit night," Colby said.

"Snitches get purl stitches," I added.

Colby turned my way and mouthed, "Nice!"

"Was Lance honestly a TV star?" Lark asked.

For some reason, everyone looked at me. "I don't think 'star' is quite the right word. From my clearly expert Google-searching skills, Lance worked fairly steadily, and his ghost show was on a streaming service. But I have no idea if that's enough to live on in LA, let alone be considered a celebrity."

"LA is ridiculously expensive. I moved up here to escape the SoCal cost of living and not have roommates," Lark said. "But my rent keeps increasing, and I don't want to move again. Or find a couple of roommates."

Everyone grumbled for a moment about inflation, but Olivia brought everything back to the murder.

"So what was Lance like when he lived here, Mrs. Sullivan?" Lark asked.

"You can call me Estelle, you know. I'm retired. I'm not a math teacher anymore," Mrs. Sullivan said. "And Pearl is my only former student here, so it's not like the name is ingrained in you."

Pearl looked awkward. "I barely scraped by in high school. Academics weren't my thing," Pearl said.

"But you did well for yourself, despite your challenges," Mrs. Sullivan said. "Traditional schooling isn't for everyone. You went to the craft college, correct?"

Pearl nodded. I realized she was working on the same shawl with a bat pattern from the taproom a few nights back, but she'd unraveled at least a few inches. "My classes in textiles and fashion are what got me into knitting. Although I used to adore weaving, as well."

As she knit, Pearl said, "I appreciate how knitting and yarn-based crafts have traditionally been female spaces and a place for women to gather and talk."

Beside me, Jonah raised his eyebrows. "Should I leave?"

Pearl laughed. "No, no, knitting should be for everyone. Especially now that we don't need to knit socks for a whole family."

I glanced at Jonah's project: a pair of striped yellow socks.

"I always appreciated knowing students found niches for themselves," Mrs. Sullivan said. "I'm not surprised that Lance tried the Hollywood route, just like I'm not surprised Rex Abbot found acclaim as a writer. Rex was a fantastic writer even as a teen, which wasn't easy for him since that wasn't what his father valued."

"Oh?" Lark asked.

"Rex's dad was the sort of macho, stereotypical man who would mock a small boy for crying, like when Rex broke his arm when he was about five and his dad ridiculed him in public. I remember how angry it made my husband. My husband was one of the ER doctors at the hospital in town, you know, and said the break would've made a grown man cry, let alone a small boy."

Had Rex inherited his dad's temper? I hadn't seen it, but I barely knew him.

The shop door opened, and Fiona from the Haunted House B&B entered. "Am I too late?"

"No, come join us! Let me get another chair." Pearl sprung up, brought out a chair from the back, and then made Fiona sit on the couch.

"You look like you need a comfortable spot to sit," Pearl said. She sat down on the hardback chair from the staff room.

Fiona rubbed her stomach. "But sometimes, standing up from sitting is hard."

"When are you due?" Pearl leaned toward Fiona as her fingers kept steadily knitting.

Colby glanced at me. "Baby fever," she said. "There's no cure."

"I have two cures at home. You're free to borrow them for an afternoon," Jonah said.

Lark laughed. "Don't tell Pearl that."

"Don't tell me what?" Pearl asked.

"Jonah might need a babysitter."

"You can always ask me," Pearl said. "Your little girl is such an angel."

"She only looks like one," Jonah said. He shook his head with a smile as he worked on his socks.

"That's mean." Pearl shook her head.

"Don't get me wrong, she's bright, funny, and she always runs headfirst into the world without it slowing her down. But four-year-olds have such big feelings. Coming here and talking to adults for a few hours each week is a lifesaver." Jonah took a sip of wine.

"Raising a kid poorly can hurt their future, which is my biggest worry. I don't want to ruin my kid's life," Fiona said. She held a skein of bright yellow yarn, and Pearl had been patiently teaching her how to do a garter stitch, which is the basic stitch all knitting is based on. "I just hope I don't make any parenting mistakes—oh, this is definitely muddled now."

"Just keep practicing and your knitting will improve. It just takes time," Pearl said. She helped Fiona untangle her yarn.

"You should know that you'll make mistakes as a parent. I've made some doozies. But I do my best, which involves listening closely to what my daughter isn't saying. Having a tantrum over how I cut her cheese slice is rarely about the cheese. Maybe she's tired, overwhelmed, or feels like she's not being listened to." Jonah sounded like he knew what he was talking about.

Jonah and Fiona talked about child-raising theories.

Ash looked at me. "Please bring up a new topic."

I glanced toward Colby. "We could ask Colby about her and Hayes' plans."

"Not you, too. My mother keeps asking about grandkids." Colby's eyes stayed on the striped pullover she was making for her husband.

"Do you even see Hayes enough for that?" Ash asked. "He travels, what, six or nine months of the year?"

"Yeah, but he's making bank for when we decide to try for real instead of practicing whenever we have the opportunity." Colby smirked at her sweater.

The door opened, and my hope that the situation would turn less fraught crashed and burned.

Chapter 19

Taylor from the film crew.

Why was she here? Was she honestly joining us for the knit night?

I glanced at her usual leather tote, which didn't have any yarn poking out of the top. But it was big enough to hide a project deep inside.

Taylor pulled one of her black ghost meters out of her bag. But something told me it was just a pretext. Maybe because she didn't have the air of intensity she'd had at the taproom.

Was Taylor looking for a reason to come here? But why? It was a store, and the knitting night was open to everyone.

Pearl abandoned her knitting and walked up to Taylor. "Can I help you?"

"I'm from the ghost-hunting show, and one of our venues fell through, and I wanted to see if your store could be an option."

Ash leaned toward me. "My taproom is the place that fell through. No way I am letting them in my baby after they destroyed your shop."

Colby snorted. "What ghost would haunt a knitting shop?"

"A cozy one," I said.

Pearl trailed along as Taylor walked around the yarn shop, doing her thing.

"The store isn't haunted," Pearl said.

"My scans show something different, but it feels like this whole town is full of deep, dark secrets."

Fiona laughed, and Taylor looked her way.

A snide look slid off Taylor's face. "You own that B&B with all the kitschy ghost stuff. Our footage from there was lame. You know, Lance was so annoyed with me because I was supposed to book us to stay at your hotel, but I booked at Sleepy Hollow instead."

"You were lucky we had a last-minute cancelation for two rooms," Marion said. "Where did the rest of your crew stay?"

"At that motel up by the highway. They needed space for the van."

So Taylor, or whoever booked the film crew, had stuck Bill and Jill in the old-school motor lodge that desperately needed a remodel.

I glanced at Marion, who made eye contact with me with a look that I'm pretty sure said Lance and Taylor would've been welcome to stay elsewhere. Then she glanced back at the peacock-blue lace shawl she was knitting.

"Why was Lance so interested in the Haunted House B&B?" I asked. Even though I suspected I knew. Although seeing your childhood home turned into a B&B would feel odd, and would staying in it feel weird? I tried to imagine my grandparents' house turned into an inn.

"Who knows. Lance always knew how he wanted things to be and didn't want to listen to anyone else." Taylor put her bag down on the floor and turned to wave her scanner away from us.

Peaches darted over and stuck her head in Taylor's bag.

Taylor turned back around and saw the Jack Russell half inside her bag. "Get out!" she screamed.

Peaches scampered away with something black and shiny, most likely a makeup bag, while Taylor chased her.

"If you chase her, she'll think this is a game and run faster. If you ignore her, she'll drop that unless there's food inside," Lark said.

Despite being Peaches' owner, Pearl just stood and watched. She squeezed her hands, adorned in bright red-and-purple hand warmers, in front of her chest instead of trying to stop her dog.

Lark put down her knitting project and joined the Peaches hunt. She showed Peaches a treat, and the Jack Russell stopped at her battered Doc Martens. Peaches sat, still holding the pouch.

"Trade," Lark said. Peaches dropped the bag in exchange for a biscuit, and Jack ambled over to get a treat, too.

Lark handed the bag back to Taylor, then gave Jack his treat. "You're such a gentle giant versus this naughty little girl."

Jack gazed back, probably hoping for a second biscuit.

Taylor had grabbed her bag and inspected it. "This better not be ruined. I bought it in Milan, and it's irreplaceable."

"It's just dog slobber. It'll wipe off," Lark said.

Taylor unzipped the bag and glanced inside, tilting it so no one could see inside. "If anything is damaged, you'll have a serious problem."

Lark looked like she was gritting her teeth. "It would be best if you left the store. We'd hate for you to risk getting injured on the premises."

"And continue ruining the knit night vibe," Colby muttered.

Ash snorted, and Taylor stiffened.

"This town is so lame," Taylor said. She snatched her tote off of the floor, shoved her smaller bag inside, along with the ghost-hunting equipment, and marched off.

Lark carefully picked her knitting project, and once she'd walked over and watched Taylor march away from the store, Pearl returned to her shawl.

Mrs. Sullivan—I mean Estelle—had taken over helping Fiona, and Fiona was smiling.

"This is starting to make sense!"

"Pearl's right that practice will help. It's like most things in life—very few things immediately make sense, and even if you're naturally good at something, repetition always helps," Estelle said.

"How many squares do you think I'll need before I can sew them into the blanket?"

"Well, dear, that depends on how large of a blanket you want to make."

Colby eyed Estelle. “Do you miss teaching?”

Estelle tilted her head slightly to the side. “Sometimes. I don’t miss the daily grind, but I do miss the rewarding sides of it.”

“If you ever want to be a drop-in math tutor in our after-school club, we could use you.”

They talked briefly about Colby’s after-school study program in the library, with Colby, coworkers, and volunteers helping teens with their homework. “We have a reading specialist who shows up a few days a week to help with papers, along with a local historian who is shockingly good at college essays. A math specialist would be a miracle.”

Estelle laughed. “I wouldn’t call myself a miracle, but if you can assist with transportation, I’d love to try.”

“And we should put together a senior stitch group at the library,” Colby said.

“They could always meet here.” Pearl’s tone was snappish.

Colby dropped one of her needles and raised her hand. “It’s not a competition, Pearl. But my coworker is always looking for programming ideas. Our senior tech class was a huge hit.”

Pearl turned back to Fiona. “How’s that knitting square going?”

Fiona held it up. “Good, except I have a few holes?”

“I can show you how to fix them. There’s a way to insert a knitting needle in the row below the error and unravel to that point.”

“Or just leave it since it’s Fiona’s first square. I’ll show you how to avoid making unintentional yarn overs, and you can use that square as a washcloth or rag. You’ll need plenty of them when the baby comes,” Mrs. Sullivan said.

Knitting night continued, but when it hit nine I was happy to walk Colby and Mrs. Sullivan to Colby’s car before heading home with Jack.

As I walked, I thought about how it’s so much easier to fix small knitting mistakes than most problems in life.

Chapter 20

Jack and I took the slow route home from knit night, and when we arrived home I left my knitting project on the table by the stairs and turned onto the main floor.

I had a project and one thing I'd learned long ago: if you want to research something, head to the library. And the collection in this venue was exactly what I needed.

I'm pretty sure the library in my grandfather's house would be the family room flowing into a dining room on a foursquare blueprint. The fireplace in the front room makes it cozy on winter nights, and the bookshelves lining the walls are a curated look at my grandparents' favorite books over the years. I paused by the shelf of signed Ursula K. Le Guin novels, which had been my grandmother's favorites, then headed through the wide doors into the second room, lined by bookcases, with a dining table in the center. The table gave it a library reading room feel with the added bonus of being a good table for holiday meals. We'd always used the small table in the breakfast nook for every day.

The bookcase closest to the door to the kitchen had a few shelves of photo albums and, if I remember correctly, yearbooks.

I scrolled through the shelves and bingo.

All four of my mother's yearbooks were on the shelf, alongside Hudson's and mine.

Getting my high school yearbooks each year had felt momentous. I realized I hadn't even looked at them since I'd started college. They didn't feel as important as I thought they'd be, although I knew I'd never get rid of them. That being said, an unwillingness to get rid of books is a family flaw.

I laid all four of my mother's yearbooks down on the table and started with the beginning: her freshman year. I flipped back to the index and noted the pages where my mother was mentioned.

Fingers crossed, whoever created the index had been diligent.

My fourteen-year-old mother had looked so young. Her school photo was black-and-white, but I knew the thick hair flowing onto her shoulders was golden blond with natural streaks from spending the summer in the sun, helped with a few sneaky sprays of hair lightener. The photos were full of nineties style. Lots of flannel and baggy jeans.

My mother has been on the cross-country and track teams, plus freshman basketball.

Wait, my mother had played basketball?

I scanned her various club photos. Even at fourteen, she'd been a focused student, working on extracurriculars for her eventual college applications. I wondered what she'd felt like when she'd finished med school. Had she reviewed her life and decided the years of single-minded focus had been worth it?

I looked up Rex and Lance in the index and noted their page numbers. They were both juniors. And like my mother, they were on the track team, although Lance played football in the fall and basketball in the winter, while Rex was on the fall cross-country team. He blended into the background of the cross-country photo, standing in the back row like he didn't want to be noticed. My mother stood in the center of the front row, looking lean in her singlet and running shorts. Was she intentionally the focal point? Had she purposely sat in the center, or had the photographer moved her there?

I stopped at one of the photos in the junior section of the yearbook. Three teen boys in the hallway of Elyan Hollow High School, with lockers in the background.

I looked at their names: Lance, Rex, and a boy named Matt. They looked chummy, but social media had long ago taught me that photos don't always tell the truth.

I put this yearbook down and scanned through my mother's sophomore yearbook.

It felt similar to my mother's freshman year, but I noted she wasn't on the basketball team. Maybe she'd found something to fail at; then I chastised myself for being mean.

But one picture brought me to a halt.

My eyes lingered over the group prom photo from my mother's sophomore year. In the center yearbook section of full-color pages, eight students stood together, including my then fifteen-year-old mother, adorned in a long dark purple dress with a yellow rose corsage pinned to the chest.

Plus, Rex is dressed in a ruffled-down tuxedo shirt and black jeans.

And Lance in a traditional tux with a yellow rose boutonniere.

Plus, Pearl and a couple of people I didn't know. I read their names, and none rang a bell.

I looked back at the flowers. Pearl's corsage was red, while the girls I didn't know wore pink and white corsages. Rex's boutonniere was red, like Pearl's corsage, while the other two teens wore pink and white, matching the other two girls.

My mother and Lance were the only two with yellow flowers.

Had my mother gone to the prom with Lance?

Was I the stereotypical baby accidentally created on prom night?

I snapped a photo of the picture with my phone and moved on. There were photos sprinkled through the index, and I stopped in surprise.

Unless the photo was a lie, I hadn't realized my mother and Pearl had been friends. There were plenty of people in high school I'd considered friends, but we'd drifted apart immediately after graduation and they show up occasionally in the personal social media feeds I rarely check since I'm always burned out by the shop's accounts.

Pearl had never mentioned being friends with my mother, but maybe she thought I knew. Or didn't think it mattered. Perhaps this photo showed a friendly moment between two classmates who lived very separate lives. After all, if social media has taught the world anything, it's that anyone's life can look a certain way with curated photos, regardless of the truth.

My mother and Rex were in a National Honor Society group photo together, and my mother, Lance, and Rex were stretching together in a candid picture for the track team. The caption under one photo mentioned that the men's 400-meter relay team had won the district and taken third at state, and Rex was in the photo, along with three boys I didn't know.

I paused again at another photo. Lance, with his arm around my mother's shoulders, at the annual senior awards and scholarship night. Rex was in the background talking to my grandfather.

I glanced at the list of awards. Rex had received a small four-year scholarship from the bookshop, which my grandparents funded off-and-on over the years, and it always involved an essay. He'd also received the local booster's annual scholarship for student-athletes and another from a regional grocery chain. Lance had received one lone scholarship from the local mill.

Which, I remembered, his father had managed. Something told me that the scholarship had been rigged.

Overall, they seemed like reasonably successful high school students. But my eyes went back to the photo.

Was this a photo of two teens in love? Or had someone asked them to pose and Lance had thrown his arm around her shoulders to pose?

My eyes went to Rex's list of scholarships. His refusal to have anything to do with the bookstore for years after receiving a scholarship stung.

But my grandfather had always spoken fondly of him, so he hadn't taken it personally. He must understand why. Maybe that was why he hadn't taken the declines personally.

I looked through my mother's junior and senior yearbooks, noting a few more group photos that included my mother and Pearl. My mother was clearly pregnant in one as she talked intently with Pearl, unaware the camera was focused on them. It wasn't a particularly flattering one of Pearl. The weird angle made her look rounder than normal, but my mother's smile looked radiant.

My mother looked back to normal in her senior yearbook, and her listing on the awards and scholarship page took up more real estate than everyone else's. Valedictorian. Most inspirational member of the track team. Multiple scholarships from local organizations that paid for books and lodging alongside her full-ride to the University of Oregon and let her save her college fund to offset medical school.

Pearl wasn't listed on the awards page, but she had a senior photo and was in the large group photo of that year's graduates. Mrs. Sullivan had mentioned that Pearl went to the now-defunct craft college, and from their conversation at knit night I suspected Pearl struggled in the traditional academic environment my mother had diligently excelled at.

I put the books away since this wasn't helping me figure out who killed Lance.

I glanced at Jack. "Ready for your evening constitutional?" I asked. He stood and took a moment to stretch out both back legs before sauntering to the door.

"That's a yes," I said. I grabbed his leash from its hook.

When I held out his halter, he darted forward and stuck his head through it. "Such enthusiasm," I said.

For his last walk of the night, Jack and I usually take a slow few-blocks stroll through the neighborhood. Jack sniffs his usual collection of shrubs, presumably checking on the newest updates in the dog news network.

The night was clear, and I checked out the constellations as we moved at a snail's pace down the sidewalk.

Jack's head snapped up, and he growled down the sidewalk right when something whizzed at me.

I ducked, and something thudded behind me.

"What the . . ." A figure in black disappeared around the corner.

Jack was sniffing behind me, and I turned and saw the projectile thrown my way.

"A caramel apple?" I said as Jack took a lick. I pulled him away. "You don't know what's in that."

He glanced at me like he was saying, "Apple and caramel, human, duh."

My mind whirled as I made Jack walk quickly back to the house.

Was this a stupid teenage prank? Would I find video footage of me online tomorrow, ducking an apple?

Or was this more sinister?

Was someone trying to warn me off?

Chapter 21

It was chilly enough that I wore my favorite light hoodie but still warm enough to sit happily outside Morning Broo. I grabbed a couple of cappuccinos and marionberry muffins while Colby watched Jack. When I came outside, carrying our breakfast, Jack was sitting intently watching Colby as she told him about the plot of the new middle-grade book she'd acquired for the library but was reading first "for research."

"And you won't believe what happened next," Colby said. Jack's eyes didn't waver from her face.

"Coffee delivery," I said.

Colby looked solemnly at Jack. "I'll tell you about the climax and resolution next time we chat, so you'll have something to look forward to."

Jack laid down, and Colby turned to pick up her muffin.

"I don't usually like muffins, but these are so good," Colby said. "So why are we joining the banana pants running group tonight?"

I told her why we were joining the Hunt 'n Run and also what I wanted to achieve since Colby is goal focused like that.

"So we're investigators masquerading as runners. I take it a fedora would be too much?"

"Feel free to run in one if you'd like."

Kristobel, the owner of the Bone to Be Wild pet boutique next door to the coffee shop, walked over. "Can I borrow Jack for a few minutes? I need a dog model."

"And Jack's a world-class model when he wants to be," I said. "You can use him if he'll consent to pose. But you'll have to discuss the particulars with him."

Kristobel took off Jack's red-plaid scarf and left it on the corner of the table before leading Jack away. Jack glanced at me a few times as he followed her like he was making sure this was okay with me 'cause he wasn't sure. I kept half an eye on them as Colby and I talked.

Over in front of Bone to be Wild, Kristobel had tied a different bandana around Jack's neck. She showed him a treat. Jack straightened up, ready for his close-up.

I glanced at Colby and then looked back in Jack's direction. "I'm not claiming this is the best investigative path ever, and I don't know if it's Miss Marple approved, but it seems like a way to find out more about Lance." I still hadn't told anyone, including Colby, my biggest fear about Lance.

"I'll be there tonight but won't be wearing bells. Or a fedora."

"I'll buy our beers afterward."

"And dinner."

"Deal. You drive a hard bargain."

A few minutes later, Kristobel and Jack came back. Jack wore a black bandana with orange pumpkins, and I suspected his belly was full of organic dog treats.

Kristobel handed over a bag of pumpkin-shaped treats. "Jack drove a hard bargain. Did you know he prefers peanut butter treats to sweet potato?"

I laughed. "Yep. Do you want the scarf back?"

"That's part of Jack's payment. Just tell people where it's from if they ask."

As Kristobel walked away, Colby shouted, "Hey, where'd your dog get that scarf? He earned it modeling."

"Not just modeling, but modeling at Bone to Be Wild!" Kristobel called over her shoulder.

"We always knew you didn't have such long legs for nothing," Colby told Jack as he sprawled across my feet.

We chatted briefly, and I tucked Jack's old bandana into my bag. Colby headed to the library while Jack slowly stretched to prepare for our two-block walk to the bookshop.

"Not a bad morning's work. You earned a new scarf and bag of treats. And I have a running buddy tonight, so you can nap at home." Not that Jack would've run with me regardless.

Jack held his head high as he walked alongside me.

Opening the bookshop went smoothly, almost like the world had returned to normal. A few orders had been placed for signed festival books and some new releases. Plus, it was time to get the romantasy boxes ready to ship since we'd already sent out the coffee- and tea-themed packages. So, when the store was quiet, I had plenty to accomplish.

The door jangled midday, shortly after I'd sent Milo on his lunch break. The man I'd seen several times, including going to Evelyn's office upstairs and once in the shop when he'd interrupted Jack's staring contest with this ball, strolled in.

He was casual again, in a dark gray T-shirt that brought out matching notes in his stormy blue eyes and dark brown cords. Rangy, I decided. If I was describing him in a novel, I'd use words like "rangy build" and "high cheekbones under stormy eyes."

I needed to get a grip.

"Back for more books?" I asked.

"Not exactly," he said. "Evelyn told me about your involvement in the murder case. I'm Sam Maki, by the way."

"I'm Bailey."

"I know. Evelyn's told me all about you."

"That sounds terrifying."

Jack trotted up to Sam and leaned his head into Sam's thigh. Sam promptly scratched behind Jack's ears, thereby sealing their lifetime friendship.

"You can't blame my sister. She's pretty fired up on your behalf."

Wait, sister? "I didn't know you and Evelyn were related."

Sam smiled. "We started out as stepsiblings when I was three and she was eight; then her mom adopted me and my mom adopted her. It's easiest to just say Evelyn is my sister."

Their family tree was almost as interesting as mine. "But you kept your last name?"

Sam nodded. "We debated changing it to the way Evelyn uses both of our moms' names, but I really wanted to keep it. It's one of the last things I have of my dad, who died when I was a baby."

"I'm sorry about your father."

"He's the one who named me Samu, which is basically the Finnish version of Samuel. Evelyn's mom really wanted to Americanize my name, but thankfully, my mother was on my side, and she backed down."

"Samu," I said. I felt the sounds of his name as I said it.

"But please call me Sam." He flashed his thousand-watt smile at me again. His smile was legitimately unfair. Almost too perfect, except it was slightly crooked.

"Back to why I came. I saw the name you were doodling and guessed it was related to the murder investigation. So when I needed to take a break yesterday, I ran the name for you."

I'd been around Jack enough to pick up some of his world-class side-eye. "Ran the name? Like through a police database?"

"Looked it up using completely legal means that use a few tools that rely on a simple web search," Sam said.

"That sounds sketchy."

"Let me try again. Let's say I have tools that are basically super Google, and I used them to search the internet for you. I'm a white hat hacker if that helps."

The opening was impossible to resist. "White hat? Your head is bare."

"It's also called ethical hacking. It's complicated, but corporations hire people like me to test and ensure their networks are secure. I occasionally do research for Evelyn, too, if that makes you feel any better."

That did, actually, since I doubted Evelyn was interested in lawbreaking. "So what'd you find?"

Sam placed a manilla folder on the counter between us. "It feels so old-school to carry around paper folders. Like I'm a spy passing secret info. I need a cloak."

"A white one," I joked. "And shouldn't this have been dropped in a garbage can with a sliver of microfiche or something to keep up the spy vibes?"

"Maybe." Sam opened the folder. "I'm guessing you're interested in Matt Leverton, who was in school with Lance Gregory."

"Exactly."

"From what I can tell, Leverton was convicted of larceny, criminal mischief, and drug possession as a teenager. He was caught breaking into the high school, which led to the larceny charge, and he had drugs on him, hence the possession with intent to distribute charge. But from what I've gathered, no one thought he'd done the crime solo. But he refused to turn on his friends, even when offered a better plea deal."

Sam pushed a collection of newspaper articles my way. I scanned the headlines.

Local Teen Convicted of High School Break-In and Graffiti.

Teen Facing Criminal Charges After High School Break-In.

High School Broken Into; Vandalized; Led to Drug Bust.

"You're sure this is Leverton?"

"The local paper didn't list his name because he's a juvenile. But one of the county court records was available online when it should've been sealed or at least redacted. Plus, a few Facebook posts from graduates of Elyan Hollow High talked about Matt. Check out this photo."

Sam showed me a Facebook printed-out that included a photo of Matt, Lance, Rex Abbot, and a fourth teen I didn't recognize. The text read: *My high school friends. Who would've thought one would end high school in jail and another would be a star?*

"It's not the only social media reference to the crime," Sam said.

"Did you find what Leverton is up to now?" Had his teen conviction scuttled the rest of his life?

"It looks like Leverton is doing okay. He's a mechanic in Wilsonville, Oregon."

Sam handed me a photo printed out from a company website. Wilsonville isn't too far south of Portland, although in a different direction than Elyan Hollow.

Something told me Matt Leverton's classmates would recognize him. He had a few crow's-feet around his eyes that matched his friendly smile. His dark hair was cut short versus the shaggy Kurt Cobain–like style he'd worn in the nineties.

I glanced back at the old photo. Cardigan? Check. Baggy jeans? Check. Matt had definitely been channeling Cobain's iconic look.

But despite the changes, you could see the man he'd become in his teenage face.

Wait. I recognized Matt's face. He'd come to the library event on the day of the murder with a small child. A girl who'd been wearing a green dress over purple-striped leggings. Her long brown hair had been shiny and pulled back from her face with a yellow headband.

Had he been leaving the maze when I arrived? While holding the hand of the little girl?

Had Matt run into Lance? And did their discussion spark into an argument?

But would Matt attack Lance in front of his daughter? From the few glimpses I remembered, Matt had been patient with her. I was sure I'd seen him holding her hand while walking out of the event.

"Do you think he's involved?" Sam asked.

"No idea, but I've seen him before," I said. "Thanks for this. I feel like I should pay you for your time."

"Why don't you pay me by letting me take you out for a beer one night? Or coffee?"

"That's not exactly how paying people back usually works."

Sam smiled at my words. "Is there anything else you want me to look up using my super special spy skills?"

"Can you find photos of the *Gone Ghouls* showrunner?" So I could compare them to the photos in Lance's folder.

"Do you have his name?"

I shook my head.

"It's okay. I can find that online, too. So, are you up to anything special tonight?" Sam asked.

"I'm dropping in on the Hunt 'n Run club." I explained the point of the club.

"Do you run with them often?"

"Nope, but I'm hoping it'll help me figure out what happened to Lance," I said.

"I'm not going to insult your intelligence by trying to tell you what to do, but remember this: if someone was desperate enough to kill Lance Gregory, you don't want to make them desperate enough to kill you."

On that happy note, Sam left.

Chapter 22

Not long after Sam left, my grandfather walked into Lazy Bones. I wondered how he felt coming into the shop now, having run the shop for decades before passing the torch to me. When I tried to check in with my grandfather about changes, he was willing to be a sounding board, especially on financial matters. But he was always ready to tell me that the decisions were mine.

But it must feel like coming to a place that used to be home but is subtly changing constantly.

"Captain!" I said. Jack stood and barely stretched before ambling over for a head scratch like it'd been days since they'd last seen each other. For my dog, that's a sign of excitement.

"Have any good ARCs come in?" my grandfather asked. He referred to the advance copies of books that publishers send us. We can also be approved for e-ARCs, but there's just something special about reading on paper. It's less distracting than reading on a device, so a book will never notify you about a new email or alert you that the book is running low on battery.

"A mystery arrived that might be perfect for you. I put it aside on my desk upstairs. The rest are in the usual spot in the break room."

We had a designated spot for ARCs, and my employees knew they could grab any ARC they wanted from the shelf. I always knew we had a shop bestseller on our hands when one of us would read an ARC and be so excited when telling the rest of the staff about it that everyone would argue about who got to read it next. Eventually, we'd pack the advance copies into online orders as bonus books. Which has to be one reason our online business has flourished with repeat customers. Because who doesn't like free books?

I left the shop in Milo's hands and followed my grandfather into the back.

"Captain, question for you," I said. I stood in the doorway to the back in a spot where I could keep an eye on the shop's front door.

My grandfather looked up from the back of the ARC he was scanning.

"You invited Rex to speak at Lazy Bones over the years, right? Why did you keep inviting him when he kept saying no? Weren't you offended?"

My grandfather leaned against the worktable. "As far as being offended, no, although I was slightly disappointed. But we're a small store, so I wasn't surprised when his publisher sent him on tour that they sent Rex to the big stores with a greater return on investment."

"That tracks."

"And since Rex didn't have family left in town, I couldn't blame him for not coming here."

"Even though the store gave him a scholarship?"

My grandfather raised his eyebrows at me.

"I looked through my mother's high school yearbooks and noticed the shop listed on the senior honors page."

"Rex is probably the most successful, book-wise, of anyone we awarded that scholarship to. But we weren't looking specifically for aspiring authors. A couple of the winners were readers who became high school English teachers. One went to law school. I've lost track of most, to be honest. Although I always appreciated the ones who dropped by the shop and told us how they were doing."

Milo came back into the store, and my grandfather beamed. "Milo! It's been ages."

As they chatted, I got ready for my late lunch and left the shop in Milo's hands.

I texted the Haunted House B&B that I was on my way. Fiona's husband, Donovan, met me at the door of their inn. He was bouncing on the balls of his feet as he said hi. His T-shirt had a drawing of Beethoven, and I wondered if he stuck to a wardrobe of music-inspired T-shirts and jeans during his job as a music therapist.

Donovan brushed his dark brown hair away from his face. "Fiona showed me the footage of Lance trying to move the bookcase."

"It seemed a strange thing to move."

"It is unless you know there's a door behind it. But not like a regular door, a hobbit-sized one. We debated setting it up as a kid's hideout but decided it would be easiest to block access for now."

The books and decor on the bookcase had been stacked in a couple of boxes on the opposite side of the foyer.

"Once Fiona comes up, you can help me do the honors," Donovan said. "She should join us in a minute. Do you need anything? Coffee? Fizzy water? We just restocked the drinks fridge."

Over a couple cans of sparkling water, Donovan and I chatted about town.

"I can't wait for Halloween. I hope we're overrun with trick-or-treaters," Donovan said. He bounced on his feet a few more times.

"We get tons at the shop."

"But you're right downtown in the middle of the action. We'll have to make signs so people know we're stocked and ready for Halloween in style."

"Just don't make a 'free candy' sign 'cause that'd be creepy."

Donovan laughed. "I'm thinking maybe we should offer something for parents, too. Like a mini-martini."

Fiona came up from the basement apartment. "I'm sorry for the delay. It feels like I'm in my second year of pregnancy and moving at a quarter speed these days."

"Second year." Donovan laughed. "You're on the home stretch, sweetheart. Just one more month."

Donovan and I each took an end of the bookcase and moved it away from the wall, leaving it in the center of the room.

The door behind it was about three feet high, with a curved top. It looked handmade, with careful craftsmanship. Although the sides were straight, it had a strong hobbit door vibe with its rounded top. It was an odd architectural choice.

But it was unbelievably charming. I couldn't believe Fiona and Donovan had willingly covered it up.

"If this was a family home, that would be the perfect children's hideout. Imagine coming in here with a snack and ukulele and feeling like this was your private world," Donovan said.

"It looks like you'd also like it as a hideout," I said.

Fiona and Donovan laughed.

"You got me," Donovan said. "You want to do the honors?"

"Sure."

Fiona handed me a flashlight, and I hoped this was worth the effort and wasn't a wild goose chase.

I opened the door and shone the flashlight inside, then crawled inside.

The room had a sloped ceiling that spanned the length of the staircase. I stood up when I entered. Donovan followed me inside.

"We thought about taking this down and adding shelves or something to turn it into a charming nook," Donovan said. "Let's see if the light works in here."

He flipped the light switch, and the bulb overhead flickered on, bathing the room in a weak light.

"It's a fun space."

"Imagine it with a beanbag chair and a lamp." Donovan had switched back into energy mode, and I was tempted to ask if he had an eco-mode setting.

But why had Lance tried to enter here?

Was it just nostalgia? Had this been child Lance's hideout? Did he escape here from a family of older sisters?

Had he brought his friends here?

I shone the flashlight into the corners, with dust particles and a tiny spiderweb catching in the light. Maybe Lance had wanted in here to set up a ghost scene. I could imagine his words: this was my childhood hangout, and it's the reason why I became a ghost hunter. . . .

I paused. Was one of the floorboards slightly raised?

I knelt in the slanting area of the room. The board was a short piece, about a foot long, leading to the wall.

Donovan looked over my shoulder.

"I don't remember the floorboard sticking out. Maybe the house settled? But other than ensuring this was empty, we didn't do anything with the space."

I gently grasped the board's edge with my fingertips and pulled it outward. It lifted easily.

Someone had created a little cubbyhole. I pulled out a yellowed paperback of *The Count of Monte Cristo*, a spiral notebook, and a small brown cardboard box, the type you get at jewelry stores.

"Is that it?"

I handed Donovan the flashlight and crawled backward. He took my place and checked out the cubby.

"Darn, that's it." Donovan turned and called out over his shoulder, "Fi! Bailey found pirate treasure!"

"Ohhh!" Fiona said through the hobbit door.

When I'd pulled out the floorboard, I'd noted the paneling above it looked odd. So I took the flashlight and crawled back to the hole. I stuck my fingers under the panel, in the gap created by the floorboard, and pulled.

The paneling came forward at an angle. I switched my hand to the right side and pulled again, and the panel creaked open.

"You have a tunnel!" I said. It was about three feet tall, although when I aimed the flashlight inside, the tunnel was taller than the door.

"What?" Donovan pushed up next to me. We gazed into the dark abyss, which sucked up the beam of the flashlight. The air smelled damp, but not moldy.

"There are a handful of tunnels leading out to the river. You know those circles in the retaining wall along the beach? The ones with the grates? That's where the tunnels meet the river."

"FI! Bailey found a rumrunners tunnel *in our house*!"

"What!"

I glanced at Donovan. "Some of the tunnels connect with each other. You could visit one or two of your neighbors this way, provided the tunnel hasn't collapsed, or they haven't barricaded the entrance in their house."

"Should we keep this secret?" Donovan said.

"Maybe for now," I said.

We left the cubbyhole, crawling back out into the light in the reception room of the inn.

"What's this about a tunnel? I can't believe you guys are having all of the fun without me."

I explained the legend of the tunnel system to Fiona. "It makes me wonder if the original owners of this house were bootleggers during prohibition."

"We could host our own speakeasy!" Fiona said.

"With a secret password people will need to know, else we won't let them enter!" Donovan said.

"The historical society might have more information, although some of the houses kept their tunnels secret." Had Lance known about the tunnel? Was there a reason he wanted to access it?

A secret tunnel could've looked great on his TV show. But if that was the case, why not tell Donovan and Fiona about the tunnel and convince them to let him reveal it on air?

Donovan led Fiona into the room, helping her navigate the small doorway, to show her the tunnel.

"It's so awesome!" she squealed from inside.

As they explored, I thought about how the air in the tunnel smelled fresh enough that it could lead somewhere. Maybe to the river.

But maybe somewhere else.

The thought gave me chills.

Donovan and Fiona rejoined me. "I can't believe we have our own smugglers tunnel!" Fiona said. "A tunnel and pirate treasure we still need to check out. This is the best day, ever."

"'Treasure' might be an overstatement." I put the small stack on the table and started with the paperback. A faded movie theater stub from the Popcorn Palace was stuck in the pages about three-quarters of the way through.

A stamp inside said: "Property of Elyan Hollow High School."

I put the book down and opened the spiral notebook. The first few pages held notes about *The Count of Monte Cristo* like Lance had been keeping a reading journal for class. His handwriting was neat, although the ink had faded slightly, probably due to his using a cheap pen on cheap paper. At least I could still read it.

But I stopped at a new page.

The word "February" was circled, and he'd counted backward.

My birthday was in February. On February 29, so I usually could only celebrate my actual birthdate every four years and everyone always divided my age by four and pretended I was that age. Like when I turned eight, everyone joked I was two since it was only my second birthday. When I turned twenty, my cake at home had been adorned with the sort of "5" candle found in the grocery store's children's party decorations section.

Underneath the dates, Lance had written *May?*

Was this note about me? Had Lance known about me and traipsed away, pretending he hadn't left a sophomore in high school pregnant when he graduated?

I flipped through the rest of the pages. A few had been torn out, the long, faded scraps of paper still stuck in the spiral rings. Nothing else interested me.

And nothing in the notebook felt worth coming back for.

"Now for the final item," Donovan said in a deep voice like he was narrating a documentary.

The box.

Donovan moved it to the center of the table, upping the suspense for Fiona and me.

"You do the honors, Bailey," he said.

I reached and slowly opened the box.

A tarnished silver charm was nestled inside. It was the type of charm one would find on a charm bracelet, shaped like the caduceus, aka the two snakes twined around a winged staff used as a symbol for doctors in the United States.

One of my mother's favorite jokes is that the caduceus is a misused symbol based on a lack of understanding of the actual symbolism and that the medical profession should use the rod of Asclepius instead.

Why did Lance have a caduceus charm? As far as I knew, he hadn't wanted to study to be a doctor. But there was so much I didn't know about him.

Maybe the name Haunted House B&B was appropriate, although not in the way they expected.

Maybe this house was haunted by faded memories waiting to pounce into the light of today.

Chapter 23

I'd dropped in on a college running club a few times as an undergraduate, but I generally preferred to go solo or with a friend like Colby. I enjoy the time to think and feel in tune with myself instead of trying to be social. Colby and I could run for miles without talking.

Joining up with a group of overenthusiastic runners was like dropping Jack into a pen of playful golden retriever puppies. In one aspect, we were the same. But the bustle and energy was overwhelming. But I still pulled on my favorite green running shorts and a navy tank and headed out, leaving Jack napping on the couch.

"I'm so glad you joined us!" Kristobel from the Bone to Be Wild dog boutique said as I walked up to the parking lot outside the Outdoor Spirits Sporting Goods on the edge of downtown. They have a decent selection of workout and outdoor gear, plus popular bicycle and gear rentals during the summer. "It's good you didn't bring Jack, although I miss seeing his fuzzy face."

I noted Kristobel's light green shirt, which read STAY PAWSITIVE alongside a dog print. Her running tights had a dog bone pattern.

"Jack's a lover, not a runner," Colby said. I turned to see my friend decked out in her usual warm-weather runners' capris and a slightly loose tank top. Her shiny black hair was pulled back into double French braids, which almost made me jealous since the best I could do since bobbing my hair was to pin the top back or wear a headband, like now.

"He is the sweetest boy. When we got Great Pyrenees at the rescue, they were always the fluffiest, most stubborn loves," Kristobel said. I was pretty sure she referred to the dog rescue she'd run before moving to Oregon. "Colby, I wanted to talk to you about a project I have in mind with the local animal shelter. Because who can resist a readathon for dogs or cats fundraiser? . . ."

As they talked, I moved over to the curb to stretch. Kristobel regularly fundraised for no-kill shelters in her shop, and asking Colby to throw her efforts behind a readathon was a surefire way to success.

Evelyn's brother Sam walked up, dressed in the same Ironman finishers shirt I'd seen before and navy-and-red shorts.

Sam smiled at me. "Come here often?"

"It's not one of my usual haunts." I glanced at the store, hoping he'd see the wit of my impromptu pun.

He laughed. "It's my first time. But it seems like a good place to get to know my neighbors."

"And if you don't like them, you can run away," I said. Had Sam known about this club before I told him about it?

Had he come because he'd know I'd be here?

"That's a benefit. So, how far do you usually run?"

We talked about training plans, and I finally got an answer to one of my questions about Sam.

"I'm not sure if I'll do another Ironman, but I'm registered for the regional triathlon series," he said.

Would it be stalkerish if I looked up his past results? I'd decide later, although I was tempted to crack out my phone and google him on the spot.

Colby walked back up. She eyed Sam and then glanced at me.

"Colby, this is Sam, Evelyn's brother. Sam, this is Colby."

They shook hands. "So, come here often?" Colby asked.

Sam laughed. "I was just telling Bailey I'm new to town and came out to meet people."

The organizer called Sam over, and as soon he was out of earshot, Colby glanced at me. "Evelyn's brother?"

"Blended family."

"Explains why they don't look anything alike."

This was an understatement, but I still said, "Not everyone in a family looks alike. Your parents used cookie cutters to produce Danby and you, but I don't look like my mom."

"You sort of have her smile."

"Yeah, but her other kids are clearly hers."

It was just about to hit 6:00 p.m., and we'd self-sorted into speed groups, with Colby and me in the eight-minute mile cluster, when Rex walked up to the parking lot, dressed for running.

"Rex!" one of the guys greeted him. "I'm so glad you could make it. Guys, you won't believe this, but this man was one of my high school teammates. . . ."

"Rex couldn't show up for his bookstore event, but he can arrive here mostly on time?" Colby muttered beside me.

"At least he made it to the panel." Silver lining.

Rex's eyebrows raised when he saw me, and he nodded hello. I gave him a solemn nod back.

Was he surprised I ran? Or just surprised we'd run into each other again?

The organizer called for everyone's attention. "Okay, Hunt 'n Runners! Some of you are new or haven't been here for a while, so let me remind you of the drill! Alex is our rabbit today, and he left five minutes ago. He's dropped a trail of flour at each intersection, telling you where to go. So let's go hunt down our rabbit!"

The group took off, with the fastest group leaving first, followed by the seven-minute milers, and then the group that included Colby, me, Rex, and his friend. Groups followed us, and for the first block, we were all close, but as we followed the first flour hash and headed up the road toward the highway, gaps started to emerge.

"You sure this is a good pace for you?" Rex's friend asked.

"I think so, but I can always drop back if needed."

The friend sounded chipper despite climbing uphill. "I caught a glimpse of Lance last week, but we didn't get a chance to talk. I can't believe what happened to him."

"Did you see Lance much over the years?" Rex asked.

"No, he fell off the face of the earth as far as I was concerned. But from what I remember, he'd burned every bridge possible by the time he graduated, so I wasn't surprised. How about you? Weren't you both in LA?"

"It's a giant city, and we ran in different circles. Although I did get coffee with him once or twice. Hey, weren't you friends with Lance's sister? Melly? Is she still around?"

"She and her wife moved to an island near Seattle a few years ago. Whidbey, I think. The twins show up in town sometimes, and Ally pops by occasionally. What about you? How long are you staying?"

Colby and I started to outpace them, probably because they were talking so much, and I didn't hear Rex's response. But I wondered: Was Rex here because an old high school friend invited him? Or did he have to come to also find out the lowdown on Lance from his old high school buddies?

The running club had one thing going for it. After chasing the flour arrows through town and back again, eventually ending at the sporting goods store, everyone met up at the Elyan Mortuary & Deli for a recovery beverage.

Aka a beer. Although Ash also sold a handful of sports drinks she kept on hand for the runners since some people don't want a pint after running. A few people snagged sparkling water, and the Boorito cart boomed with food orders. So, as Ash poured our pints, I added my and Colby's food orders to the virtual queue, wondering how long it would take.

"Did you know a group in Spain, I think, did a study of athletes and found that a light lager was more effective than water as a recovery drink?" Ash said as she handed over our beers.

"Sounds like an excellent excuse," Colby said.

Ash stuck her tongue out at Colby, and they both laughed.

Rex walked up, still in his running gear, like everyone else, although he'd added a black hoodie.

"What'd you go for?" Rex asked, and motioned at my pint.

"It's a locally made hefeweizen," I said.

"I'll take one of the same," he said.

Ash raised her eyebrows at me, then turned to pull his pint.

"Bailey!"

Oh great.

Of course my uncle Hudson had to make an appearance. He was dressed for work in a dapper gray suit with a snowy white shirt beneath. No tie, so it must've been a casual day for him.

"How is the financial analysis of the festival coming along?" he asked.

It would be such a relief to tell him it wasn't his business. But I took the coward's way out, yet again, and simply said, "Our sales were stronger than last year."

"But were they high enough to make it worth holding the festival?" Hudson asked.

"That's something the business will discuss later once I've had a chance to look at the month and get feedback from my grandfather." My subtle dig hit home when Hudson processed what I said.

"Just because you and Dad like the bookstore doesn't mean it's worth maintaining."

"I think the shop is a great asset to the town," a voice said next to me.

Hudson's eyes narrowed in annoyance.

"The festival was wonderful, and it's nice to see so many people embracing books," Rex continued.

Hudson's eyes widened when he recognized who he was talking to.

"Mr. Abbot! I don't know if you remember me, but I used to run into you in the bookshop when I was a kid. Liz is my older sister." The grating note in Hudson's tone made me want to shower. Granted, as I'd just run for an hour, I needed one.

Based on the way Rex's face closed off, he felt the same way. "You were lucky to grow up around such a cozy shop. I was always jealous of Lizzy for belonging to the shop when I just visited whenever I could, feeling like an outsider. But your father always welcomed me, and that's the value of bookstores. They're welcoming places with access to the best thing in the world: books. And stories. They allow kids in small towns to dream of the wider world, and when the magic is right, they bring people home."

"We have an exceptional library with excellent funding," Hudson said. "Bailey should've become a librarian like her friend."

I held in a snort. Hudson had ranted against the last library levy, which had passed with eighty percent, ensuring long-term access for locals of all ages.

"I'm happy she didn't since her lit festival brought me back to town."

Was Rex telling the truth? Had it really been the festival that brought him to town? Or did he have other, secret reasons? The sort that would lead to Lance's demise?

"Rex, it's so nice to see you!" A guy in his forties walked up. They gave each other hugs, part handshake with a one-armed hug.

Rex motioned to me. "Have you met Bailey, Lizzy Briggs' daughter?"

The man turned to me. "You know, I've seen you around, but I hadn't connected you and Lizzy. Which is stupid of me since I was good friends with your mother when we were kids. Is she still in Portland? I'm so impressed she finished medical school since that was all she talked about as a teen. Me, I wanted to become an architect but ended up in logistics."

"Yep, she's still in Portland." We talked briefly about my mother and her family.

Hudson hovered, trying to worm his way into the conversation, while I eased my way out of it. I slowly drifted back to my friends as Colby and Sam debated the proper pronunciation of "data."

"Do you have an opinion?" Sam raised an eyebrow at me in a roguishly charming way.

"I think I should stay out of this debate," I said.

"Just get over it, because you know I'm right." But I could tell Colby was mostly joking.

Evelyn walked up with a pint of ale. "Are you two finally done debating? You're as bad as some of my law school classmates."

"You're just jealous because we're usually the two that get into stupid debates. It drives our mothers mad," Sam said. "The no debates at Thanksgiving rule is always broken."

"Usually by you," Evelyn said.

"Says the person who started the 'is a hot dog a sandwich' debate last year. I know you saw the meme and thought it was the perfect way to shake things up when Mom asked you about your dating life."

As Sam and Evelyn bickered, I thought about family. Something told me, minor debates aside, Sam and Evelyn brought out the best in each other. I can't say the same thing about Hudson and me since every conversation feels like a land mine. Especially since he didn't know the bookshop ownership had already switched into my hands.

We really needed to tell him, although it had been my grandfather's decision to wait and see how the transition went before letting him know. My grandfather had decided this to give me a gentle out in case I decided running the shop wasn't for me after all.

But it was the type of secret that would ruin a holiday dinner in a way a debate about what constitutes a sandwich won't.

Unless your family is intense and looking for ways to ruin holidays.

"Anything between bread is a sandwich," Colby said.

"But hot dogs are in buns," Sam said. "Not slices of bread. What constitutes a slice of bread?"

Evelyn looked at me. "And think this is how you're coming down from your runner's high."

My phone beeped. A text from Boorito telling me my order was ready.

"Saved by the Boorito cart," I said. Evelyn tagged along with me.

"Have you heard from the police in the last few hours?" she asked as we joined the short line to pick up food from the bustling cart.

"No, thankfully. What can I expect if I am arrested and this goes to court?" I asked.

"That's a hard question to answer. So many of the end results in our courts depend on the skill and dedication of the defense attorney, plus how well funded the defense is, which sucks. Everyone deserves a fair shake. As I mentioned, my friend Calla is an absolute pit bull, and the local DA wouldn't know what hit them, so you'd be in good hands."

As long as I could afford her.

"You sound passionate about the topic. Did you consider going into public defending or something?"

"It crossed my mind. I've even reviewed a few basics in case I need to stand in for you again."

Our food was ready, and Olivia waved when she caught sight of me. "I can't believe we're so slammed I can't even run orders out!" she said.

"If it slows down, come see me in the taproom," I said.

Evelyn and I carried the food back to the table, where Colby and Sam debated something new.

"Save your breath to cool your bowl," I joked as I handed Colby's pollo bowl over to her.

She laughed.

As we ate, a group with Rex grew and moved closer to us, not unlike patches of seaweed floating in the ocean.

Ash must be ecstatic that her taproom was slammed tonight. The last time I glanced at the bar, she was swapping out a keg while one of her bartenders poured a series of pints.

A voice from the crowd caught my attention.

"Lance basically had to leave after graduating, right?"

"He didn't have to flee. Everyone loved him."

"Nah, I only think he left 'cause his parents did. Otherwise, he would've been here yearly, telling us stories about Los Angeles." Wait, that sounded like Pearl. I glanced over and saw her holding a can of sparkling water. She'd opted for lemon this time.

I wanted to keep listening, but Rex asked me, "Do you run with that group often?"

I shook my head and hoped he couldn't tell I was about to lie. "Colby and I felt like dropping in. We usually run together a few days a week in the morning. Plus, we paddleboard and cycle."

"Do you have an end goal for this, or do you just like to be active?"

"No, not working out makes me anxious. I've debated signing up for a triathlon but have yet to work up the nerve to do it."

"Why not?"

"I don't really like the whole competition aspect, but it'd be fun to finish one."

Rex half smiled. "You didn't inherit your mother's killer instincts?"

I held my hands out in a "no idea" gesture. But I was lying. I definitely hadn't inherited those traits from my mother.

"Hey, Rex." One of the guys from the running group walked up.

"Do you know Bailey?" Rex asked. "She's Lizzie's daughter."

"Lizzie Briggs? I haven't thought about her for years." He turned to me and gave me a once-over with a frown. "Huh, I wouldn't have guessed you were her daughter. You're way too old, making me feel ancient, and you don't look anything like her."

Yes, please remind me that I don't look like my mother. The voice in the back of my mind asked if I'd looked like Lance.

And that was a no, too. Although Lance might have dyed his hair, we may have had our original hair colors in common.

Rex nodded toward a woman walking inside the tap room. "Hey, Ally Gregory is here. Do you remember her? Lance's older sister? She wants to—oh, that's her now."

A woman with long gray-streaked brown hair walked up. She was a few inches taller than me, maybe five foot eight, with a curvy figure, dressed in a flowy espresso brown cardigan over a black tank and jeans.

"Ally," Rex said.

"I'm surprised you remember me," Ally said. They gave each other a slightly awkward hug.

"And this is Lizzie Briggs' daughter, Bailey."

"I always liked your mom." Ally was clearly trying to be social but struggling.

"Are you in town 'cause of your brother?" one of the guys asked.

I flinched but also appreciated the question since it meant I didn't have to ask it.

"Yes, I came to identify him and start the funeral arrangements. One of my sisters flew to LA to pack up his apartment."

"I'm so sorry for your loss," several of us murmured in unison as if we'd practiced it.

Rex nodded at me. "Bailey helped Marion pack Lance's things at the Sleepy Hollow."

Ally's gaze swiveled to me. "You did?"

"Marion wanted a second person, and I helped document everything, just in case there were any questions."

Ally nodded. "That's a smart idea, and I'll pretend it doesn't offend me a tiny bit. Out of curiosity—did you see a pocket watch?"

I paused, thinking back to the belongings we packed. I shook my head. "No, I don't remember one. Maybe he left it in LA?"

"Oh no, Lance always had it with him. He called it his good luck charm. The police don't have it, so I hoped it would be with the rest of his stuff."

"I'm sorry, but I didn't see it," I said.

Ally's eyes went vague, like she was viewing the past instead of focusing on anything in the here and now. "Lance inherited that watch from our grandfather since he was the only boy in the family, which annoyed my oldest sister, who really wanted it. And she'll want it for her oldest son, even though Lance has a son, so it should go to him."

"Lance has a son?" I asked.

Ally nodded, and tears gathered in the corners of her eyes. "He's ten. He lives with his mom in Colorado these days. He's a good kid and turning into quite the mountain biker. But Lance hasn't been much of a dad. He tends to fly his kid to our parents' house during his visitation. My parents spoil him even worse than they spoiled Lance, so it's probably good that he's mostly with his mom. She has a good head on her shoulders."

"Doesn't Lance have an older kid?" one of the guys standing nearby asked.

I hadn't realized we had a crowd listening in. But we were in a bar, so it's not like this was a private conversation. But it always makes me feel skeeved out to realize people had been listening in on me.

"No, just the one. Lincoln. He's going to be heartbroken," Ally said.

At the same time, the man said, "There was a rumor, but maybe it was about someone else."

"Is there anything we can do for you?" someone asked Ally.

"Turn back time?" Ally said.

She looked at me. "I heard there's good food here."

I pointed out the QR code on one of the tables and explained she could go order in person or online. It felt like we were alone for a moment despite the busy bar.

"I went into the Haunted House B&B a few days ago."

Ally looked up from her phone order. "I can't believe my childhood home is an inn now. But it's a huge place, and I'm glad someone loves it. I thought about booking a room, but I'm staying with a friend in Scappoose instead." She referred to a bigger town almost ten miles downriver from us.

"It's a beautiful place. That hobbit closet under the stairs must've been a blast when you were a kid."

Ally's smile was sad. "It was, but Lance got all of us girls kicked out of it, under punishment of having to clean the bathrooms or worse."

"Youngest child?"

"Spoiled only boy. Lance never fully grew up," Ally said. "But you can blame my parents for that. They always swooped in to save their baby, even when they should've left him to figure things out like they did for the rest of us. They practiced tough love for the four oldest and decided to forget all that when it came to the youngest. Whether it was giving him the coveted hangout space or covering up a minor fender bender.

"Don't get me wrong. I loved my brother, and his visits were always a delight. He was great with my kids, and he was great at subtly breaking up the inevitable family bickering. He excelled at reading people—he could be amazingly insightful. But Lance never really grew up. Without my parents' help, he couldn't have really afforded to live as he chased his dream."

"He sounds complicated." And he was good at reading people if he could minimize family drama for his own benefit. Which is a skill I'd love to acquire.

"That's Lance in a nutshell, especially since he didn't always use his power for good."

"You must have loved the tunnel as a kid. Did you ever see where it went?" I asked.

"Tunnel?"

She looked at me skeptically as I said, "The one that leads somewhere from the hobbit closet?"

Ally shook her head. "There's no tunnel."

"I saw it today."

"Are you sure you went to the right house?" Ally asked. She suddenly pursed her mouth. "You know, that could've been Lance's reason for wanting to keep the closet all to himself. And it could explain how he kept sneaking out as a teen."

"If there's anything I can do for you, let me know," I said.

"I'm going to go wait for my food."

Ally left the bar, and I returned to Colby, Evelyn, and Sam. About ten minutes later, as I walked home, I wondered if Lance was my father if my mother hadn't told him about me since she didn't want his family involved. Did I have four aunts that I didn't know? And cousins?

And maybe a younger brother named Lincoln?

When I got home, Jack was napping in the living room, with only a solo light glowing in the dark. Jack stood and slowly stretched as he walked off the couch before coming to greet me.

"It's good to see you're so excited to see me," I said. I gave Jack a thorough head scratch, as was his due.

When I held up Jack's halter, he shoved his head through it, and we went for a short walk. Although my mind was still whirling like I was running a marathon. Jack sniffed his favorite trees and shrubs, and I wondered what the dog news network had posted.

"I wonder what neighborhood secrets you've learned but have never told anyone," I told him.

Jack ignored me and kept sniffing.

The house was still empty when we returned home. It was rather late for my grandfather to be out. I'm not his keeper, but it seemed like he'd been going out more recently.

Before taking a much-needed shower, I pulled my phone out of my bag.

I clicked on my mother's number, which rang twice before going to voicemail.

She'd declined my call.

I tried to keep the annoyance out of my voice as I said, "Mom, it's Bailey. A lot of things have been happening, and we need to talk. Please call me back ASAP."

After I hung up and tossed my phone on my bed, I realized that while Elyan Hollow loves to celebrate ghosts as part of Halloween, we had plenty of real ghosts of unsettled issues lurking in the shadows.

And did one of those ghostly shadows kill Lance?

Or was it chance he died in his hometown? Taylor, at least, had come to town because of him and the ghost show, and she clearly carried a major grudge against him.

I kept seeing Lance's past like a specter, sneaking up behind him.

But whoever had caused this tragedy was all too human.

Chapter 24

It was Friday morning, so it was time for the highlight of my week: stand-up paddleboarding.

It was my week to drive, so I picked up Colby and headed down to the marina. I glanced at my friend as we took our paddleboards out onto the water.

"This might be our last paddleboarding Friday of the year," I said. The air felt cold, too cold, but I knew I'd warm up as we started paddling.

"Unless we head out for a few more weeks in wet suits," Colby said.

We did our usual route. The light waves lapped against our boards, making me stay light on my feet to keep my balance, all while keeping my knees slightly bent. The morning was peaceful, and being out reminded me that somethings in the world will always feel right, no matter what else is going wrong.

We paddled to the center of the harbor and stopped, floating on the waves. Colby dropped into a downward dog on her paddleboard, then lifted one foot into the air. She glanced over at me, her balance rock solid. "I booked a last-minute flight last night," she said.

"Where are you going?" I held a warrior pose. Colby transitioned to a low lunge.

"I'm flying out this evening to visit Hayes since his contract was extended a few weeks. Hayes wanted me to tell you that he's sad he missed your festival. And that he's loving the books you recommended to him. He will message you next week and ask what he should order next." Colby's husband, Hayes, traveled for weeks at a time. He'd stopped by the shop and picked up a couple of books before his most recent trip. I'd once recommended an e-reader to Hayes since it takes up less space and weight when traveling. But after spending his days looking at computer screens doing whatever he did as an IT consultant, he wanted something without a screen to help him unwind.

"It's really not fair that Hayes likes your book recs better than mine," Colby said. She fluidly transitioned to a high lunge like she was on dry land versus on an unstable paddleboard rocking gently in the river.

I wouldn't touch the book recommendations debate with a ten-foot pole. "Do you need a ride to the airport?"

"Danby already offered to drive me. I think she needs an excuse to go somewhere in Portland, but she knows our parents want her to stay in town. They still don't trust her."

"If Danby changes her mind, let me know."

"If you could find out where Danby's sneaking off to, let me know," Colby said. "I feel like she's hiding something."

When she'd gotten into a legal jam, Danby's family hadn't helped her avoid the consequences, which I respected. They'd worked as a group to ensure she didn't get into trouble again. "You need to trust Danby to make her own decisions."

Something told me Danby would eventually rebel if she felt smothered for too long.

"She's doing so well; I just don't want her to ruin it."

It sounded like Lance's family kept him out of trouble instead of letting him face the consequences of his actions. And had those actions led to his death a few decades later?

I told myself to focus on my workout and enjoy this moment in the sunny but cold late September air.

Everything else would work itself out.

Life always keeps moving, after all.

With everything that had happened, losing myself in books should've been an easy escape. Find a new life, maybe somewhere magical, to explore for an hour. But even though Lance's death made me too anxious to relax, I could focus on the shop at least. The usual opening tasks, in conjunction with my morning paddleboard, made me feel grounded.

At lunchtime, Danby showed up, and I left the store in her hands for a few minutes as I headed to the office to scarf down my lunch. Jack stayed with Danby, helping her keep an eye on the shop. From the security system monitor, I saw Danby stop and pet him, then help a customer who'd walked up to the register with a stack of books.

When I returned downstairs, multiple people were browsing, and Danby was reorganizing a display by the register.

"Full disclosure: your sister asked me to snoop and find out if and why you've been heading into Portland. But as I told her, it's not my business."

"But you thought I should know. Thanks for being up-front," Danby said.

"Just know that Colby cares. She's committed to ensuring you succeed, even if it runs the risk of running you off."

"Aw, you said the quiet part out loud." Danby checked off titles on the list of books to restock on the shelves.

"By the way, the film crew is returning tonight," I said.

Danby turned and focused on me with a laser glare. "You're kidding, right?"

"I told them they could hold a séance. I'll be on-site, and they promised not to destroy anything this time."

"You know that's a terrible idea, right?"

"Yes, but I hope it'll help me figure out what happened to Lance."

"With a fake séance?" Danby continued to look at me like I was the biggest idiot in Elyan Hollow.

"I really don't want this hanging over me."

This made Danby pause, and I suspected she understood at a deep level, as she knew what it was like. Although I was a murder suspect and she'd actually done a prank gone wrong that had resulted in property damage, with no deaths or injuries, except to her own pride.

A while later, the door jangled again, and Sam walked in. Jack headed to him right away for an ear scratch.

Sam looked as casual as ever. But this time, as he said hello, he pulled a tablet out of his messenger bag and showed me the screen.

"A photo of the *Gone Ghouls* showrunner as requested," Sam said. "I can send over his bio and a few other details."

It wasn't the man from the photos with Taylor, which made me feel slightly better about the world.

Chapter 25

I went home after closing the shop to eat dinner, put a fresh bandana on Jack, and we walked back downtown.

The TV show's van promptly pulled into the parking spot in front of the store at 8:00 p.m.

Letting the ghost hunters back into the bookshop was a bad idea.

But I let them in anyway.

"I swear we'll be careful," Jill told me, and Bill nodded in agreement. They lugged in their gear while Taylor followed with her ever-present tablet and a leather tote over her shoulder.

I'd already shifted a bookcase aside and set up a round table in the store with three chairs.

"Where's the tablecloth?" Taylor snapped at Jill.

"What tablecloth?" Jill pulled a microphone out of one of the bins.

"The one I told you to bring. We need to set the right ambiance."

"I don't work for you," Jill muttered, and turned to grab something else out of a bin.

Taylor glared at her and started to open her mouth, but Bill spoke.

"Let's just get this filmed," Bill said. "It'll look better without a tablecloth. With one, it'd look like we were trying to fake effects, like a Victorian psychic's parlor tricks."

I wondered if Taylor wanted a tablecloth to cover for shaking the table or causing "paranormal" events. Because I was willing to guess the show regularly created fake footage.

Taylor glared at Bill and put a couple of fat white candles on the table.

"You have holders for those candles, right?" I asked. "Cleaning candle wax off a table isn't my idea of a good time. We have some battery-operated candles. Much cleaner." It would also reduce the likelihood of Taylor burning our store down.

"We will obviously need real flames," Taylor said. She stalked to the back of the store.

Jill glanced at Bill. "We're almost done with this contract."

"Just stay focused," Bill said.

I suspected they'd been repeating that mantra to each other since coming to Elyan Hollow.

Clarity, the owner of the apothecary, knocked on the door. Taylor pushed past me to let her in.

I paused by Bill. "Would it be easier on you and Jill if I just kicked all of you out?"

"Don't tempt me," Bill said.

Clarity fussed over the candles while Jill and Bill set up their cameras and audio equipment.

Taylor shifted a candle, and Clarity immediately moved it back.

"It'll look better on-screen if we move it to the left," Taylor said.

"But if you want the spirits to come, you need to follow my instructions." Clarity sprinkled a bag of something shiny on the table.

"That better not be glitter," I said.

Clarity didn't respond, so I knew she'd just released glitter into my store.

I glanced at Jack, who was watching things from the sanctity of his dog bed. All I needed was a glitter-covered Great Pyrenees to make tonight absolutely perfect.

"What exactly are you hoping to achieve?" I asked.

"A séance, duh. Hopefully, we can get Lance to answer questions," Taylor said. "This bookcase is in the way."

Taylor stepped toward the display of signed books from the festival.

I jumped in her way. "You will not touch or move anything in this shop. Period. If you damage these signed editions, you will have a serious problem."

Taylor raised her hand like she was trying to shoo me away.

"Remember the agreement we signed, Taylor," Bill said. "And if you want a positive recommendation, don't destroy our filming sites."

"Like I'd ever want a recommendation from you," Taylor said.

"You do know we're asked about your performance, right?" Bill said.

My eyes narrowed at Taylor. Had she been upset about a possible poor report from Lance, and snapped? But that seemed unlikely, although it might have been the last kicked pebble that caused a rockslide.

When I hired a new bookseller, I always looked at how they treated their potential fellow sales associates, especially when I wasn't around. When my grandfather owned the store, I realized how people treated me—especially when I was a lowly teenage employee—gave me insight into how they'd deal with people they saw as "beneath" them. Taylor should learn that treating people she saw as "unimportant" would come back to haunt her.

Or she could follow my theory and try to be as good of a person as possible all the time, not just when it felt convenient. Not that I don't stumble occasionally.

Which I proved when I metaphorically poked Taylor. "What do you think Lance could tell you?"

"Other than his killer?"

"I don't know; I just keep getting an image of photographs."

Taylor's eyes widened, then narrowed. "Did Lance show you photos of me?"

"I can honestly say no, Lance never did."

She stared at me and I kept my gaze level, daring her to break eye contact first. She broke first and turned her head away.

"I knew that snake was taking photos of me last month in Arizona when my boyfriend visited," Taylor muttered.

"Why would he do that?" I asked.

"Because he wanted to get me fired and wasn't against playing dirty. But what I do on my own time is no one's business," Taylor said. "Let's get back to work."

Maybe the photos were of the someone special in Taylor's life when he'd come to visit her on the road. Or he'd been someone she'd met while filming. Maybe Lance had just been a voyeuristic creep.

A while later, we were ready to start. I sat at the table with Clarity and Taylor. The candlelight sparkled on the glitter sprinkled across the tabletop. Bill stood with his camera focused on Taylor while Jill knelt with her microphone out of the frame.

"We're here today, in Lazy Bones Books, to see if we can reach—" Taylor broke off. She cleared her throat and looked directly at Bill. "Make this look good."

"I'm doing my job." Bill's tone was brisk.

Clarity glanced at me, raised her lip slightly, and then shook her head.

I wasn't the only one annoyed with Taylor.

"Let's start over."

Jill counted down from five, and Taylor looked at the camera again. "We're here today to see if we can contact our dear departed show host, Lance Gregory, who was killed six days ago."

Taylor held up a pocket watch in the candlelight. "I have one of Lance's most beloved possessions here, hoping it will draw his spirit here."

My gaze snapped to Taylor. How did she get Lance's pocket watch? I'd definitely send the security footage of tonight to Detective Whitlock.

"The three of us are going to hold hands and see if we can make contact." Taylor held out her hands, and I shifted forward to clasp hands with Clarity and Taylor. I closed my eyes, wishing I was anywhere else.

"Lance? Are you there?" Taylor asked. Her voice sounded quivery, like she was on the verge of tears.

"Do you smell something? I think I smell pine, like the cologne that Lance used to wear," Taylor said.

I barely opened my eyes, letting me see Clarity grimace through my slitted lids.

Taylor started to shudder. One of her feet kicked the table legs, making it shake. She spoke in a deep voice. "I've been wandering in the darkness, but now I'm here."

Jack walked up next to Taylor and barked at her. She jumped.

I couldn't help it. I laughed.

Taylor jumped up. "Your stupid dog just ruined that take."

That take? There would be more than one? Jack walked around the table, his tail wagging gently. He pawed me, slapping my leg with a demand for pets.

Clarity stood up. "You're a fraud."

Taylor's nostrils flared.

"I came today because you made me think you were honestly trying to hold a séance and contact Lance from beyond the veil. But you're a fake. You can no more contact a spirit than I can walk out of this shop and fly to Jupiter. I will not stay here and let you ridicule my beliefs while capitalizing on them." Clarity purposefully turned her back on Taylor, implying Taylor wasn't worth anything.

Taylor's face went red under her thick stage makeup. She clenched her hands.

Clarity marched to the door, and Taylor followed her. "You don't get to just walk away from me!" Taylor yelled.

I glanced at Bill and Jill. "What a time to be out of smelling salts," I said.

"I'm going to make sure our showrunner sees this footage," Bill said.

Taylor stopped in the doorway and then turned back. She marched over, picked up her tote bag from the side of the room, then grabbed Lance's pocket watch and dropped it inside.

"You are all going to regret sabotaging me," she said. Taylor turned and marched toward the door.

Jack barked once as Taylor flounced out of Lazy Bones.

"At least she didn't destroy anything this time," Jill said.

I turned the shop lights back on, then blew out the candles. Together, we slowly put the store back to rights. I tried to use a dust-buster on the glitter but suspected I'd find it in the store for years.

Once the TV show's van was packed back up, I set the security alarm and locked the store behind them. Then Jack and I walked home.

"That was interesting," I said. Jack ignored me to sniff a planter box.

Taylor sometimes felt like two people in one body to me, with two different personalities. Or maybe she was always playing a role and didn't know who she was deep inside.

Or she knew and the charming side of her was simply that: an act to hide the ruthlessness inside.

Given how Taylor had threatened us all, I could see her going a step forward and snapping. Especially if Lance had dismissed her and turned his back.

Since Colby had flown out last night, I went for my Saturday morning run solo. Which I enjoy occasionally since I get to follow my own pace without matching my friend. Although I missed her company as well.

Jack didn't budge from his early morning sleep session since he only runs when he wants to, and when he does it's usually only a few steps, provided treats or squirrels are involved. Or maybe sketchy birds.

Since it was quiet before the town woke up, I cut through downtown on my way to the park, which I'd circle, then climb up toward Highway 30 before running parallel to it for a mile before heading back to the river and returning to town on the river path for a five-mile run.

I paused when I came up to the front of Lazy Bones.

Someone was huddled in the doorway.

Elyan Hollow's homeless problem rarely results in people sacked out in doorways, or at least not for long. We're more likely to have people without a place to go crashing on a friend's couch or camping. Should I call the community resource officer's number? He partnered with a town social worker to help get people services.

But then I paused.

It wasn't just a person in the doorway.

It was Taylor.

Whom I'd last seen when she stormed out of Lazy Bones.

And she didn't look good. I should check her pulse. But I couldn't bring myself to touch her neck. My eyes kept staring at the red line circling Taylor's neck. It was just like the one I'd seen on Lance.

My hands felt shaky as I pulled my phone out of my running belt and dialed 911.

Chapter 26

The police showed up and cordoned off the street around the bookshop entrance. The door was locked, and I took one of the officers into the shop through the back door so we wouldn't walk through the crime scene.

I held my hand out toward the shop. "So far, everything looks like it did when I left, so I doubt Taylor came back inside. The door is still locked, and the alarm system was on when we entered."

"Can you wait here?" the uniformed officer asked.

I nodded, then texted Evelyn about what was happening.

Seriously?

she texted back, then sent a follow-up:

I am on my way. Don't say anything.

Come in through the alleyway,

I responded. Then, I made a cup of my favorite black tea, hoping it would calm my nerves. Although I kept seeing Taylor's face in my mind, and the red line on her neck. Had Lance and Taylor been killed in the same way? With the same weapon? A knock sounded at the door as I added a splash of oat milk from the fridge. I opened it and found the uniformed police officer in a showdown with Evelyn.

"That's my lawyer," I said, and he let Evelyn inside.

She wore black workout capris and a fitted cherry shirt under an open white hoodie. "The silver lining is that Sam was making me go for a run. Now I can go for a leisurely walk instead of trying to keep up with him."

"You're welcome?" I said.

"And Sam requested I tell you to let him know if you need anything, like bail or a ride home from the pokey. Or did he say big house?"

"As always, Evelyn, you're immensely reassuring."

She laughed, but then her face took a serious note. "How about you make me a cup of tea as you tell me exactly what happened."

I'd just told Evelyn about calling 911 when Detective Whitlock came in the alley door.

The detective was dressed as always, in an Elyan Hollow polo shirt and cargo pants, but the dark circles under his eyes were new. And he smelled like he'd been mainlining coffee.

Detective Whitlock cut right to the chase. "Please tell me about this morning."

So, I summarized the turn my tranquil morning had taken.

"When's the last time you saw the victim?" he asked.

I confirmed with Evelyn and gave Detective Whitlock a quick rundown of the séance. "When Taylor left the shop, she carried a leather purse." Or pleather, but I didn't think the detective would care. "I don't know what was in it, except she had Lance's pocket watch."

The detective's eyebrows raised slightly. "What's this about a pocket watch?"

I explained how Taylor brought it for her séance. "It must be the one Lance's sister asked me about. It was some sort of family heirloom that Lance kept with him. It sounded meaningful to his family." It was the type of item that potentially had more sentimental value than monetary. But who knows what it's worth if it's an antique.

The question that bothered me last night came to mind: How had Taylor gotten Lance's watch? And how long had she had it? If it wasn't in her bag, could it be connected to her death?

But why would it be? It was just a watch. Maybe it was worth something as an antique, but something told me the sentimental value to Lance and his family was higher than the monetary worth.

"And Taylor thought it would help her contact Lance from the great beyond?" The sarcasm in the detective's voice made me want to smile.

"I had a similar reaction. All of this was caught on the shop surveillance footage," I said.

Evelyn gave me a sharp look like I should've run that by her first.

"You recorded it?"

"We have a security system in the shop to deter shoplifters. It allows us to see what's happening in the aisles while at the register or in the back. I left it running every time the film crew was here."

"So you recorded the TV crew both times they filmed." Detective Whitlock studied me.

I nodded. Evelyn shifted beside me, and I could feel a wave of annoyance flowing off of her.

"I'd like copies of the footage."

I glanced at Evelyn.

"Do you have a warrant?" Evelyn asked.

The two stared at each other in a silent battle of wills. Detective Whitlock was several inches taller than Evelyn, but something told me she wouldn't lose this fight.

"You know I don't have a warrant. But I'm sure I can get one, and you should weigh the pros and cons of forcing me to do so."

"Okay, Ms. Briggs will get you a copy of the footage from last night's séance, which wouldn't be helpful for your investigation, as the victim left the store alive."

"The film crew also recorded the scene," I added.

Evelyn's gaze snapped my way, and I'm sure everyone in the room could read the "stop talking" message she sent me. But it's not like I was directing trouble toward myself, just toward the film crew.

"I'll go take care of the footage," I said. I fled upstairs to my office. I used the shop's computer to save the relevant security footage of last night's scene.

When I downloaded the footage from the front door camera and saved it, I took a moment to scroll through the feed. A cat wandered by at one point, but other than a few shadows of passing pedestrians, downtown Elyan Hollow had been quiet.

And then, a little after 4:00 a.m., a body fell backward into the doorway.

Taylor.

She curled onto her side while the shadow of her attacker presumably stood just out of sight of the camera.

Nothing in the image proved I'd harmed Taylor, but the reverse was also true: nothing in this ruled anyone out.

I averted my eyes from Taylor's final moment, and once I'd double-checked it had been saved, I turned the footage off. My stomach felt off like I'd never be hungry again.

I took a moment to create a new address with my backup email to a free storage service, uploaded the footage to a folder in the new account, and sent a link to the detective. It was probably paranoia telling me to keep my regular account separate from this legal situation.

I left the office and walked down the stairs, where Evelyn was flipping through a novel. "I sent the footage," I said.

"Thank you, Ms. Briggs." The detective left, and I could breathe a little easier.

Evelyn put the book down and turned to face me. "Let's discuss how to talk to police," she said.

Today should be a prime shopping day since it's a Saturday leading up to Halloween, with an afternoon parade and a few kids' events. Instead, access to my shop was blocked off, and my annoyed lawyer-neighbor had gone into full lecture mode.

As I walked home, I passed by the Eye of Newt Apothecary.

Clarity stepped outside and waved me down. "What happened at your store? I've heard rumors of a death?"

I made eye contact with Clarity. "Taylor was found dead outside my shop."

Clarity held eye contact with me. "You're serious?"

I nodded and tried to let the bleakness inside me flow out.

She folded her hands together on her chest, palms down. "May Taylor's family take comfort in their time with her and in the memory of her good works."

I suspected a final touch of sarcasm in the words "good works," but the rest of Clarity's statement felt genuine.

"Given what happened last night, don't be surprised if the police want to talk with you."

"Me? Why would I harm Taylor?" Clarity asked.

Because you thought she was a fraud who didn't respect your beliefs. Instead, I said, "Because we were amongst the last to see her."

"Except for whoever killed her."

"Exactly."

I continued on my way, and when I glanced back after a few storefronts Clarity was still standing outside her shop. She'd turned to face the direction of the area the police had protected with their yellow tape.

Where had Taylor gone last night after she'd flounced out of the shop? Downtown Elyan Hollow is quiet, but maybe she'd run into the wrong person at the wrong time? But as the words crossed my mind, I knew that was too unlikely, given everything that had happened.

Did she follow Clarity home? But if she had and then confronted her, how had she ended up outside my shop?

Was there some reason Taylor had returned to Lazy Bones?

If I could figure out why, would I know who killed her?

As I stepped onto the front porch of my house, I wondered if I went back to sleep, could I pretend this morning had never happened?

Chapter 27

Saturday night. I should be out doing something. But going to clubs isn't my style, and I'd need to drive into the city to find one.

I could head to the taproom since Ash is always happy for me to hang out, and once they closed their cart Olivia and Mila would happily prop up the bar with me. But I still felt unsettled after the morning. The most I could do was take Jack for a long walk full of sniff breaks.

Plus, my grandfather had texted this afternoon and asked me to be home for dinner. Feeling like a teen again, I said of course we could eat together.

After my interview with Detective Whitlock and Evelyn's lecture, I'd gone home to shower and pick up Jack. Tara usually manages the shop on Saturdays, but her sister was still in the hospital, so I was supposed to fill in. I'd debated telling Milo to stay home. That we would keep the shop closed today. But instead, I'd gotten creative.

Milo and I had been able to pull a table and a few stacks of books out of the back door of the shop and around to the front of the building, where we set up outside of the police perimeter, selling a handful of books on display and running inside for titles or taking online orders until we were able to open for real for the afternoon. Today hadn't been a total loss financially, but the word was still out on the full cost of the day.

Someone who should have had a long life ahead of her dying on the sidewalk outside Lazy Bones should have a lasting impact.

So, while we took the long way, Jack and I headed home. We had to wait for the train, full of young children and their parents, to roll by. I saw another group with a map of the *Haunted Hounds of Hamlet Bay* filming sites. In other words, a typical day in Elyan Hollow's spooky season.

As I walked inside, I smelled the siren song of zesty tomato. I dropped my bag in the living room and followed Jack to the kitchen.

"Captain, oh captain, your world-famous lasagna," I said.

"That's stretching my fame a little bit." My grandfather was sprinkling croutons into a bright red salad bowl. The light was on in the oven, with the lasagna bubbling inside. The egg timer on the counter showed five more minutes until pasta time.

"Can I help?"

Jack collapsed next to the kitchen table with a loud thump.

"No, I just need to toss the Caesar, and we'll be ready to eat."

Homemade Caesar salad?

"Is something wrong?" I asked as my grandfather split the salad between our plates.

"No. We have been like ships at night, and I wanted to check in. It's been a while since we've had more than a passing chat."

As we ate, I said, "You've been out a lot recently, Captain."

My grandfather's face flushed slightly. Wait, was he embarrassed? "You've noticed."

Yep, definitely embarrassed.

Wait, was he dating someone?

"I've been spending time at the Sleepy Hollow B&B. And Marion and I have gone into Portland for dinner a few times."

My grandfather was dating Marion?

But the little voice in my mind told me it made sense. Marion had been a widow for at least ten years, and my grandfather had been a widower for five. So it's not like they were rushing into anything. And as much as I didn't want anyone to replace my grandmother, if my grandfather was going to spend time with anyone, I was glad it was Marion.

"Do I need to have a talk with Marion about her intentions toward you?" I finally asked.

My grandfather laughed. "We're not exactly serious yet, but we're seeing where things go. You know she's been a friend for a long time."

She'd been close to my grandmother. "I know. And I like her."

Maybe this dinner was part check-in with the granddaughter about stumbling over dead bodies, part discussion of his dating life.

Which was much more exciting than mine at the moment. I really should take Sam up on his offer of grabbing a drink. Although Sam and I might need to leave town if we wanted one-on-one time to talk.

My grandfather and I had just finished eating when there was a knock on the front door. Jack let out a couple deep woofs as he ran to it, letting whoever had dared to approach know that he was on duty. My grandfather followed to answer it while I cleared the table.

The sound of my mother's voice caught my attention.

"Traffic wasn't too horrible. I'm glad Laurel and Ryan are attending the same party tonight, so Spencer could be on kid duty."

I wiped my hands and then walked out into the dining room.

My mother smiled when she saw me, and I remembered the teen girl from her yearbook photos. Between her being a teenager when she had me and looking young for her age, most people from the outside would guess we were sisters. Or maybe cousins since we don't look anything alike.

"Bailey, I listened to your voicemail, and when I called him this morning, your grandfather told me about Lance's death and everything. And it's time I told you the truth."

"We don't have to talk about it," I said. The thought of Lance being related to me made me feel sick inside.

"I should've been honest with you from the start. And you're not the only person I lied to, at least by omission. Because when I found I was pregnant, I didn't tell your father."

Lance.

"He was off to follow his dreams, and I didn't want to admit I was pregnant. I ignored it. Then, when I had to face the reality—"

She'd faced reality while he'd striven to see his name in the Hollywood lights.

"And I was selfish. I didn't want your father to have any claim on you. You were a Briggs."

I spoke. "I get it. Lance is my father." Or was, given his death.

My mother stopped and stared at me for a moment. "Bailey, no. Lance . . . why would you think that? No."

She paused and took a deep breath, like saying the words was difficult. Which made sense since they'd been a secret for decades.

"Rex Abbot is your biological father."

It was my turn to freeze for a moment. "Rex?" I finally said. I remembered Rex's face when I introduced myself at the opening reception. The ways his eyes had widened. The way he kept trying to talk to me.

Rex, really?

"Rex was always coming into the bookshop when I worked there on the weekends," my mother said. "I knew him from school, of course, and we'd been on the track team together for years. He was always so nice once you got past the shyness, and teenage me thought he was gorgeous. I was smitten."

"Umm . . . what about the prom photo where you and Lance wore matching flowers?"

"What's this?"

I pulled up the photo on my phone. My mother's face lit up in a grin when she saw it. "I'd forgotten about this. We all went as a group, and Lance's mother bought a mix of corsages. The girls divvied up the flowers based on which would look best with our dresses, while the boys chose theirs randomly.

"That was such a lovely night," my mother said. "We went out to eat at the old Wisteria Dining Hall, and I thought it was so elegant, and I was so sad when it closed. Rose drove us all in her mom's old Volkswagen bus. We danced all night, went to Rose's house afterward, and watched movies. It was the first time I saw *Rocky Horror Picture Show*. The boys didn't spend the night—just the girls—but I walked outside with Rex that night."

Was that a euphemism?

Dear lord, I really am a prom baby.

"That was the night I told Rex I liked him, and he told me he liked me back. We only kissed, but clearly, over the next few weeks before school ended, we got . . . closer."

Okay, maybe I was a high school graduation baby. Which was better? Or maybe it was worse than being a prom baby?

The doorbell rang again, and Jack woofed twice as he ran to the door. My grandfather followed along behind him.

The rumblings of deep voices at the door made me stiffen.

Rex was here.

"Lizzy!" Rex smiled when he saw my mother. She blushed, and I'd never seen that look of embarrassment intertwined with pleasure cross her face.

"I go by Liz these days," she said.

"Actually, I heard it's Doctor Liz." Rex's tone was lightly teasing, and my mother flipped her blond hair over her shoulder.

Wait. Were they flirting? Jack wandered back to my side and pushed his nose against my hand.

My mother's face turned serious, and her tone matched. "I told Bailey the truth."

Rex turned his gaze on me. "I've wanted to tell you since I came to town, but I couldn't figure out how to say it. When I missed my event, I was walking, debating how to tell you. Then you were freaked out after finding a body, so it wasn't the right time to break the news."

And Rex had tried to stop me from talking to the police.

Because he thought I'd done it? Or had a flare of fatherly concern made him get involved?

Or had he wanted the police to leave because he'd done it?

But if he had, why would he have harmed Taylor?

"I should've told you years ago," my mother said. She was looking at me, so she must be directing her words my way instead of at my grandfather. "When I see your younger siblings with their dad, I think of what I denied you, and it's not fair. To you or to Rex."

I shrugged. "It is what it is." Should I feel angry since my mother had denied me a chance to get to know Rex when I was a child? But had he even wanted me in his life? Would he have shown up on the occasional weekend or holiday like a whirlwind, leaving the work of raising me to my grandparents?

Or would he have wanted to fully step up? Become part of the foundation of my life?

I'd never know, but something told me that might be for the best.

"Who'd like a drink?" my grandfather asked. I felt like I could breathe again. He and Rex decided to opt for whiskey, while I said I'd brew peppermint tea for my mother since she planned to drive home because she wanted to spend Sunday with her kids.

My grandfather and I walked into the kitchen together. "Are you all right?" he asked.

I set the kettle to boil, then turned and looked at him. "I have no idea."

"If you'd like, I can kick both of them out of the house," my grandfather said.

"No, it's fine. At least for tonight."

When I carried my mother's tea and my can of sparkling water back into the living room, my mother and Rex sat facing each other. And I realized this was the first day, other than that fateful moment in the bookshop as a toddler, that I'd been in the same place with both of my parents at the same time.

And I still wasn't sure how I felt about it.

Chapter 28

At about 9:00 a.m. on Sunday, just after I'd finished whisking my matcha, a knock on the front door sent Jack sprinting with a few deep woofs. Jack stared at the door handle, daring it to turn.

I followed along more slowly and looked outside before opening the door.

Detective Whitlock.

"Let me call my lawyer," I said. I stepped outside, leaving Jack inside. He barked twice to let me know he was, once again, questioning my decision-making.

The detective held up his hand. "I just have a quick question. When was the last time you saw Clarity Blooms on Friday night?"

I paused. "Why? Is Clarity missing, too?"

Could Clarity have made a run for it yesterday after she found out about Taylor? But that didn't make sense since Clarity had seemed shocked to find out Taylor was dead.

Had Clarity really been angry enough to harm Taylor because of the fake séance?

"Please answer the question." The detective looked exhausted. Two murders in a town with a low crime rate must be working him over.

Even though Evelyn would tell me to wait for her, I spoke. "She left at the same time as Taylor, which should be on the footage I handed over. I didn't see her again Friday night, but I did see her when I walked by her shop on Saturday morning. Clarity came out and asked me what was going on."

"How did she react?" The detective leaned against the post by the top of the stairs.

"She seemed shocked." And slightly sarcastic. "I really believe the news of Taylor's death was a surprise to her. She wasn't overly upset, like she was faking a show of grief, but it surprised her."

"You're sure you haven't seen Clarity since?"

I shook my head. "I was at the shop during the day yesterday but didn't see Clarity again. But I also didn't seek her out."

"Her shop was closed yesterday," the detective said.

Could Clarity and Taylor have fought after they left Lazy Bones? But I couldn't see Clarity killing anyone. Could they have fought and then Taylor escaped and ran away, only to collapse by my store? I've heard people can survive being strangled, but their throat swells, and they collapse later. Or maybe the fight had triggered something else in Taylor.

The memory of the shadowy figure near Taylor when she collapsed made me shiver.

"Can you think of anything else I should know?" The detective had gone the Hail Mary route, lobbing a ball in my direction, hoping I'd turn it into a lead.

"Did you know, Detective, that when Lance was a teen, one of his friends—Matt Leverton—was convicted of larceny and drug possession in juvenile court? But everyone thought he didn't commit the crimes alone."

"So?" The detective didn't look impressed.

"Everyone suspected Lance might have been the friend that Leverton protected."

"And so?"

"Leverton was at the festival," I said. "And if he's been holding a grudge against Lance for that crime, this might have been his first time to get vengeance."

My words sounded overwrought and like I'd totally lost the plot.

Or was trying to push culpability to any possible suspect.

A connection clicked in my mind, and I scolded myself for not realizing this sooner. "I might be able to prove Leverton was around," I said. "The rest is just speculation. I'll be right back."

This train of speculation that could make it look like I was trying desperately to push suspicion away from me, but I couldn't stop myself. I dashed inside and pulled my tablet out of my bag and brought it back outside. I scrolled through the library story hour event photos. I stopped on one that showed a couple of children sitting, listening attentively, with a few adults off to the side in the background.

Including Matt Leverton.

"That's him."

"You're sure? Do you know him?" The detective sounded skeptical, but I was pretty sure there was a note of interest layered in his voice.

I shook my head. "We've never met, but there's a photo of him on his work website in Wilsonville; if that's not him, it's his doppelgänger. Let me see if he's in any of the other photos."

Matt was in the background of a few shots, almost like a wraith.

"Send those to me, and I'll look into this." The detective handed over his card again, and I used his email address to send the photos with Leverton in them.

As Detective Whitlock walked away, I wondered if I'd thrown an innocent guy to the metaphorical wolves. Just because he'd gotten into trouble once years ago didn't make him more likely to be guilty now. I stood by one theory: this might have been Matt's first chance to get revenge if Lance had caused Matt to go to jail years ago.

However, that didn't explain Taylor's death.

As I closed the door, one nebula of an idea that'd been floating around crystalized into a cohesive thought: even though I wasn't sure how I felt about him, I didn't want Rex to be the killer.

* * *

After talking with the police, I needed to do something. Ideally, something taxing. The sort of thing that would help the stress coursing through me flee my body and leave me, hopefully, calm. Shooting for happy might be a leap too far.

Colby was still gone, visiting her husband, who was on a three-month assignment in the Midwest, so I debated the merits of a solo run or bike ride. I ran yesterday, so I knew I should do something else that worked other muscles.

But then I figured out what to do. I pulled on my favorite workout gear and apologized to Jack, promising we'd go for a walk later.

He yawned in response and flipped onto his back, his four paws sprawled at an awkward angle.

The Monster Smash Gym & Yoga Studio is just a few blocks from the Outdoor Spirits Sporting Goods store on the edge of downtown. I jogged over, which was always a good warm-up. I've been a gym member for a few years, although I barely visited this past summer, maybe once a week. I'm more consistent about lifting during the winter when it's cold and wet and long bike rides seem depressing, if not dangerous on slick roads.

After stowing my wallet and keys in a locker and a second quick and furious warm-up on the rowing machine, I was ready to lift weights.

I'd first started lifting at the Monster Smash as a teen. I was smart enough to know that, while I wanted to push myself today, I wasn't physically ready to set any personal records. So, I carefully worked on a series of snatches, reminding myself how the movement would flow. "Form first," I chanted mentally when tempted to add a couple of extra ten-pound plates to the bar.

"Looking good, Bailey," the gym owner said as he walked by. From previous experience, I knew he'd tell me if my form was terrible.

I moved on to one of the squat racks, and as I was loading a couple of twenty-pound plates onto the bar, a familiar face walked in.

Rex. Here. Seriously?

Was he following me?

He looked surprised when he saw me, then beelined my way.

"You're a member?" Rex asked. I nodded, and he said, "I shouldn't be surprised. I heard you're into triathlons and running. I picked up a guest pass for my visit since I didn't want to drive out of town to work out."

"It's a good gym." The owner is serious about keeping the gym friendly to everyone, especially women, newbies, and anyone who doesn't fit into the stereotypical "gym bro" mode. "The TRX class is awesome if you want to switch things up."

"Yeah, I did TRX after I tore my ACL," Rex said.

"That must've been tough. I've yet to injure a knee, although I almost shredded my ankle a few years ago and broke my wrist in a bike accident." The words felt awkward, another example of the emotional distance between us. My grandmother had practically moved into my college apartment when I'd broken my wrist, even though I'd been able to take care of myself. A brief wave of grief passed through me, both about my grandmother and because I'd never know what she'd think of Rex being my father.

As we talked, I felt prickles on the back of my neck. Like someone was staring at me. I used the mirror on the wall to check out the rest of the room.

Detective Whitlock. Staring at Rex and me. He clocked when I noticed him, and he glanced away.

Of course he'd be a member here. It's the only gym in town.

But was he working out this morning? Or had he tailed me? Did he think I'd lead him to the killer but instead saw an opening for a bonus workout?

The detective wore black exercise pants and a light gray T-shirt with sweat stains, which could be one clue about why he was at Monster Smash.

I couldn't resist it. I walked over to the detective. "Are you following me?" I asked.

The detective motioned to the set of dumbbells on the floor in front of him. "Meal break workout."

Rex had trailed after me. "Bailey, do you need a spot?"

"No thanks," I said. I slouched back over to the squat rack.

Those weights weren't going to lift themselves.

But it was hard to get back into my flow when I kept catching glimpses of Rex and Detective Whitlock working out.

And it didn't help that both were keeping an eye on me.

Chapter 29

As I left the gym, I swung through town to walk past the bookshop. A quick peep inside through the window showed me that Milo and Danby had everything under control. Danby waved at me and then gave me a shooing motion, which made me laugh.

So, I mixed things up and ordered lunch. A turkey and bacon sandwich on telera bread from Ahead of the Carve, the butcher-slash-sandwich shop a few blocks from the bookshop, sounded good. So I walked that way. I still felt restless, although my workout had helped me move from overwhelming to slight.

I missed having Jack alongside me, too.

Once I had my sandwich, I headed home. My route took me past Stitch Craft, and Lark waved me inside. Despite the siren song of my sandwich, I walked inside.

Mrs. Sullivan was sitting on one of the couches, teaching three women how to knit.

"Good call on introducing Estelle to us," Lark said. "She's an amazing teacher."

"Bailey!" Mrs. Sullivan waved me over. So I headed that way. Peaches came over to say hi but turned away when she realized I didn't have Jack or treats.

"Check out how well these beginners are doing," Mrs. Sullivan said. The retired teacher motioned to the two women working on knit rectangles while she knit a small hat in an orange yarn that would fit a plum.

"I've been telling them that knitting is just simple counting," Mrs. Sullivan said.

"I'm terrible at math," one of the women said.

Pearl walked up, bumping me slightly as she came to a stop. "I'm also horrendous at math, and if I can knit, you can, too. You might just need a different perspective."

Lark pulled me aside and invited me to a party she was throwing next week, then asked, "Are you okay? Can I do anything? The past few weeks must've been so traumatic for you."

"I'm okay." Mostly.

"I keep hearing that you've been arrested or are going to be."

"You have to love a small-town gossip network," I said. "I haven't been arrested, but I'm sure you'll see my mug shot across everyone in town's social media feeds if I am."

"People who know you don't actually think you did it. But everyone's concerned. I mean, two deaths? Even if they weren't locals."

Mrs. Sullivan must've been listening in. "Of course Bailey didn't do it, and anyone who says she did must have their own dark secrets to hide."

Lark and I turned to her, and I realized I was standing with my mouth open, so I closed it.

"Don't act surprised, girls. Everyone has secrets in their closets, but thankfully, very few people are willing to kill to keep them quiet." Mrs. Sullivan kept knitting like this was everyday chitchat.

The feeling of dread in my stomach blossomed in my stomach like a corpse flower. I said a quick goodbye with an excuse of needing to go eat and fled home.

Thankfully, no one yelled, "For shame!" or "Murderer!" at me as I scurried out of downtown.

* * *

When I was a few blocks from home, I turned and took a different path than usual. One of the regulars on my library delivery route had the last name Leverton, and he lived on this street. He was usually my last stop on my way home, but he hadn't been on my list for the past few weeks.

I paused by a slightly run-down bungalow, once painted a cheerful green. The house wasn't a wreck, but it'd needed some TLC. The inside had always been spotless. But I'd been careful on the front steps because the last before the top felt soft in the middle, like the wood was ready to collapse.

A man was in the yard, fixing the handrail to the newly rebuilt stairs to the front porch.

Not just any man.

Max Leverton.

I tried to act casual and snapped a photo. I texted it to Detective Whitlock and added a message:

Matt Leverton is on Elm Street.

Matt looked up and made eye contact with me.

I smiled, like I was happy to see him. "Hey! You came to my festival last weekend."

"Your festival?" Matt asked.

"The Spooky Season Lit Festival. I organized it. I run the local bookshop." And, clearly, I was a world-class babbler.

"Good for you." Matt looked back at his construction project, dismissing me.

Nevertheless, I persisted. "You were there, right? With a child?"

"Guilty as charged. My daughter enjoyed the picture book readings."

"So you're local? You should come by the store, then; we have a fantastic children's section."

His face relaxed as he straightened, and his eyes gave me a once-over. "I'm just in town to help get my grandfather's home ready to sell. I'll be around a few more weekends. I take it you live in town?"

For the love of dog, did he think I was flirting?

"Your grandfather? Julian? Is that right? I delivered books to him from the library. Is he okay?"

Matt shook his head. "He had a stroke."

"I'm so sorry to hear that." Here I was, pestering Matt in the midst of a family tragedy.

"He's in rough shape. So we're getting his house ready to sell, since if he recovers enough to leave the nursing home, he'll move in with my sister."

"Please tell your grandfather that he's in my—in Bailey's—thoughts," I said. Being in Matt's position was one of my biggest fears. I should walk on but paused. This might be my only chance to talk with Matt. "You know, I think you were one of my mom's classmates."

"I highly doubt that."

"No, you were a year or two ahead of Liz Briggs, right?"

"For real? Your mother is Lizzie Briggs? That makes me feel ancient. Although I shouldn't be surprised because there are a few late twenty-somethings of my former classmates running around." Matt leaned against his partially built railing. Thankfully, it held.

I eyed him as I said, "Did you hear what happened on the Saturday of the lit festival? So tragic."

"Lance Gregory's death? Yeah, I heard." Matt stood up straight and his gaze turned back to his railing. Talk over.

I might as well continue playing the ditz role. "I found Lance's body, and now the police think I killed him."

"That must be so tough for you." Matt pulled his phone out of his pocket, signaling he was done conversing with histrionic booksellers.

"Which should interest you 'cause I know you and Lance had a history, which includes you going to juvenile hall."

Matt stood still. He didn't turn and look my way.

"From what I heard, you had a bad history with Lance. Maybe

the sort that would cause someone to want revenge. What were the charges? Theft? Drugs?"

Matt shoved his phone back into the pocket of his dark brown work pants. He leaned over and picked something up.

I stepped into the yard, stopping a few feet away.

"What do you think you're doing?" Matt asked.

He was a head taller than me, with developed chest and arm muscles. And he was holding a hammer.

I raised my hands in a calming gesture. "I don't want to hassle you, but I want to understand what happened all those years ago. I have the feeling that if I can get an accurate sense of Lance's character, it'll help me figure out what happened."

Matt stared at me; the coldness in his face reminded me of the moody teenager in grunge fashion from his yearbook photo. "Do you know what I was convicted of stealing from the high school? My own camcorder. I'd worked at the local Plaid Pantry over the summer to buy it. And a teacher took it and didn't want to give it back."

"Why did the teacher confiscate it?"

"I was accused of using it to videotape girls in their locker room. Which was BS. But there was footage from the locker rooms on the camera so the school started the process to expel me. I realized later what had happened, how Lance was always borrowing it and recording himself. He had access to the coach's office in the gym, which had a door to both locker rooms."

A picture was starting to emerge in my mind. "So you broke into the school to get it back?"

"Lance convinced me that we could get it back, and I thought I didn't have anything to lose. I followed him to the school, although I knew it was a terrible idea. I thought we were just going to get my camcorder. But then Lance broke into a locker and stole someone's pot stash. We saw a police car when we left the school, and Lance dropped his backpack at my feet and ran."

"Sounds like it must've been a pretty big stash." The articles Sam had found mentioned drug charges.

"The locker belonged to a pretty big stoner. It was barely over the limit to be charged with intent to sell, but the local DA threw the book at me, and my public defender rolled over." Bitterness infused Matt's voice, but I couldn't blame him if he was telling the truth.

"Why didn't you tell the police about Lance from the beginning?" I hoped he could hear the honest question in my voice.

"Who do you think people would've believed? The rich kid, or me, the knucklehead who was always doing stupid things? Don't get me wrong. I helped Lance break in, so I wasn't innocent. At first, I didn't turn him in because that's not part of the code, and I thought Lance would do something to help me."

Something my grandfather said pinged at my brain. "Was there some sort of bullying incident with Lance that led to a broken nose? Like some kid snapping at him?"

Matt's laugh was bitter. "Oh man, I'd forgotten about that. Poor Paul. Looking back, I can see how Lance subtly bullied Paul for years. I didn't even realize at the time how terrible it was. Eventually, Lance realized that Paul and one of our classmates had been sneaking off together at lunch, and Lance followed them with a couple of friends. Lance and crew found the two kissing in the woods near the high school and started laughing at them. Paul tried to punch Lance, and Lance ended up punching Paul in the nose. There was so much blood. By the time teachers got involved, they believed the story Paul had tried to attack Lance without provocation and he had defended himself. Despite being the one with a broken nose, Paul was expelled, and Lance wasn't even punished. The girl—I can't remember her name—was hassled afterward so much that her family moved."

From the way he told the story, Matt had been a participant but clearly wasn't taking responsibility for his part.

Matt shook his head. "Yet another story of Lance ruining other people's lives while skirting responsibility."

"You were in the maze the day Lance died. I saw you."

"Yes, with my daughter. Do you really think I'd kill someone in front of her?" He ran a hand over his shaved head. "You know, I'm not the only classmate Lance screwed over who was also in town that day. I even saw one near the maze."

"I'm sorry for bothering you."

A police car pulled up to the curb beside us. Two uniformed police officers emerged.

"Matt Leverton?" one asked.

"What if I am?" Anger pulsed in his voice. I stepped away from him.

"We'd like to talk with you."

Matt looked at them for a moment, then dropped the hammer by his feet.

The police led Matt away, and they argued next to the police car. I walked home, feeling like I'd just ruined Matt's life.

Leverton clearly still had a grudge against Lance, but two things struck me. One, I believed that he would've avoided getting into a fight in front of his daughter. I didn't know how he'd react if Lance started something, but something told me his first instinct would've been to get his daughter away from the situation.

Two, Leverton didn't know Taylor and didn't have a reason to harm her.

But who had it in for both Lance and Taylor?

Other than me. I still looked like the number one suspect.

The film crew had the closest connection to Lance and Taylor in town. But it seemed like their only goal was to do their job and leave with as little drama as possible.

Could they feel stuck? If an ironclad contract kept them involved with the show, losing half of the crew must've sunk the entire project and set them free. That being said, if they needed the paycheck, that was an incentive to keep the show going. They had plenty of personal reasons why they were justified in disliking Lance and Taylor.

Bill and Jill both seemed calm. Considerate, even though they'd been there, Lance destroyed my shop, and they hadn't stopped him. But who knew what hid behind their "just here to film a show" façade.

* * *

I was finally home with my sandwich. I took it and Jack out to the backyard. Jack promptly trotted down the steps and collapsed into his usual spot beneath the Japanese maple.

I sat down at the table on the porch and pulled out my phone for internet research while eating. I logged on to the library's site and pulled up the local newspaper archives.

From reading between the lines, Rex's dad hadn't been a nice person. But that didn't mean he didn't have a different public persona that allowed him to hide his authentic self from the rest of the community.

Since I didn't know his first name, I searched on Abbot.

A handful of results showed up, and one of the photos caught my eye, so I clicked on it.

Roy Abbot.

Rex's dad.

From the photos, Rex looked a lot like his father. Same face shape, with a square jaw. The images were black-and-white, so I couldn't tell if they had the same eye color.

Roy Abbot had been in the paper several times over the years, usually for Elyan Hollow Police–related reasons. They'd gotten a new set of police cars, and Roy was pictured next to them.

His retirement merited a short mention. Barely a paragraph without a photo.

The last entry listed was his obituary.

I scanned it.

He'd served twenty years as a local police officer and just retired when he'd had a heart attack.

He'd been preceded by his wife, and he left behind one son, Rex, who lived in California.

The obituary didn't contain anything new to me, but I realized what was missing: emotion. The obituary beside Roy's mentioned how the deceased was a beloved and devoted father and grandfather who had volunteered with rescue horses and the local food pantry. The reader got the sense the world was now a sadder place.

Versus Roy's obituary, which was just a short recitation of facts.

A disquieting thought infiltrated my brain. Lance clearly liked to pick at people's weaknesses. Had he met with Rex in the hay bale maze and, unable to help himself, said something that made Rex snap? Coming to his hometown had clearly made Rex nervous, although I was a major reason why.

I put my phone away and pulled an ARC from a new-to-me writer I was reviewing for the shop. But I found it hard to focus.

I still felt like the net for Lance's murder, and now Taylor's, was closing around me.

Chapter 30

When I finished my sandwich and abandoned my attempt to read, I realized it was only the afternoon, despite feeling like it held a week's worth of drama in a few short hours.

Since Jack had stayed home while I visited the gym and town, I decided it was time to stretch his paws. As I loaded my bag with sketching materials, he brought me a pumpkin-themed bandana from his bin.

We took the long way to my favorite spot along the Columbia, passing by a guided tour of the *Haunted Hounds* filming sites. I wished I could feel carefree like that, out for a fun afternoon revisiting happy memories of my childhood.

After I set up with my sketchbook, Jack looked at me, and I gazed back into his steady brown eyes. His eyes are naturally rimmed in black like he's wearing perfectly applied eyeliner. Today, it made him look extra soulful. Sometimes, it made him look emo, especially when paired with his black skull bandana.

"Okay, Sherlock Bones, I need your help," I said.

Jack continued to gaze back, not even reacting to the nickname.

"Did Rex kill Lance?"

Jack looked away.

I'd always been curious about who my father was. And now, I knew.

But I also knew he could be a murderer.

When I was a kid, I'd dreamed about meeting my dad. The missing parts of my life would click together. We'd be BFFs. We wouldn't argue like my mother and I did, especially in my early teens when she'd gotten married and started a life that only included me on the occasional weekend and odd holiday. Part of me still ached when I remembered that time and how I felt less than. My grandparents had done their best to mitigate the pain, and I'd been an obnoxious, hormonal mess who'd eventually settled down and apologized to them for being a knucklehead.

The shock of reality made me wonder what I would've thought as a kid if I'd known who my father was. Would I have been intimidated to know half of my genes came from a well-known horror writer? Working in a bookshop and meeting authors has shown me that writers are people, too. Most are fantastic. Many are wonderfully neurotic, or at least claim to be. All of them love books.

What had Rex thought when his publicist had asked him if he wanted to be a guest of honor at my inaugural literary festival? Had he known the request came from his daughter?

Was that why he said yes? Was that his incentive to return to town?

Or had it dawned on him later?

Regardless, I'd wanted to put my hypothetical father on a pedestal as a kid. Knowing who he was, I could already see some flaws. And some strengths.

Just like everyone else.

I don't know what I expected, but I did have a few unexpected things in common with Rex. Being athletic without the killer, win-at-all-costs mindset. While one could argue my love of literature came from growing up with my grandparents, Rex and I had the desire to create in common.

But there was one sticking point of seeing Rex as a suspect: Why would Rex harm Taylor?

Had Taylor and Rex even met? They'd been staying at the same

B&B. Then I remembered her walking up to him in the opening reception and interrupting his conversation. Going from staying in the same inn and intruding on a conversation to murder seemed like a giant leap.

A voice interrupted me and made my heart start pounding.

"This is your spot, huh?" Rex asked.

"Yep." I forced myself to take a deep breath.

"It was my spot once, too. Back when I was in high school, I wanted to get away from everyone. It's weirdly appropriate that it's your spot now."

"For all I know, multiple people could claim it as their own," I said.

Rex sat down next to me.

I glanced at Rex. "During the festival launch party at the B&B, Lance had a photo of me."

"I saw." Rex unrolled his shirt sleeve from beneath his elbow. He slowly buttoned it around his wrist. "Lance must've stolen that from my room on Friday afternoon."

Rex glanced at me, and I got a sense of a deep sense of turmoil inside of Rex. "I snapped that photo when I'd come home for my mother's funeral. You and your mom were in the bookshop. I hadn't even known you existed. And there you were, reading picture books."

"As my mother said on Friday, she didn't tell you she was pregnant."

"Looking back, I made the wrong choice. Being blindsided wasn't an excuse."

"My grandparents were excellent parents to me," I said. "I didn't want for anything."

"Your mother didn't raise . . ." Rex's voice trailed off.

"It was always best for me to think of my mother like an aunt." A somewhat distant one. "She left Elyan Hollow for college and then medical school. By the time she finished her residency, everyone decided I was set here."

"Do you get along with your stepfather?"

"He's less my stepfather and more my mother's husband," I said. "I've always known I didn't fully fit into the picture of her new life, especially once she married one of her fellow residents. Adding a teen to their picture-perfect image would've crushed their vibe."

"I'm sure there was more to their decision than that," Rex said.

He must have really cared about my mother to be so willing to defend her.

"If she'd asked, I wouldn't have wanted to leave. But it would've been nice to have an actual conversation about it."

"I doubt if any of this was an easy decision for Lizzie," Rex said.

I shrugged. "There's something I've been wondering."

"Okay."

"Why was Lance in your room at the B&B?" How had Lance even had the chance to steal the photo?

Rex's eyebrows scrunched together. Maybe he'd thought I'd want to ask something personal. Have a cinematic moment, although he'd already missed a "Bailey . . . No, I am your father" moment.

"Lance saw me when I checked in, and I made the mistake of letting him in when he knocked," he said. Rex looked into the distance, down at the river. A small boat bobbed on the waves. "Lance spent years trying to make it big in Hollywood. He had a little success but never reached the heights he dreamed of. I don't know if you know this, but I cowrote one of the screenplays for one of my book adaptations—"

"*The Brothers of the Forgotten Castle.* I remember when it came out—my grandfather had me draw a castle for the book display in the shop. He was so excited about the film. We went on opening night."

"That's right. Lance tracked me down after that was announced. I passed on his name to the casting director but made sure Lance knew I wasn't involved in that process. But Lance always hoped I'd help him get his big break. On Friday, while I was unpacking—"

Wait, was Rex the sort of person who used the dresser drawers in a hotel instead of living out of a suitcase like a normal person?

"I emptied out my messenger bag to organize the bookmarks and postcards I planned to bring to the events. The photo must've fallen out of my notebook. I didn't realize it was gone until I saw it in Lance's hand at the party."

"You must've been annoyed."

"Shocked, more like." Rex glanced at me, then turned to face the river again. "Lance fooled me when he came back to my room when we left the party. I wanted the photo back, and instead, he must've stolen my watch. And to think, when I first opened my door to him, I'd hoped he'd finally grown up. But as usual, he was only looking out for himself."

"What did he want?"

Rex folded his other sleeve up to just below his elbow. "Lance wanted to interview me on his ghost show. He wanted to recruit anyone that would get them even a tiny bit of buzz, including me, to get the show noticed."

Asking a horror writer to be on a ghost show did make sense, but I also understood Rex's hesitation.

"Why did Lance show the photo to me?"

"My guess is that he knew you were Lizzie's daughter. You'd met him at the bookshop, right? Your name was written on the back of the photo. I wonder if his next step would've been to try to blackmail me to be on his show by threatening to tell you. It wouldn't have worked since one of my main reasons for saying yes to the festival was to meet you. Like I said, he was always looking for angles."

"You avoided booking events at Lazy Bones in the past." I studied the side of his face. I didn't see much, if any, of myself in him. His face was more square and his nose had a subtle bump. His hair was slightly darker, but I caught a touch of red in the sunlight, like mine.

"When my first book came out, I considered doing an event here. A sort of 'look, I made it.' But I wasn't ready to face the demons of my past. I don't mean you—but my parents. My father had died a few years before my debut came out, and I was still dealing with the emotional fallout."

"Your father was a police officer?"

Rex's eyes widened. "How did you know that? It's one reason I hovered when you spoke to that detective. I didn't want you to get yourself into trouble by accident. The detective on this case seems like an okay guy, but still, I'm wary."

"My lawyer friend Evelyn basically said the same thing."

"Most of my father's coworkers were nice to me. One even helped my mother escape. He got her into a domestic violence shelter outside the county, and they planned to help her move out of state. But she was diagnosed with cancer and came home, and a year later, she was gone."

Rex looked down at his scuffed day hikers. "If she'd gotten away and been diagnosed just a few years later, I could've helped her. Kept her from moving back in with my dad."

"Even though his coworkers knew?" I asked.

"I heard the local police chief wanted an excuse to fire him by that point, but it was easier to expect him to retire when he hit twenty years of service. And domestic violence wasn't treated the same then as now. Since my mother wasn't willing to press charges, nothing happened."

We sat in silence for a moment. To my surprise, it felt natural versus awkward.

"So, what's next?" I said.

"What do you mean?"

"We shake hands and move on with our lives?" Rex's presence was still unsettling to me.

And I really hoped he wasn't a murderer.

"We could get dinner, maybe? You could introduce me to your girlfriend," Rex said.

Wait, what? "Umm . . ."

"I won't judge. She seems nice from the little bit I've seen of her."

"Do you mean Colby? She's my best friend, but she's not my girlfriend. Her husband would take exception."

"Ah, I misread that situation."

We were quiet for a moment. I realized Jack had shifted, so his chin sat on Rex's thigh.

"Your dog's a sweetheart," Rex said. He scratched Jack behind the ears.

"Only to people he likes," I said. Jack had liked Rex from the get-go, I realized.

My phone beeped. My grandfather asked if I wanted to grab dinner with Marion and him.

The woman my grandfather was now dating looking for a second chance.

Also, it is a long-standing part of my family foundation versus my newfound paternal side.

A glint of bronze caught my eye as I slid my phone back into my bag. I used my pen to hook it and pull it out.

A pocket watch?

Was Lance's pocket watch in my bag?

And then the picture shifted into a perspective.

And I knew who the killer was.

At least, I suspected.

Now, how could I prove it?

Chapter 31

A few of the rumors I'd heard about, combined with one of the photos I'd seen in my mother's yearbook, had changed my entire perspective of the case.

It's like drawing. Maybe you see a beautiful bouquet of flowers. If you sketch them straight on, they're pretty. But if you alter the angle and change up the lighting, suddenly, you have something unique that hints at something profound.

Something darker.

I went home, photographed the yearbook page in question, and called Mrs. Sullivan, who confirmed my suspicion.

I then texted the snap of the photo to Detective Whitlock, along with my theory of what happened.

Then, with Jack alongside me, I headed back downtown.

I had a murderer to unmask.

I emailed Detective Whitlock my suspicions as I navigated through the crowd in town to enjoy the Halloween festivities. I paused when the train crossed in front of me, noting it was full of kids.

But I ignored the festivities and headed to Stitch Craft.

Pearl sat on a stool at the end of the counter behind the register, knitting what looked to be the final ruffled edge of the spider shawl, and I walked straight to her. I didn't bother saying hello.

"You know, Pearl," I said. "There were a lot of rumors that Lance fathered a child as a teen."

Pearl knit a little faster.

"You've always been a bit baby crazy. You don't just coo over them in your shop, but seem a little . . . obsessed."

"I've always wanted to be a mom," Pearl said. "It's all I've ever wanted, but it didn't happen. It caused my marriage to wither until my husband left for someone who wasn't defective and could have babies. I don't really like to talk about it."

"And when I saw you at the taproom before the murder, you were about halfway done with the spider shawl. But then, at the knit night after the murder, you'd restarted it. And you're always proud about not needing to restart projects. You brag about fixing them, or at the very least offer to show people how to unravel to just before their mistake versus starting over. Remember when you insisted on showing me how to unravel the row behind a dropped stitch on a scarf? Restarting would've taken more time."

"So, I messed up a knitting project." Pearl looked at me. "It happens."

"I think you strangled Lance with your circular needles."

"Really?" Pearl's eyes focused on the ruffle edge she knit.

"And I think you bore Lance's child as a teen. I saw a photo of you and my mother in your yearbook when she was pregnant with me. At first, I thought it was just an unflattering angle of you, but then I realized that you were pregnant, too." Mrs. Sullivan had even mentioned a second girl being pregnant, but I hadn't realized it was at the same time as my mother.

"Your mother was a month ahead of me," Pearl admitted. "We were the two pariahs, the two pregnant sixteen-year-olds. My parents flipped out and almost sent me away to my grandparents. They let me stay in town but forced me to give my daughter up for adoption. They decided the embarrassment was an appropriate punishment for me."

"You wanted to keep your baby?"

"I've never understood how your mother left you behind. You,

you're wonderful. And if I could've raised my daughter, I bet she'd have been equally amazing."

"And Lance was the father?"

Pearl looked at me, and I could tell she wanted to lie. But then she let out a deep breath. "I never told anyone, but somehow, that was the rumor. People guessed. And it was true. I can only assume someone saw us together, although I didn't realize then that Lance was just using me. He didn't love me, not the way I loved him. When people asked him, he denied that he could be the father of my child. Even when my dad confronted him in the street. And, of course, everyone believed Lance. They thought he was so much better than me. My parents punished me again, even though I didn't start the rumor."

I was trying to sketch the final details that would turn this image from a smudge into a fully rendered image. "And you couldn't have more children?"

"I hit rock bottom after being forced to give up my baby. I barely finished high school, and my parents promptly kicked me out. I couch-surfed for a while, finally ending up in Seattle. But I was self-medicating, first with alcohol, then with drugs. The rest of my behavior wasn't much smarter, and I caught an infection. I didn't know it'd caused me to become infertile. Not until long after I'd gotten back on track." Her smile was seeped in sadness.

"I've been sober for twenty years. I managed to get a degree in textiles. I even managed to start this shop. I didn't tell my husband about my past until the fertility tests. He was disgusted with me. He left me then and served me with divorce papers without speaking to me. He's blocked me everywhere, but his second wife's social media is wide open. They have two kids. He's living his dream while I'm limping in the shadow of mine."

Pearl's hands stilled. "I've done everything I can to find my daughter. I've signed up for every genealogy site I can find and uploaded my DNA. I've done everything possible to make myself available, but I've yet to hear from her."

"After everything, you moved back to Elyan Hollow?" I couldn't imagine coming back.

"It wasn't my first choice, but my then-husband got a job with the county. He thought this town was charming and the perfect spot to start a family. And I realized, for better or worse, this town is part of me. So I opened my yarn shop and held my head high when everything else imploded. But staying in town might help my daughter find me. I'm sure her birth certificate will mention Elyan Hollow."

"You came to Rex's talk but left early when Rex didn't show up." And Matt Leverton must've seen her near the maze. The classmate he'd mentioned had to be Pearl.

Pearl finally put her knitting project down. Something about her looked defeated like she'd given up the last bits of hope in her life. "You're right. I'd dropped by Rex's talk, but I left when he didn't show. I ended up knitting in the pumpkin maze. It's so nice there when it's quiet. And then Lance showed up."

"And you confronted him."

"You know the night Lance came into the taproom? You were there with Colby? He was faking it when he didn't recognize me that night, and I called him out. He finally asked about our daughter, and I told him the truth: my parents made me give her up for adoption. And he . . ." Pearl wrapped her arms around herself in a hug.

"He what?"

"Lance said that was for the best. That I hadn't been mother material then, and I clearly wasn't any better now. He was so smug and turned away from me like I was nothing. Like I didn't matter, I was still the same stupid high school girl he'd used and discarded like trash. I just snapped. My knitting was in my hand, and then the circular needles were around his throat. Then he was on the ground, and he wasn't moving."

Pearl picked up a bottle of water and took a sip.

I glanced down at my phone, which was recording.

"Why did you put Lance's pocket watch in my bag?"

"It was in my cardigan pocket, and your bag was open. I needed to get rid of it. I thought you'd be smart enough to find a spot where no one could find it since you're a suspect in the murders. I really wanted to keep it. It was a family heirloom, and it could've been the only inheritance my daughter received from Lance."

Pearl stepped toward me, and Jack growled loudly.

Pearl stepped backward. "There has to be a way we can work through this. It's not like anyone will miss Lance, and murders go unsolved every day."

Yes, but the police didn't suspect me in those murders. And no matter how terrible Lance had been and how poorly he had treated Pearl, Lance hadn't deserved to be murdered in the hay bale maze. Ridiculed in the public square, perhaps in a set of stocks with a sign, yes.

"What about Taylor?"

Pearl shook her head. "That stupid girl. She'd figured out there was something more between Lance and me, and she kept taunting me about it. Then she decided to blackmail me, and it was too much."

"You left her in the front of my shop."

"Not on purpose. I couldn't sleep and went for a walk. The town is so peaceful at night. Taylor was filming something near your shop with her phone, and we argued. I didn't mean to harm her."

For the first time, I felt like Pearl was lying to me.

"How could Taylor have blackmailed you?"

"Lance must've said something since Taylor claimed she had a video of Lance talking about me having a long-lost child. She said I was pathetic. But I told her to take a good long look at herself, and she laughed at me."

Being laughed at might have been what made Pearl snap.

"You just happened to have an unused circular needle with you when you ran into Taylor?" I asked.

"I always have knitting supplies with me."

Another lie, since Pearl had opinions about how to store circular needles when they weren't in use to keep the flexible cable that connects the pointed ends from getting bent the wrong way. Using a craft tool that's meant to create something new to kill someone felt like it should go against the knitters code.

"You have to turn yourself in, Pearl," I said.

She shook her head. "We can just pretend this conversation never happened." Pearl stepped toward me again, and Jack growled.

The front door jangled, and when I turned my head Pearl rushed past me, bumping me into a display and causing skeins of yarn to go flying, as she ran toward the door.

Jack barked as Pearl tried to run out the door. But she bounced off the poor woman who'd just walked in and banged her head into the doorframe. She fell straight down onto her face.

As I called 911, I looked at the spilled skeins of orange and black yarn, then at the woman Pearl had run into, who simply looked confused. The woman took a few steps backward and leaned against one of the couches.

Pearl groaned as I asked the 911 operator to send the police and an ambulance. Jack stood, staring at Pearl. When she twitched, he growled. She stayed still, either knocked out or afraid.

I sat on the couch in Stitch Craft as a pair of uniformed police officers led a handcuffed Pearl out of the store. She had a bruise on her forehead, but the paramedics who'd come and left didn't seem concerned. But I was willing to bet the police officers would take her to the ER just in case.

I wasn't sure how to feel. On one hand, I felt sorry for Pearl. The wounds from her past had never healed, and I believed her when she said she'd snapped.

But that didn't excuse her from attacking Taylor.

And she'd hidden the pocket watch in my bag. What would her next step have been? An anonymous tip to the police?

Detective Whitlock walked up. He still looked tired, but I suspected there was relief layered underneath. While Elyan Hollow's murder rate had skyrocketed this year, at least the clearance rate was one hundred percent.

A small, smug note might be swirling around in my mix of emotions. I'd been right all along. Lance's past had caught up with him. If Pearl hadn't slipped Lance's pocket watch into my bag, I might not have put the clues together and figured out what she'd done.

"I helped you solve a murder," I said. While I wasn't exactly happy with everything, a few notes of pride made me feel steadier. Like the world would make sense again.

"Don't get overconfident," Detective Whitlock said. He sat down on the couch next to me. "We found a recording of Lance and Pearl saved on Taylor's phone, with Pearl insisting on speaking with Lance outside the taproom. When Lance ignored her and left, Pearl told him he'd regret walking away from her again. And the same incident was caught on the taproom's security feed. Plus, Taylor had a clip of Lance talking about Pearl being, let's say, troubled."

I stopped myself from pointing out that I'd solved the case without the footage.

"Therefore, Pearl was on my list to question. And we pulled camera footage from the surrounding blocks from Friday night that we're still analyzing. While the footage from around your store wasn't conclusive, it didn't rule Pearl out. We knew she was around when Taylor died. While we found footage of you and your giant white dog leaving downtown, we didn't see anyone that looked like you returning to the area."

I glanced at Jack, who was lying on the floor at my feet, but with his head up so he could keep an eye on everyone. "It's nice to hear you're good for something, Jack. Growling at killers is more productive than barking at birds."

I was babbling and should stop talking. I felt unsteady, like Pearl's confession had turned the floor beneath my feet into a churning river on a windy day.

"What's this about growling?" Detective Whitlock asked.

I told him about Pearl stepping toward me after she confessed to Lance's murder and how Jack growled at her after she'd run into the doorframe and sprawled on the ground. "But I hope she wouldn't have harmed me. She was always a friend," I said. But I could hear the doubt in my voice, and I realized I wasn't sure. Pearl had killed once to cover up her involvement in Lance's death, so what was to say she wouldn't keep going?

"Good job, Jack," Detective Whitlock said. Jack gazed back at him but didn't leave my side.

"Detective, I have something you'll want." I explained about finding the pocket watch in my bag. He put on gloves and put the pocket watch into an evidence bag. He wrote on the bag.

"I never touched it," I added. "I used a pen to pull it out of my bag and then drop it back in."

Hopefully, it would have Pearl's fingerprints on it.

"If I'd analyzed all of this faster, I would've taken Pearl in for an interview without you putting yourself at risk," the detective said.

"I never want to be involved with a murder ever again," I said.

Chapter 32

Halloween night

The pinnacle of our annual Halloween festival. Main Street was shut down to cars, and we'd set up a Lazy Bones stand by the front of the store to greet the horde of trick-or-treaters streaming through town. A few people ducked into the shop to browse books, and Milo had been ringing up a steady stream of customers.

I left the candy disbursement in Tara's and Danby's hands and took a break to visit the Happy Campers S'mores cart down the block.

Their menu looked fantastic, but I wrinkled my nose when I read the description of the candy corn s'mores. I debated the classic or one with a drizzle of peanut butter.

And peanut butter won out.

"Let me get this."

I hadn't even realized Rex was behind me. He ordered a classic, and we shuffled to the side as one of the cart workers assembled our s'mores and toasted them with a crème brûlée torch.

"I'm moving back to Elyan Hollow," Rex said. "At least for a few months, although I might buy a home here, or maybe in Portland."

I looked at him. Half of his mouth twisted in a smile.

"When I was younger, I couldn't wait to leave. But over time, especially in the past few years, I started to miss the town. And I realized that while reinventing yourself is fun, you still carry the baggage from your earlier self. And it's time I faced my past."

"Was Elyan Hollow really terrible for you?" I asked.

"Looking back, I can't really blame the town. My home life . . . wasn't good. But there were bright spots. Your grandfather recommended books to me, and he'd loan me ARCs and ask for my opinion on which books to stock. I knew he did it since he knew I couldn't afford to buy many novels. I had good friends, like your mother. Some of whom I turned my back on when I shouldn't have. Like when I came home for my mother's funeral and saw you."

Rex continued, "That was a dark weekend for me, on the whole. You know, I wrote my first novel that summer, and it was a reaction to the grief and the realization that I'd never see her again."

I remembered the dark, oppressive king in the novel whom the forgotten brothers in the story had fought against. It was the tidbit a literary critic could turn into an entire essay.

I could feel Rex staring at the side of my face, but I watched a girl dressed up like Tippi Hedren from *The Birds* as she pretended to be frightened by a girl dressed up like a parrot.

A couple of people decked out like zombies walked past us, followed by a man walking a dog the size of a box of tissues. Which made the dog's costume that looked like an order of small fries especially perfect.

"There's something I'd like to show you," Rex said. He fiddled with his phone for a second. He turned it around to show me a photo of a woman. "This was my mother."

She had the same shade of chestnut hair as me, along with similar hazel eyes. We both had heart-shaped faces, although her chin was sharper. She was dressed in an orange running singlet with a medal around her neck. I squinted at it.

"Is that a marathon finisher medal?" I asked.

"Yes, that photo was taken after she ran the Boston Marathon. In some ways, my mother was the toughest person I've ever known. She ran at least ten marathons."

She'd run a recognized marathon with a good time to qualify for the Boston Marathon. Not everyone can do that.

"I'd like the opportunity to get to know you." Rex seemed like he was ready for me to crush him.

"Let's take it one dinner at a time," I said.

Rex smiled. "Sounds good."

"Rex, your s'mores are ready," a man at the cart said.

Rex and I sat down together at an empty bench and chatted.

As a child, I'd always wondered what visiting the Halloween festival with my father would be like.

I hadn't pictured artisanal s'mores in my daydreams.

Once upon a time, Samhain was a Celtic Festival on November 1. People believed the souls of the dead returned to their homes. People would dress up in costumes and light bonfires to confuse the spirits.

In Mexico, today is Día de los Inocentes, when families bring offerings of toys and sweets to the graves of their deceased children. Tomorrow, November 2, is Día de los Muertos, aka the Day of the Dead, when people bring food and offerings to the graves of their loved ones or set the offerings up in altars in their homes.

As per my grandfather's tradition, I'd set up a bonfire on the sandy bank of the Columbia River in Elyan Hollow. We'd forgone costumes, and my friends were decked out in cozy sweaters or hoodies since the weather had turned chilly, reminding us winter would be here soon.

Lark showed up, accompanied by her new dog, Peaches. She'd agreed to take custody since Pearl was in jail, most likely indefinitely. Peaches wore a butter yellow sweater with a knit shark fin on the back, and she looked around eagerly, ready for trouble.

Peaches wasn't the only attendee who looked festive. Olivia had painted her face to look like a sugar skull, and she'd brought a container of cookies to pass around. Evelyn had brought a large thermos of hot chocolate, while Ash had hauled down a few growlers of beer. Sam had shown up, looking adorable in a charcoal sweater.

"Let's schedule that drink," he told me, and we made plans for next week.

Colby and Hayes walked up next, holding hands, with Danby trailing behind them. Hayes was back in town for a few weeks, and Colby glowed.

Danby beelined to Ash, but Colby chased her down. "I better not see you drink a beer," Colby said.

"Chill, I told your sister I'd bring her that retro gum she's been looking for. One of my distributors knew how to find it." Ash pulled a small brown bag out of her messenger bag. Colby snatched it before Danby could touch it and pulled out a red package of gum.

"Gum? You've been trying to track down gum?" Colby stared at Danby.

"Let your sister be," Hayes said. He wrapped his arms around Colby's waist, and she leaned against him.

"Here's to the end of another Halloween season," I said. I held up a cup of cocoa.

We toasted, and as I looked around, I felt lucky to be here at this peaceful moment of time, with the sound of the river lapping on the shore next to us, and the scent of woodsmoke in the air. This year's Halloween festival hadn't gone to plan. Despite the heartache, I'd gained so much, even if I was still figuring everything out.

But if I felt like I had everything under control, life would boring.

Acknowledgments

While writing a book is a solo process, many people provide help along the way. My list of people to thank includes:

Alexa Butler and everyone at Beach Books. Including Ann, who let me shadow her at work and showed me the ins and outs of their ordering system.

Larissa Ackerman and Jackie Dinas at Kensington for championing the idea of a quirky Halloween bookshop in a Halloween town.

Robin Herrera for our regular writing sessions and for her feedback on *Chaos at the Lazy Bones Bookshop.*

Melanie, for loaning her name to Melanie Wilde and for giving me feedback on the opening chapters.

Bill and Jill Cameron also loaned their names to the book, and I hope I've done them justice!

Frank Zafiro for always being willing to discuss the minutiae of police procedural, and for this book, how to annoy a real-life detective if he stumbled into a murder-mystery party while investigating an actual crime.

While I wish I could claim the "snitches get purl stitches" quip as my very own, I have to give props to Jeana for coming up with that gem.

My agent, Joshua Bilmes, and everyone at the JABberwocky Literary Agency.

My editor, John Scognamiglio, and everyone at Kensington who took this novel from a Word document to the finished book you're reading right now.

Annie Bloom's Books in Portland, Oregon, aka my "home" bookstore. I've been a customer there for longer than I've been a published writer, and it will always be one of my favorites. They partner with me for preorder campaigns and events, and it's lovely to have their support. Books Around the Corner, formerly in Oregon and now in Forks, Washington, for the Halloween-themed bookstore inspiration. Bookstore and booksellers every, and not just for their (amazing) support of my books, but for providing spaces for readers everywhere.

And the readers who've embraced the Ground Rules series and hopefully enjoyed their journey to the Lazy Bones Bookshop and Elyan Hollow.

Like many authors, I borrowed from real life to create my fictional world. On that note:

If you want to visit Elyan Hollow, you'll struggle to find it on a map of Oregon. But St. Helens, Oregon, and Sand Island inspired the town, although my book version differs from real life. St Helens' annual Halloween festival runs from late September through October every year.

You can visit the filming sites for several movies in addition to celebrating Halloween.

Tots Book Bank is inspired by the Children's Book Bank in Portland, Oregon, as well as similar organizations across the country that get books into the hands of children.

The cigarette machine-adapted-to-toy-dispenser concept is borrowed from Green Beans Books in Portland, Oregon. So, if you think the idea sounds fun, stop by their shop to check one out in person!